Artful

Deception

A NOVEL

BY

JAMES J MCGOVERN

ISBN: 978-1466312296

To My Family

Lynn, Keri, Katie and Bryan.

With love and thanks.

"There are no facts, only interpretations."

-Nietzsche

ACKNOWLEDGMENTS

I want to thank my family for putting up with me for the three and one-half years it took me to write this novel. They all deserve medals! I also want to thank my daughter, Katie, for her exceptional work creating the cover. My gratitude and thanks to the Isabella Stewart Gardner Museum for permission to reprint Vermeer's "The Concert".

James J. McGovern
Marshfield, Massachusetts
July, 2011

JAMES J MCGOVERN

PREFACE

This is a work of fiction. Although certain real locations and public figures are mentioned, all other characters, places, documents and events are totally imaginary. Names and specific details about some individuals in the story were changed to protect their anonymity. All others are either the product of the author's imagination or are used fictitiously. Any resemblance to actual persons, living or dead, events or locales, is coincidental and unintended.

Chapter One
Sanibel Island, Florida, October 3, 2007

Sitting at the Hurricane Bar and Grille on Sanibel Island, an idyllic seaside paradise on Florida's West Coast, Ted McGrath, a retired FBI agent originally from South Boston, Massachusetts, stared at the high definition television hanging on the wall above the bar. It was World Series time and one of the teams, the Boston Red Sox, a team he was intimately familiar with. It was the second time in three years the Sox had been able to stay in the hunt into early October, having beaten the Cleveland Indians to win the American League pennant. McGrath had retired from the Bureau in late summer 2007 and moved to Sanibel shortly thereafter, buying a two-bedroom condo with a view of the Gulf of Mexico.

He loved Florida, and not for one minute did he miss the long, snowy New England winters. He enjoyed fishing for grouper and sheepshead off the pier at the western tip of the island, a six-iron shot from the Sanibel Lighthouse. Like clockwork, he would arrive at the pier every morning, rain or shine, cooler and rod in hand, ready to land a keeper.

McGrath was a large man. His neck made him look like a bulldog with its rolling creases at the nape, tanned by the Florida sun. His rough Irish skin had a constant ruddiness, the result of his other hobby, hanging out in gin mills. Standing in his shorts and tee shirt above the pilings, he would make small talk with his fellow anglers to pass the time, an ever-present cigar in his mouth and Red Stripe in his hand. In between often-exaggerated fish tales, he would ramble on about "the case". Each morning, as he stood on the pier and looked out on the churning blue-green waters of the Gulf, McGrath daydreamed about "the case". It was a high profile robbery that happened years ago in Boston. At the time, he had been the lead agent for the Boston field office of the Federal Bureau of Investigation.

Tonight, as was his routine, he arrived at The Hurricane at 6:30 PM and ordered his first beer from Jerry, who McGrath had learned, once lived two T-stops away from his old home in South Boston. Picking up the icy bottle, he emptied it in several gulps, the bottle never leaving his lips. As he looked up at the game, he was happy to see that the Sox had scored two runs in the first inning.

It was unusual for him to speak to anyone at a bar. His one exception was Jerry the bartender. Jerry knew he was from Boston but didn't know much more about him, other than what he liked to drink and eat. When Jerry asked him what he did for a living, he told him he was a retired FBI agent and then started to talk about "the case". It had something to do with a robbery at a museum in Boston back in the early 90s. Jerry would learn that it wasn't just any run-of-the-mill robbery. It was the largest art heist in the history of the United States and maybe, the biggest of all time anywhere. It also remained unsolved.

Chapter Two: "The Case" Boston, Massachusetts, Early Sunday Morning, March 18, 1990

8:14 AM - Before the good citizens of Boston even had a chance to grab their umbrellas and put on their rain coats and head to 9:00 o'clock Mass, a frantic call came into Boston Police District B-2, located on Dudley Street in the historic Roxbury section of the city. The rain and mist of Saturday night continued to fall, making for a miserable start to a day meant for celebration. The city was slowly starting to awaken from the March 17th St. Patrick's Day festivities. The annual, St. Patrick's Day parade in South Boston was scheduled to kick off at 1:00 PM. this year on March 18th. Boston's finest were determined to make sure it went off without a hitch.

The caller, obviously shaken, had the clear, yet unmistakable sound of panic in her voice. The 911 operator wasn't sure what she was saying. It was something about either an on-going break-in or a B&E overnight at her location.

At 8:16 AM, cruisers were dispatched in haste. "Attention all units, please be advised of a probable B&E in progress at 280 The Fenway." Officers in cruiser 5623, hearing the radio call, raced to the location, believing there was a B&E in progress. Officers in cruisers 1033 and 4710, operating under the same belief, sped through the rainy streets. Sirens blared and blue lights from the cruisers' wigwags flashed in the murky air. Turning the corner onto The Fenway, long time partners Tommy Folan and Micky Bradley were the first to arrive on scene: the renowned Isabella Stewart Gardner museum. When the call came over the radio, the two were talking about how lucky they were not having to work the parade in Southie. A few minutes after arriving on scene, they wished they had been scheduled to work the parade route.

Pulling up in front, the cruiser's tires almost jumping the curb, the two quickly got out and ran up to a female and two males who identified themselves as museum security employees, Karen St. Pierre, Edward Franklin, and Larry O'Dea. They were standing at the black iron front gate of the museum. Raindrops glistened from their distraught faces, for they knew, in all likelihood, based on what had taken place moments before, something had gone terribly wrong during the 11:00 PM to 7:00 AM graveyard shift. Despite repeated attempts to rouse the guards who had worked the shift, neither one had responded to rapping on the employee entrance door and window. Although without first-hand knowledge, St. Pierre, O'Dea and Franklin feared the worst. "I arrived at 6:45 AM, my usual starting time," Franklin explained, "but could not gain entrance. I waited outside until approximately 7:25 when Ms. St. Pierre arrived. The guard station is located right inside the Palace Road entrance on the right side of the building. We knocked on the door and window as loud as we could and then called the security desk telephone without any response. We then decided to call our Supervisor, Larry O'Dea, who arrived minutes later. When we again got no response from the guards, that's when Karen placed the 911 call." While Franklin spoke, they all walked with Folan and Bradley around the corner onto Palace Road, a quiet, tree-lined, one-way street. The employee entrance door, in keeping with the overall design of the Venetian mansion, mimics the heavy wooden doors of Old Venice, ornate with long, black exterior hinges and a small, protected window located at eye level.

Taking the key from O'Dea, Folan opened the outer door, doing so extremely carefully, so as not to disturb any possible fingerprints, and to make sure no one was in the vestibule. Stepping into the confined, box-like space, he opened the inner door with the same care. Folan and Bradley, weapons drawn, walked carefully into the museum's security area, a glass partitioned room with a chest-high security desk. The light above the desk was on but the guards were nowhere to be seen. Except for a low humming sound coming from a security monitor above the desk, dead silence. Sensing something was seriously wrong, all three museum employees started to get knots in the pits of their stomachs as they walked cautiously behind Folan and his partner. With adrenaline flowing, the long time partners were on high alert and tightly wound since they had no idea who or what they might encounter.

All of a sudden, Folan's radio screeched, causing him to yell, "Son of a bitch," when another patrolman, who was checking the main entrance, radioed to report it was still locked and secure with no evidence of forced entry. Everyone else jumped out of their skin and caused the three museum employees' hearts to skip a beat. As they stood in the guardroom and caught their collective breath, it became apparent that no B&E was in progress and that the two guards had either left the building or were still inside but unable to respond. Not wanting to contaminate what they believed could be a crime scene Folan and Bradley secured the immediate area near the security desk. Seeing debris on the floor Folan crouched down to take a closer look. It was a doorknob and splinters of wood that had obviously come from the door to his left.

O'Dea, who was looking over Folan's shoulder, seeing what was strewn on the floor, picked up the phone and dialed the museum director's home number. Folan overheard him giving the shocking news to his boss: "My guards are missing. It looks like someone came in through the Palace Road entrance and we don't know if the overnight guards are dead or alive. There has been no response from them despite our repeated attempts. There is significant damage to the security area. This could be very serious." Folan looked at Bradley and without saying a word, radioed for additional aid including detectives and crime scene specialists.

The first order of business was to get more officers on scene to secure the building. Folan also realized they would need the specialized expertise of the Federal Bureau of Investigation. Unaware that the initial dispatch had also been picked up by the Bureau's radios, as Bradley and Folan entered the Palace Road entrance, an FBI agent was speeding to the museum.

Chapter Three: "The FBI Agent from Southie"

FBI agent Edward "Teddy" McGrath, a life-long resident of Boston rushed to the scene as he picked at his early morning coconut donut. Most of it, not quite having made it into his mouth, was strewn down the front of his shirt and onto his lap. Wisps of grey smoke from the Churchill cigar that dangled from the right corner of his mouth swirled in an upward spiral, dissipating as it made contact with the yellow, nicotine stained headliner of the Crown Victoria.

McGrath loved being an FBI agent and had wanted to become one since he was thirteen. He was inspired by a visit to Washington, D.C. years before. His father Patrick had developed a relationship with an older, very distinguished local South Boston Congressman by the name of John McCormack. It just so happened "Old Jawn" had risen through the Congressional ranks to become the Speaker of the House of Representatives. He had invited Patrick and his sons to Washington to tour the Capitol building during cherry blossom season. Ted had celebrated his thirteenth birthday during the visit. The two boys and their Dad were awed by Washington and could not believe the beauty of the Nation's Capitol building. As the three walked through the halls adorned with portraits of members of Congress past, trying to find the hearing room where they were to meet the

Speaker, they became mesmerized. They could all feel the "power" of Washington in the hallowed halls. It was palpable and intimidating! Finally locating Hearing Room 207, they opened the massive wooden door as quietly as they could, taking seats in the back. The room was overflowing and extremely hot and humid. Ceiling fans tried to cool the room without any effect. The McGrath's were dressed in their Sunday best. Speaker McCormack sat in the middle of a long table at the front of the room, while other men and women sat to his left and right.

Each had a microphone in front of them and as each spoke, flashbulbs popped from cameras pointing at the witness who had his back to the gallery. About twenty minutes had gone by when McCormack, speaking into the microphone with a gravelly, strong Boston accent said: " Mr. Director, the Chair and all members of this committee very much appreciate you taking time from your hectic schedule to address some of our concerns about certain policies of your agency. We are comforted by your reassurances that you will look into the issues that have been addressed today by this committee. Thank you. This meeting is adjourned." As the last word sounded from the speakers, McCormack banged a gavel on the table startling both Ted and Tom. "Patrick, I'm so glad you and your boys could make the trip. It's wonderful to see you. This must be Tom and Ted" as the tall, stately Speaker shook their hands. "I would like you all to meet someone. Mr. Director, this is my good friend from home, Patrick McGrath and his sons Tom and Ted." Ted realized that "Mr. Director" was the same man that had been sitting alone at the table with his back to them during the hearing. "Hello Mr. McGrath and boys, it's very nice to meet you, I'm Director Hoover of the FBI," as he handed Ted and Tom pins, each with the Department of Justice logo. "As Speaker McCormack will tell you, the world is a dangerous place and we at the FBI are dedicated to making it safe for you and other families. We provide justice to all and enforce the law. It's a very rewarding career and the two of you should really consider becoming agents and serve your country. Just remember, as we all go through life, we are judged on how we treat others. Good luck to all of you and I hope to see you in Washington again someday."

Chapter Four: "Two Sketchy Guys"
The Isabella Stewart Gardner Museum, Boston
March 11, 1990

It was one of those early spring days in dreary March that teased the winter-weary citizens of

Boston. A record high of 67 degrees brought joggers out along the Charles River and couples to the Public Garden. Jack and Linda Casey were in the city to forget the brutal winter that continued to blister their home state of Maine. Leaving the Ritz-Carlton on Arlington Street, they headed to one of Linda's favorite places, the world-renowned Isabella Stewart Gardner museum, one of the world's most beautiful. Quaintly nestled in the "Fens," it sits just a stone's throw from Fenway Park, the home of Mrs. Gardner's and the Casey's beloved Red Sox.

Entering the foyer, the Casey's walked to the museum's brilliant, sunlight-drenched inner courtyard. A fountain in the center, set below the glass enclosure three stories above, provided a wonderful warm feeling of spring. Picking up the museum's guide brochure, Linda and her husband were ready to enjoy their day. It was 11:20 AM. The brochure provided the museum's visitors with the locations of priceless works of art and a brief description of each. There was a portrait by Manet located in the Blue Room; numerous works by Degas in the Short Gallery, Flinck's "Obelisk," Rembrandt's "A Lady and Gentleman in Black," "The Storm on the Sea of Galilee" and his self-portrait, and Vermeer's "The Concert," on display in the gilded Dutch Room. Linda's two favorite paintings were "The Storm on the Sea of Galilee," Rembrandt's only seascape, and "The Concert," Boston's only Vermeer. As the day progressed, it had become balmy in the sun-filled museum forcing the Casey's to head back to the hotel earlier than they had planned.

March 18, 1990, 10:23 AM

When McGrath finally arrived at the museum, a Boston patrolman standing out front directed him to the Palace Road side entrance. Folan met him there and with perfunctory introductions, McGrath asked in his usual gruff tone of voice: "What the fuck do we have here?" Folan, clearly not impressed with the manner or attitude of the fed, started to explain that his partner, along with several other Boston police officers and museum security, were inside. He said, "From the looks of the guard room and our inability to locate the two security guards, the situation appears very ominous. We have no clue where the guards are or whether they're still in the building. At this point we also don't know if anyone else is in here." Standing there in the rain, McGrath appreciated the gravity of the situation. No one knew whether the two guards were dead or alive. Unsnapping his 9MM Glock holster, he started to walk into the Palace Road entrance behind Folan, in the direction of the glass-enclosed guard desk.

All of a sudden, Folan heard the words, "Son of a bitch" from behind. McGrath realized that he still had his morning cigar in his hand. In order not to contaminate the crime scene, he told Folan to hold on for a moment. He walked back to the entrance, and standing in the doorway, reluctantly flipped it into the bushes. "I hate when I have to toss a $5 burner before I can finish the fucking thing," he said to himself.

The first thing he saw when he entered the guard area was what appeared to be doorknob fragments on the floor outside the assistant security director's office. He looked at the door and realized someone had made obvious forced entry into the office. The door was shattered at the lock indicating someone had kicked it in; pieces of it were scattered across the floor. As he looked up towards the ceiling, he could see a surveillance camera behind the guard desk, but someone had turned it up and away towards the ceiling. He assumed it usually pointed down to the area in front of the desk.

He pushed open a door carefully and entered a small office. An empty frame rested on a small, swivel chair. Coming out of the office, he looked to his right and noticed another small room next to the security office. The door leading into that room also appeared to have been forced open. As he walked in, he noticed a videocassette recorder in the corner. A label taped to the top of it read: "Surveillance Security March 18, 1990". Taking a closer look, he could see that the tape was missing. He looked around for it but it was nowhere to be found. His initial gut reaction: "the surveillance security tape that would have captured the intruders' initial entry into the museum, as well as any confrontation with the guard at the desk, had been taken." He then turned to the computer's attached printer. What appeared to be a computer printout of all alarm and guard activity also appeared to have been tampered with. The long, perforated sheets had been torn from the printer. He grabbed what was left and made a mental note that he would later memorialize in his trusty spiral notebook: "the last time of entry was 12:46 AM". Shaking his head in disgust, he mumbled to himself, "There's no fucking report of any alarm or guard activity after that." Just then his radio went off.

Chapter Five: "These Guys Look Familiar?"
The Isabella Stewart Gardner Museum, Boston
March 11,1990

The Casey's were ready to head back to the Ritz for an early dinner. Linda first needed to use the facilities. As he waited for his wife, Jack stood in the North Cloister near the public entrance and exit. He was minding his own business. He really wasn't interested in looking at any more art or the nearby sculptures; he figured he would people-watch for a few minutes. That's when he first noticed them: two middle-aged men taking in the scenery and the beauty of the museum. Something however didn't fit. Both were dressed in heavy raincoats and one wore a hat, not the way someone would dress on this unusually warm, sunny day in Boston. It hadn't rained in three days and there was no rain in the forecast. Continuing to look, but trying not to draw their attention, he noticed something else strange about the two. The two kept glancing over to several windows that were near the entrance to the Blue Room. It looked like they were interested in whether the windows were locked and how they were secured. They were particularly riveted on a window that had been opened due to the mild weather. His gut instinct told him that these two jokers weren't there because they were patrons of the arts. Although he had been a certified public accountant his entire professional life, he was convinced that these two were there to case the museum's security.

Casey was just about to walk over to one of the museum's security guards when Linda returned. In her usual hustle and bustle way, she grabbed his hand and as they walked past the coatroom and entrance to the Blue Room they exited the museum and jumped into a taxi. Jack's brochure had fallen from his back pocket onto the tile floor five feet away. It contained a road map of the museum. It was a virtual blue print of the building, complete with diagrams of the first, second and third floors, identifying for all, priceless treasures on display in each room. As the late afternoon sun moved towards the horizon, a solitary, hazy shaft of sunlight seemed to purposely settle, in fact fixate, on the last sentence of the last page. There, in black and white, was the museum Directors' ominous boast: "In accordance with Mrs. Gardner's Last Will and Testament, the Gardner has remained essentially unchanged since her death in 1924."Sitting in the back seat of the taxi for the short ride across town to their hotel, Casey reflected upon what he had just witnessed at the museum. He felt unsettled. The older of the two men, with a unique facial feature, reminded him of someone, but for the life of him, he couldn't recall whom. The younger of the two, without the hat, had an unusual haircut that reminded him of one of the Three Stooges.

Chapter Six: "Duct Tape and Plastic Handcuffs"

Folan had continued walking into the museum and had left McGrath at the security desk. With excitement and relief in his voice, he reported, "We've found the guards. They're in the basement and both are okay." McGrath, hearing the good news, started to walk over to the basement stairs that would bring him down into a storage area located in the bowels of the museum. As he walked away, a Boston police crime scene photographer snapped photographs of the area around the guard desk. It occurred to the federal agent, as he stepped into the basement and started to walk in the direction of voices coming from the rear of the cluttered, confined space, turning left, and then right, "whoever brought these two sons of bitches down into this basement the night before, had to be either familiar with it or was schooled as to its layout."

Folan had told him earlier that according to museum staff the only lights on in the museum during the graveyard shift were at the guard station and in the cloakroom. Walking through the cramped space he figured that whoever the clowns were, flash lights would have been needed to navigate the tight, cramped quarters. As he tried to get to the source of the voices, he stopped briefly as he jotted a quick note in his ever-present spiral notepad, "basement like a maze many unexpected turns...lots of pipes and electrical wires...? No lights on...inside help." When he finally arrived where Folan and Bradley were standing, he could see a large, white male sitting on the floor next to a work sink. Folan, taking McGrath out of earshot, told him that the guard's name was Alexander Morris. McGrath peeked over Folan's shoulder and gazed at the guard, noticing that along with being handcuffed to the leg of a wash basin, he was also bound and gagged with grey duct tape, wrapped around his hands, ankles, eyes, chin and head. While standing there, attempting to figure out what the hell had gone on during the night, another radio went off.

The second guard, like Morris, was also bound and gagged with duct tape, handcuffed and blindfolded. He was found about forty feet away on the other side of the basement. McGrath told Folan that he would be right back and proceeded to walk over to the area where the other guard had been found. Again, he thought, "Whoever the assholes were that brought these two down here were either bats with sonar or knew the layout." What he saw when he arrived astonished him.

A white male was handcuffed to a pipe. He had shoulder-length, shaggy black hair and was dressed in a shirt the rock star Jimi Hendrix might have worn on stage while "Purple Haze" blared from on-stage speakers. It was really an astonishing sight to behold. His hair was black and curly, but his unkempt beard was brownish-red. McGrath also noticed that his hands appeared to be tied by police issue handcuffs coupled to a set of plastic handcuffs. The college age kid was wearing a short sleeved, blue, unbuttoned guard shirt, black jeans and a big black cowboy buckle belt. What seemed particularly bizarre to McGrath was the black cowboy hat, complete with a feather that was perched to his left on the bench where he sat. McGrath's quick assessment: "He sure as shit didn't look like someone who was responsible for the safekeeping of Millions of Dollars worth of art."

Chapter Seven
South Boston, Massachusetts, March 18, 1990

In 1938, Mayor James Michael Curley a/k/a "The Rascal King" hoodwinked the Massachusetts Legislature into making March 17th an official state holiday, closing Suffolk County offices to allow the City's predominately Irish Catholic residents to celebrate the "Holy Day" of their patron saint of Ireland. Of course, in order to keep affairs of church and state separate, as required by the Founding Fathers, the creative Mayor cajoled the Legislature into recognizing the day as one of great historical significance to the City of Boston. The official name of the holiday would be Evacuation Day, commemorating the evacuation of British troops from the city during the Revolutionary War. In fact, the first St. Patrick's Day Parade took place some 200 years before, when, at four o'clock on the morning of March 17, 1776 more than 8,000 redcoats marched through the dark, narrow streets of Boston, looking as if they were on parade.

The unofficial name of the holiday, St. Patrick's Day, became a day off for Suffolk County employees who could sleep in, take in the parade, and drink to their hearts' content. Most of the day, other than watching the parade, is spent drinking in the countless bars scattered across South Boston, or "Southie" as locals know it. Once a blue-collar, hard-working, hard-drinking neighborhood that borders Dorchester Bay, it was becoming the preferred neighborhood of upscale, young professionals who worked downtown. The morning's foul weather would not and could not, under any circumstances, dampen the spirits of the thousands of men, women and children who waited with anticipation along tenement-lined streets to watch the parade.

The parade, to most Bostonians, was a harbinger of the spring that would arrive in just four short days. It would go on at 1:00 PM rain or shine, and without delay, to the elation of the expected crowd of 500,000. Somewhere in the crowd, lurking in the shadows, watching the movement from afar, were James "The Tooth" Kelly and his sidekick, Frankie "The Shanks" Martell, two of the most feared thugs and murderers in Boston's recent history. Both were either directly or indirectly involved in most of the criminal activity that went down in Southie. In 1990 the two controlled, with ruthless terror and intimidation, criminal activity in Boston. With snitches in the private and public sectors scattered all over the city, the two knew, or would eventually find out what was going down in the city's seedy crime world. Jimmy and Frankie, if not privy to a scam, theft, robbery, cheat or bribe, would unfailingly "place the arm" on any criminal wannabe who had the stones to not include them in the spoils of any enterprise. In the end, the two leeches would take, through intimidation or murder, what they believed to be rightfully theirs'.

Chapter Eight: " Who's Telling the Truth?"

Bradley had taken a bankcard and receipts from Fager's wallet, and collected other slips of papers and his license that were on the bench beside him. All of it was placed in a bag to be examined for prints and other forensic analysis. They were going to do the same with Morris. After McGrath assisted in removing the tape and the cuffs, Fager, who was wobbly on his feet when he first stood, was brought to a room in the museum so he could speak with him in private. The Boston officers followed. Trying not to hit their heads on the overhead steam pipes and electrical wires, they helped Fager up the stairs and into a small anteroom close to the guard station. Fager was purposely kept apart from his colleague, who was taken to another room within the museum, where McGrath and Folan would question him later. All personal papers and handcuffs taken from the two guards that had been placed in plastic evidence bags and marked for identification to ensure proper chain of custody were brought to McGrath. Although now with Fager, McGrath decided to interview Morris first. He had no particular reason for doing so; he just decided to go with the first guard who was found. It wasn't lost on the veteran agent that in the immediate aftermath of the commission of a crime, time was of the essence and establishing any early inconsistencies in witnesses' stories was crucial.

McGrath was an absolute pro when it came to questioning witnesses and assessing who was telling the truth. Since Morris was the first to be found he was going to speak to him before Fager. He was anxious to start.

Chapter Nine: "Jimmy The Tooth, Frankie The Shanks And Sal The Clam"

In 1995, James Kelly's mug shot showed up on the FBI's yearly Ten Most Wanted poster. By the time it appeared, the cold-blooded killer was on the run, thanks to a childhood friend, who also happened to be a corrupt agent in the Boston FBI field office. Playing both sides of the street, the agent had leaked word to Jimmy that his arrest was imminent. He fled and has been on the run ever since. The FBI wanted poster puts the home- grown criminal's accomplishments into glowing perspective:

JAMES "THE TOOTH" KELLY WANTED FOR: RACKETEERING INFLUENCED AND CORRUPT ORGANIZATIONS (RICO) - MURDER (18 COUNTS), CONSPIRACY TO COMMIT MURDER, CONSPIRACY TO COMMIT EXTORTION, NARCOTICS DISTRIBUTION, CONSPIRACY TO

**COMMIT MONEY LAUNDERING;
EXTORTION; MONEY LAUNDERING.**

While the Irish residents of Southie were
enjoying the St. Patrick's Day Parade that
included Miss Ireland, Miss South Boston and
McGruff the crime fighting dog riding a
motorcycle, a short distance across town in the
Italian section of the city known as the North
End or "Little Italy," its residents were busy
preparing for the Feast of St. Joseph, celebrated
on the 19th of March. It, too, was a day when an
ethnic group would honor their patron Saint.
Hanover Street, the main artery that transects
the densely populated area was being carefully
decorated with bright red and green streamers
and strategically placed statues of the Madonna.

The tiny neighborhood's narrow streets make a
parking space worth its weight in gold.
Sprinkled among churches, shops and brick
tenements are several historic sites including
Paul Revere's home and the Old North church.
Although predominately Italian, in 1990, just like
Southie, it was becoming the preferred
neighborhood of young urban professionals. It
also continued to be the preferred headquarters
of the La Cosa Nostra in the City of Boston.
Outside the Italian Community Center on Friend
Street, stood a short, white haired man, Sal
DePasquale, known to his friends as Sal "The
Clam"; a consequence of his appetite for clams

zuppa and utter lack of idle conversation. Sal was a man of very few words. He only spoke business on the sidewalk in front of the Center and never, ever on the phone. If what he had to say could hurt him or a member of his organization or assist police in any way, the Clam's mouth would stay shut. He was a devoted practitioner of the "wink and blink" school of communication. Not only quiet, he was also smart and cunning. He was a master at developing alliances with other criminal groups but was brutally swift in meting out severe punishment when anyone crossed him or his organization.

Throughout the years, he had cultivated an opportunistic relationship with Kelly and Martell and in doing so, assured not only his organization's continued existence but also the growth of the trio's combined criminal fiefdom. Although always mindful of the violent history between the Irish and Italian immigrants during the early 1900s, as well as lingering distrust between the two groups, "The Clam" refused to let the past get in the way of his present intent to make money in Boston the old fashioned way: by stealing it. In order to survive as Irish and Italian gangsters had done in other cities, Kelly, Martell and DePasquale had formed a partnership that brought them wealth and power. Just like Kelly or Martell, when any criminal activity of any significance went down in the City of Boston in the year 1990, particularly when it involved money or the path to it, DePasquale, if not involved in the scam, would, without doubt, become an uninvited participant. A visit in the middle of the night would invariably result in a tribute paid to the Clam. The trio had the uncanny ability to learn of and then track down the participants of any criminal activity conducted on the streets of Boston without their blessing. No one in Boston could figure out how the three knew what was going down, what had gone down, when it was going down and by whom. It was as if they had radar; flashing green blips representing cross-town competitors in the business of crime, who, after being threatened with two-in-the hat, would turn into compliant sheep, never again to cross paths with Jimmy, Frankie or the Clam.

On Sunday, March 18, 1990, as the late afternoon sun set in the western sky and as twilight fell over Boston, all three sets of antennae started to twitch as they never had before. In the early morning hours, something big had gone down across town. Real big!

Chapter Ten: "College Rent-A-Cops"

Morris was identified as victim #1 at the scene by the Boston police officers in accordance with the Department's time-line protocol for crime scene investigation. He sat quietly at a desk with McGrath just three feet away across the table. The six foot three college student was clearly terrified. McGrath learned from Folan that he was so frightened by what had taken place during the night that he initially refused to answer any questions put to him. With reassurance that he and his family members would be safe and some artful cajoling from the chameleon-like McGrath, Morris eventually agreed to talk about the night's events.

"I arrived at the museum around 11:00 PM and entered the building from the employee entrance located on Palace Road. I wasn't scheduled to work the night shift. I usually worked the morning hours, but got called in when another guard called in sick, probably from having too much fun on St. Patrick's Day. I was a little bullshit that I got the call to work the overnight shift when I had just left the place. I needed the money so I agreed. My shift started at the guard desk on the first floor. The first thing I did was to make sure each alarm in the building was working." When asked about the alarm system, Morris explained that he understood it to be similar to other museums. "There was a standard protocol in place that we always followed at the beginning of every overnight shift. When the third shift begins, one guard is required to walk through the museum to intentionally set off all the motion detectors in the building. The second guard remains at the guard desk monitoring the computer that would sound each time the motion detectors strategically located throughout the building were tripped. As an alarm sounded, the guard at the desk uses a checklist and checks off whether an alarm is working or not. Fager made the first rounds through the museum, while I monitored the computer. At approximately 1:00 AM, we switched positions. I did the next round and Fager would monitor the computer at the guard desk on the first floor."

He explained to McGrath that the guards who worked the overnight shift weren't really there to prevent a robbery but, rather, were more akin to night watchmen, on site to be vigilant of the museum's other potentially disastrous enemy: fire. "Somewhere between 1:15 AM and 1:20 AM, after completing my rounds and as I walked down the back stairs from the second floor to the first, I received an unexpected call from Fager on my walkie-talkie. He requested that I return to the guard station. When I arrived just seconds later, I was absolutely stunned. I couldn't believe my eyes. Fager was standing behind the desk with two white guys dressed in police uniforms standing on the other side of the desk. As I walked up to them, both identified themselves as Boston police officers. One of them spoke up and said in a very calm voice: 'We have a warrant for your partner's arrest'. Without wasting any time, the shorter of the two, who was standing closest to Fager, asked him to come out from behind the desk and to 'assume the position'. Fager obliged and was then handcuffed without any protest. Without any warning or reason, the other guy then handcuffed me much to my utter amazement and in a nasty tone, said to me, 'take off your shades'. He proceeded to forcibly rip them from my face." Although he didn't ask, McGrath wondered why the college age guard was wearing sunglasses in the first place. "I was in a state of shock and thought to myself, "What is going on here? How did these two guys get in here in the first place? It is a well-known policy that under no circumstances during the 11:00 PM to 7:00 AM shifts were we to let anyone enter the museum, including police officers. I was particularly upset and scared to death since I didn't know if these two guys were in fact Boston police officers or if they were imposters, what their intentions were. I was concerned that they were not real cops and feared that they might hurt or kill us, since, except for what appeared to be fake mustaches worn by them, neither had taken any other steps to disguise their faces."

Morris explained that with both he and Fager secured and away from the only outside alarm in the museum located behind the desk, the shorter of the two, once again in a very calm voice said, "Gentlemen, this is a robbery!" "Although I'm originally from Minnesota," Morris said, "I've been in Boston long enough to know a Boston accent and one of the robbers had a very clear and distinct one." He then went on to describe how the robbers taped his and Fager's eyes, mouths and hands with duct tape.

"After binding my mouth and eyes, I was taken to the basement where my ankles were taped together. Despite the fact my eyes were covered with tape, before I was brought downstairs I realized that the other guy walked Fager down the hallway in the opposite direction and away from me. Because they did that, I never actually saw Fager being brought down into the basement but just assumed he was there too. Before they brought me down they spun me around and stopped several times. I think he was trying to confuse and disorient me. Once he cuffed me to the leg of the sink in the basement he took my wallet. I think he pulled out my driver's license because he said again in a very calm voice, 'Say nothing... we know who you are, where you live and who you hang out with. If you give us no problems, maybe we will let

---

you live."

During the walk downstairs and while taping his mouth shut, Morris explained that the shorter of the two dark-haired men asked him repeatedly if the tape or handcuffs were too tight and whether he could breathe through the tape. "The guy actually seemed to be concerned about my well-being, which was really a welcomed sign. I never saw either one of them with any weapons. They were carrying what looked like police issued, two-way radios that blared constantly. Both guys are probably in their late 30s or early 40s, one taller than the other. They were both of medium build and the taller one seemed to be hunched over slightly, like he had a back problem. He had black shoulder-length hair. It was not the type of haircut that the local neighborhood barber would give. It was fancier. He appeared to be either Eastern European or Italian, and was confident and controlling. His speech bordered on the aggressive and again, he had a definite Boston accent."

"The shorter of the two had dark, short cropped hair and had the appearance of being also of Italian descent. He was very quiet. They both had brown eyes and the shorter one had wire-rimmed glasses." McGrath sat quietly while listening to Morris, taking notes and at the same time, with complete focus on his witness, sizing up this apparent victim of a robbery. When

Morris finally finished his story, McGrath asked him if he had anything else to tell him. He thought for a moment. "While I was in the basement, after being handcuffed to the pole and after he said to me in his Boston accent that he had some work to do upstairs. I could hear what sounded to me like a metal cart being pushed across the floor directly above me. On at least two occasions during my encounters with the guy that handled me that evening, he referred to me as 'Mate'."

The last thing Morris said raised the hairs on the back of McGrath's neck. "Shortly after being brought down into the basement when it became very quiet, it sounded to me like there were definitely more than two people working upstairs." McGrath closed the door behind him leaving Morris sitting at the table. He started to scratch his head trying to take in all that Morris had told him. He couldn't get over the fact that the museum employed college students from schools in the area to protect their priceless works. These knuckleheads are unarmed ornamental slackers of little consequence. Incredible!

McGrath understood that during the day there were always enough visitors and security guards on site to minimize the risk of theft. On the other hand, overnight, when the risk of a robbery increased exponentially, the security consisted of two guards, and one solitary button to summon help in the event of trouble. Both Morris and Fager were students at the school of music located a short distance across town. Morris played the oboe in a quartet and Fager, the steel guitar in a heavy metal band. And, as McGrath just learned from Morris, most if not all of the college age security guards liked to smoke pot! As McGrath started to open the door to the room where Fager sat, Officer Folan already there, he wondered whether museum security conducted criminal background checks on each applicant for employment and if they did, to what extent? "I fucking doubt it. From what I've seen so far, it looks like whoever hired these two midnight tokers blew it big time. Instead of figuring out which college kids might be halfway responsible and actually take the job seriously, the museum appears to have done just the opposite," McGrath thought to himself.

Chapter Eleven: "The Buzzed Rocker"

Introducing himself, McGrath pulled up a chair, put his feet up on the desk and asked Fager, who grew up in New Jersey, what happened. While McGrath took notes, Fager started to tell his story. "Between 12:30 AM and 1:00 AM I was conducting my usual rounds when I needed to

respond to several alarms sounding in the
building. My partner contacted me by radio to
tell me that one of the alarms was from a smoke
detector that had gone off in the main building."

"The smoke detector alarm sounding at
approximately 12:44 AM was unusual, the others
were not. Once I dealt with the alarms and
figured out there was no fire, I continued with
my rounds and returned to the guard station to
relieve Morris. I took my seat at the guard desk
and when I glanced up at the security monitor I
noticed headlights that seemed to be coming
from a vehicle parked on Palace Road. The black
and white monitor displays four separate views
of the exterior of the building. The headlights
were in the lower left quadrant of the screen. I
continued to watch the monitor and then noticed
two white dudes dressed in what looked like
police uniforms walk in front of the headlights
and then towards the employee entrance. I
looked at the monitor panning the main entrance
and saw no one at or near it. While I continued
to look up at the monitor, the doorbell located
right outside where I was sitting, rang twice."

Although the side entrance was equipped with
an intercom, when asked if he used it, McGrath
was stunned to hear his response: "I did not use
it and never even asked them to place their
credentials up to the closed circuit monitor to
determine if they were, in fact, Boston police

officers. I was really spooked!" Fager had done none of this despite the fact that, as McGrath had just learned from Morris, it was standard operating procedure, known by all of the guards who worked the 11:00 PM to 7:00 AM shift, not to allow anyone into the museum, including police. "Without any apparent thought of the consequences for doing so, this nitwit pushed the buzzer to let these two guys in," McGrath thought to himself. "As the two of them stood across from me, I glanced at the watch desk clock that read 1:24 AM. The one and only alarm wired to the Boston police was located behind the chest high security desk and could only be seen when sitting or standing behind it. They told me they were responding to a call about a complaint of kids creating a disturbance outside the museum. I told them that my partner and I, had been watching the security monitors and that neither one of us had seen anyone outside the building, let alone anyone causing a disturbance."

Chapter Twelve: "What A Disaster"

Walking into the Dutch Gallery, McGrath couldn't believe how massive it was and how many people were now in it. It looked like the room had been hit by a tornado. The scene was very chaotic. His eyes quickly surveyed the entire room. A yellow crime scene tape had already been set up. Starting at the entrance, it meandered some fifty feet across the brick, tiled floor all the way to the left, front corner. On the floor in the right rear corner, was a large frame with a smaller frame leaning up against it. Pieces of broken glass lay scattered next to both. He then noticed a large panel at the back of the room that appeared to have been pushed open from the other side, three upholstered chairs leaning against the bottom of it. He found that curious and made a mental note to himself to put it in his notebook. On a table in the center of the room, somewhat to the left of where the frames lay on the floor, a tiny frame lay on its side. To the left of that table, he could see another large frame on the floor. Just in front of that frame was yet another smaller frame with shards of glass scattered about it. "What a fucking disaster," he found himself saying out loud. He walked over to Officer Folan to be briefed. Folan explained that museum staff had made the dreadful discovery that the canvasses from the two large frames were gone. They both then walked over to where the frames were scattered on the floor. Folan explained that museum conservators had made the dreadful discovery that the canvases from the two large frames were gone. Bending over to take a look at one, McGrath could see jagged edges of canvas around the interior of the frame. He also noticed what looked like dried paint or paint chips sprinkled about it. It was blatantly apparent that someone had taken a knife and cut the paintings from the frames. From the looks of what was left behind, he thought to himself, "Whoever did this was either in a hurry or didn't give a flying fuck about the paintings." He turned to Folan and asked, "What was in this?" as he pointed to the frame with the paint chips scattered on the floor as well as about the frame itself. Folan looked over to him and replied, "I'm not really sure. I think one of the museum guys said it was 'The Storm on the Sea of Galilee'."

"How about the other?" McGrath asked. "I don't have a fucking clue." As Folan and McGrath stood near the two large frames, the museum's long time Conservator, Charles Viser, walked over to them and shook their hands. "Your assistance is greatly appreciated. Everyone is in a state of shock. I have been the museum's Conservator for thirty-two years. Along with my two assistants, I examine, repair, and conserve Mrs. Gardner's paintings and objects of art. Since many of the paintings are centuries old and are considered priceless works, we inspect them constantly to determine if any are in need of repair. Our ultimate goal is to make absolutely sure that the collection is preserved for future generations."

With pain in his eyes, he looked squarely at McGrath and Folan and said, "Regrettably gentlemen, based upon my staff's preliminary inventory, there are six pieces missing from this one room alone: Vermeer's 'The Concert', Rembrandt's 'A Lady and Gentleman in Black', and 'The Storm on the Sea of Galilee', as well as his self-portrait, Flinck's 'Landscape with an Obelisk', and a Chinese bronze beaker or 'Ku' from the Shang Dynasty. Five Degas drawings are missing from the Short Room. Manet's 'Chez Tortoni' is missing from the Blue Room located on the first floor." Pointing to the panel that jutted several feet into the room, right behind where the two large frames lay on the floor, McGrath asked, "What's that?" Viser, a scholarly-looking short man wearing a bow tie and tweed jacket, explained in a pronounced French accent, "It is the private entrance to the gallery, one that is never used by the public. Only museum employees know that it's here and there is no reason for anyone to use it unless they work with me in the conservation laboratory," as he pointed towards the interior of the tapestry panel. Peeking behind it, McGrath could see two wooden doors both, wide open. Stepping back and gesturing up at a well-defined area on the panel, he asked, "Did a painting hang here?" Viser turned, looked towards and pointed to the larger of the two frames now at their feet and replied, "Yes, the 'Storm on the Sea of Galilee'. Rembrandt painted it in 1633. As you can see the only thing left now, is the frame, the stretch and jagged edges of the canvas."

The Director of Security, Lyle Harrison, who had been working non-stop with Viser to determine what was missing, approached McGrath and introduced himself. "Agent McGrath, I would like to show you something in the Short Gallery, located right down the Hall." They walked out and into the Tapestry Room and then into the Short Gallery. Harrison walked over to a wood paneled wall, located on the right side of the room. He pointed to the spot where the five works by Degas had been taken from the two frames.

McGrath could see where they had been due to the dark colored rectangle shapes left on the wooden wall, those areas having been shielded from sunlight. He also saw that the frame closest to the floor, although broken, was still attached to the wall, hanging from its mount. There was glass on the floor directly below that frame and as McGrath crouched down, he could see that the glass that had covered the prints was shattered.

With the help of his flashlight, McGrath continued to survey the floor, and spotted two screws-one brass, one steel. He also found a small yellow tag near a fire extinguisher. He had the police photographer take photographs of the area and of the two screws and yellow tag. Then, putting on his evidence gloves, he picked each one up, placed them in individual plastic evidence bags and marked them accordingly, always concerned about chain of custody of evidence for trials. Harrison explained that similar yellow seals were on all of the fire extinguishers throughout the museum. They were used to secure the safety pins in the extinguishers. They both then looked down at the one in front of them hanging on the wall and could see that the pin had been pulled halfway out from the safety lock. He made a note of this in his little spiral notebook as well as a note about the secret panel door he saw in the Dutch Room. Harrison then brought McGrath down to the first floor and into the Blue Room.

He again walked over to a wall, this time on the right side of the room. Standing in front of the table, he pointed to a spot where a painting had once hung. McGrath could once again see where the painting had been due to the lack of discoloration of the blue-striped wallpaper. On the table directly below, the two noticed a solitary screw and one piece of white plastic tubing. Both items were photographed and placed in evidence bags. Before they left the room, Harrison turned to McGrath and said, "The painting that was in that frame, Manet's 'Chez Tortoni', is missing, but we found the

frame sitting on a chair in my assistant's office
next to the security desk."

Chapter Thirteen: "The Ruse"

Fager continued with his story. "As soon as the
last word came out of my mouth, one of the
'cops' said to me, 'You look familiar, don't I
know you?' He then ordered me to come out
from behind the desk and told me that there was
an outstanding warrant out of the Boston
Municipal Court for my arrest. He told me to
place my hands on the wall and to stand away
from the desk. The shorter of the two then
clicked a handcuff onto my left wrist and asked
about the whereabouts of my partner and
whether anyone other than the two of us was in
the building. I told him that my partner was
doing his rounds upstairs, and that we were the
only two in the building. They then told me to
radio the other guard to ask him to come down
to the guard desk. I did what I was told. When
Morris arrived, they also cuffed him, told both of
us this was a robbery, and if we cooperated no
harm would come to us. 'Don't tell them
anything', one of them said, 'and in about a year
you will get a piece of the reward.' Before
bringing us downstairs, they took our drivers'
licenses from our wallets and then one of the

robbers said in a very threatening tone, 'We know who you are and where you live'."

While he listened, McGrath noticed that, unlike Morris, the shaggy haired rock star wannabe told his story very calmly and without any apparent concern for his personal safety after having been warned by the robbers of the consequences if he cooperated with the police. "This kid seems to be unfazed by this whole ordeal. He either doesn't care about what happened or knew that it was going to happen," McGrath thought to himself. "The guy that handled me was white and I really can't guess his age. I would say that he was about 5' 8" tall, medium build, about 170 lbs., medium complexion. He had dark eyes and black hair. He was wearing an obvious fake, black mustache. He wore gold colored, square, wire-rimmed glasses and a dark, blue nylon jacket with what appeared to be a police patch on the right shoulder. He had a badge pinned to the left breast-side of the jacket and was wearing a light blue shirt, with two round red and blue enameled pins on each collar. I noticed that the pin on the left side of the shirt had a bronze star in its center. That suspect also wore a black tie with dark blue pants, a light blue stripe running down the side of the pant leg."

When asked about suspect #2, Fager replied, "He was taller than the other guy, and was clean-shaven." He could provide McGrath with no additional identifying characteristics, much to the astonishment of the seasoned agent. When pressed, Fager explained to McGrath that suspect #2 reminded him of a character from a popular 1970s television show that popped up occasionally on late night reruns. "I can't remember the actor's name or the name of the show, but I think it was a sitcom about American and British prisoners of war held in a prison camp." McGrath made a note of that and then asked Fager if he could tell him anything else about the two thieves. His response got McGrath's attention. "I think they communicated by walkie-talkie and spoke in code, using numbers." McGrath thought, "That's odd, one of the robbers was with Fager only for a very short period of time while upstairs and in the basement. How was he able to hear any communications between the two thieves on the radios?"

He thanked Fager and then started to walk out of the room when he turned abruptly and asked whether the alarms were wired to an off-site location to alert security or police. Fager told him that only certain people in the museum, including himself, knew that the alarms were not wired to the police or an outside security company. As he walked down the corridor, McGrath stopped, looked down at his notes of his interview with Morris and read what he had jotted down in his spiral notebook: "Radios attached to robbers' belts, suspect #1 speaking into radio...could hear voices on police radio...talking in numbers... in code...too loud... turned radio off. He also wrote, "Did the thieves know that the motion alarms being recorded by the computer were not being reported to police? If yes, how did they? Public does not know the location of the security video recorder. How did the robbers know where it was located?"

Chapter Fourteen: "The Belle of Boston and the Collection"

McGrath arrived early at the museum the next morning and went directly to the Dutch Room. Before he'd left the day before he stopped at the museum's bookstore and skimmed through a book about the museum and its creator, Isabella Stewart Gardner, the "Belle of Boston." He learned that three floors of galleries surround a glass-covered garden courtyard. Isabella used the fourth floor of the building as living quarters until her death in 1924. In keeping with her promise to make it a world-class museum, at the time of her death, she had compiled an astonishing 70 pieces, including works by Rembrandt, Titian, Vermeer, Michelangelo, Degas, Whistler, and Sargent, all on exhibition for the people of Boston and its visitors. Gardner died quietly at 10:49 PM on July 17, 1924, at the age of eighty-five. In her Last Will and Testament, she declared that Fenway Court was created "as a museum for the education and enjoyment of the public forever". In fact, directly above the museum's main entrance, she had masons inscribe the words: "C'EST MON PLAISIR" or "IT IS MY PLEASURE". Her only request: "maintain the museum and its contents exactly as it exists at the time of death," a snapshot of the museum with all its treasures meticulously placed by Isabella, forever frozen in time.

McGrath shook hands with Folan who explained that the assistant director of security along with several others had made a very detailed examination of the museum overnight. In doing so, they discovered two pieces of antique furniture whose locked drawers had been forced open. However, nothing was in them so nothing was taken. Closer scrutiny of the Short Gallery established that a silk, Napoleonic flag encased in a large swinging glass-enclosed iron frame had been tampered with. In order to simulate a flagpole, a gold plated, bronze eagle, known as a finial, had been placed at the top left corner of the frame by museum staff. It was now missing. Six long steel screws were also found in a small bucket of sand next to the fire extinguisher in the Short Gallery that McGrath and Harrison had inspected the day before. The screws were consistent with those that secured the iron frame above, and in fact the number found corresponded to the number of bolts missing from the frame.

A closer look by McGrath also found that one screw was halfway out of the frame, but still firmly attached to it. The robbers apparently gave up trying to remove it. McGrath then walked over to Harrison and asked him about the flag and the eagle that had been taken. Harrison explained that the eagle was a gilded metal imperial eagle that was about 9 inches high and approximately 7 inches wide. It was perched on a slab depicting the number 1 that represented the regiment to which the eagle belonged. The eagles were made to imitate the design of the seal of Napoleon's empire and were issued to various regiments of the Imperial Army after 1804. The eagle, Harrison further explained, became more important than the flag that was given to General Petit by Napoleon in 1814. What he said next blew McGrath away.

"Napoleon's flag has been an item of controversy between the French government and the City of Boston since at least the end of the Second World War. The French wanted it back and the museum refused to give it back." McGrath and Harrison then started to walk back upstairs to the Dutch Room. While they walked along,

McGrath made a note in his notebook, "Possible French connection?"

He then asked Harrison if he had any early theories about the robbery. He responded, "Whoever did this knew what they were looking for. It appears they spent little if no time on the third and fourth floors and apparently focused on paintings on the first two. They also seemed to be primarily interested in the Dutch masters. If I had to guess at this point, I think they had a checklist for the artwork. I say that because they bypassed too many important paintings, including: Titian's 'Rape of Europa'; Allesandro Botticelli's, 'Madonna and Child of the Eucharist'; 'The Tragedy of Lucretia'; Giovanni Bellini's 'Madonna and Child' and Loschi Giorgione's 'Christ Bearing the Cross'."

"Because they skipped some works and took others, I think they probably had a shopping list. I don't believe they were art experts or art thieves. If they were, the two Rembrandts would never have been cut from their frames. I think they knew what they wanted and based on what they did in the Dutch Room, I would guess that they were probably just two common thieves or run of the mill bank robbers who were hired by someone who knew what they wanted based on their own personal knowledge and expertise of rare paintings and art." They definitely stayed away from the Italians. Their focus was obviously directed at the French and Dutch masters."

"Can I ask you something else, and please don't take offense at my question, please understand that I know nothing about art or paintings. Why are these paintings so important? Is there one that stands out from the others such that someone would want to steal it because of its value? I realize all of the pieces in this museum are of great value but is there one that stands alone? I've obviously heard of Rembrandt. Were his two paintings and his self-portrait the most valuable pieces taken?"

Harrison, not at all offended by the questions, said "Believe it or not, Rembrandt's paintings and self-portrait, at least as far as I'm concerned, weren't the most valuable pieces taken. 'The Concert' was and I'll tell you why. It all has to do with basic supply and demand. As far as we know, there were only thirty-two paintings done by Jan Vermeer and the one taken from us, in my opinion, in terms of value, is truly incalculable. Don't get me wrong, the Rembrandts have great value, but when you have only thirty-two paintings in the entire world, of a Dutch master like Vermeer, you really cannot put a price on any one, particularly 'The Concert'. All of them are considered to be technically perfect."

"Do you have any photographs of 'The Concert'," McGrath asked. "Absolutely, they're downstairs in my office. We can take a walk down." As they walked down the stairs, Harrison continued. "Let me give you an example of the value of Vermeer's work. When the Museum of Fine Arts here in Boston exhibited some of Vermeer's works, including 'The Concert,' in 1984, the museum's Curator was quoted as saying that its appraised value was one of the highest that had ever been put on a painting."

The two entered his basement office and sat down, Harrison still speaking. Opening a file drawer in the cluttered room, he removed a folder. "Notwithstanding its enormous value, 'The Concert' also has a sentimental connection to this museum because it was one of Mrs. Gardner's earliest. She purchased it in 1892, when Vermeer was a relative unknown and not particularly appreciated or valued as an artist. In fact, there is a rather humorous story behind its purchase. Mrs. Gardner and her husband, Jack, just happened to be in Paris when the 'The Concert' was placed on the selling block at the Hotel Drouot, an auction house. Two mega museums at the time, the National Gallery in London and the Louvre in Paris it is believed, were both determined to acquire it for their collections."

"The story goes that the National Gallery's delegate was under the impression that the Gardner's agent was from the Louvre, and the Louvre's straw, thought he was from the National. As a result, the two refused to continue to bid against one another. In those days, museums didn't spar for paintings, as they are prone to do today. Mrs. Gardner made out on the deal and bought 'The Concert', for the equivalent of $6,000. Before she died in 1924, the value of the Vermeer had escalated to $200,000." As he handed McGrath a photo, he asked, "Can you now see why its recovery is so important to the art world and to this museum in particular?" It was a photo of "The Concert".

His first impression: very simple, not busy. A man with his back to the viewer plays the lute. He is with two young women in what appears to be a small room with a black and white, checkered floor. The woman standing to the right appears to be singing while she glances down at a piece of paper she holds in her left hand. The other plays the harpsichord. Sunlight, coming from the left, shines through a window out of view, casting light upon the room and its occupants. The instruments are being played with fine, delicately painted hands.

As he handed the photo back to Harrison, the director said, in a sad tone, "I'm sorry to say that this is not the only important Vermeer that has been stolen. Unfortunately, 'The Concert' is now the third." Pulling out another file from the same file cabinet, he handed another photo to McGrath, "The Storm on the Sea of Galilee". As soon as he saw it, his immediate thought: total chaos; compared with the quiet, controlled, tranquil setting of the Vermeer. It was Nature in all its unchecked fury. As he looked at it, Harrison gave him some history. "It is believed to be Rembrandt's only seascape. He painted it in 1633 and used oil paint on canvas. The storm depicted is referenced at least three times in the Bible. In Mark 4:37, it is described as "a furious storm that came up as the waves broke over the boat. Luke and Matthew describe the rain during the storm that "came upon a calm sea without warning."

In the painting, a tiny vessel is being pounded by the wind and rain; white water from the ocean's spray engulfing the boat; Jesus is seated at the stern, and unlike his crew mates the twelve Apostles, he seems oblivious to the maelstrom and their inevitable drowning. The Apostles are working the sails and rigging to keep the vessel afloat. One is seasick as he leans over the port side rail in an involuntary retch.

Taking the photograph from McGrath, Harrison grabbed a magnifying glass from his drawer and handed it to McGrath. "Ted look at the rudder. Do you see his signature?" "Yes I do," he responded. "He may have been a great painter, but apparently, was not a good speller." McGrath, trying to get better focus moved the monocle closer to the photograph. "How is it spelled?" "It looks like 'Rembrant', he must have been in a hurry because he forgot the letter 'd'." Harrison was not finished.

"See the little guy in front. Do you know who that is? It's Rembrandt! He put himself in the painting." With obvious pain in his eyes as he looked down at the photo, Harrison lamented, "Sadly, I can't help but make the comparison between this horrible robbery in the quiet early morning hours to Luke and Matthew's description of the storm that came upon a calm sea without warning."

Chapter Fifteen: "The Glove"

While McGrath was talking with Harrison, the Bureau's longtime fingerprint examiner, agent Amy Maher, was carefully dusting the left front face of the VCR located near the security desk. She was a real professional and extremely meticulous. If prints were at a crime scene, agent Maher would, without any doubt, find them. When the silvery powder began to adhere to the surface, a clear, discernible print started to appear. Based upon its size, she believed it to be from a male subject. Taking her camera, designed specifically for close-up shots requiring detail and contrast, Maher quickly snapped photographs of the print, rotating the camera to obtain views from several angles. The photos would eventually be downloaded back at her office. Maher's computer was connected to the FBI's high-tech forensic laboratory in Washington, D.C. where the prints would ultimately be submitted to the worldwide Automated Fingerprint Identification System, or AFIS.

She next turned her attention to the upper surface of the recorder that had been tampered with and dusted for prints at the left rear edge, approximately 3 inches from the middle. Although a print was evident, it was smudged to such an extent that she could not discern any identifiable ridges, making it of little or no consequence. She then carried her kit up to the Dutch Room, where she was asked to dust the knob of the door located behind the private, concealed entrance to the room. Taking her head-mounted ultraviolet light from its case, she put it on and then, with her right hand, directed the narrow beam of high frequency light down towards the brass knob.

Dusting it with her left hand, ever so lightly, trying to avoid smudging any potential latent prints, Maher continued with the delicate process. She tried to place enough of the light-sensitive powder on the doorknob, sufficient to identify any evidence that might be present on the surface. It was always a delicate procedure. If done properly, with positive physical findings, she knew that fingerprints could be critical to a crime scene investigation, and obviously, extremely helpful in solving a case. Crouching down towards the doorknob in an arching motion, the light reflecting off the ornate brass fixture, the experienced crime scene analyst could make out a faint but nevertheless recognizable print. Based on its characteristics, it also appeared to be from a male subject. Maher painstakingly and methodically photographed the print. While doing so, out of the right corner of her eye, she noticed a faint, but yet, visible smudge below the thumbprint. Focusing in on it, she saw what appeared to be a small print.

It was located on the inner, back portion of the doorknob, like the shaded underside of a mushroom. She hadn't dusted the back of the knob, but it was fortuitous that some of the fine powder had found its way to the spot where the print appeared. She believed it to be consistent with the thumbprint and was of the opinion, based upon her initial observations, that it was the print of someone's index finger. She again took photos of the print, packed her equipment and was anxious to head back to her laboratory to enter the digital pictures into her computer.

Chapter Sixteen
FBI Headquarters, Boston, May 7, 2007

Since that day in March 1990 when agent McGrath first walked into the Gardner museum, seventeen springs and summers had come and gone. In those many years, he was proud of some things and not so proud of others. He had put his two daughters and son through college, divorced his wife of thirty years, gained thirty pounds, survived a bout with prostate cancer, and, last but not least, hadn't solved the Gardner robbery. With just months left before he retired, McGrath had been relegated to a desk job at FBI headquarters in Boston. In 1990, when the robbery took place, he had a full head of black hair; what was left of it was now white. Occasionally, if he were lucky, one of the younger agents would take him along for the ride when a bank robbery call came in. Most of his time, though, was spent working unsolved "cold cases" assigned to him by the SAC, Special Agent in Charge Paul M. Leary. He didn't mind the desk job, because it involved no heavy lifting and his desk was close to the men's room.

As he sat at his desk, surrounded by a cubicle covered with wanted posters, photos of missing items, crime scene photographs and a world map with little plastic colored pins spotted across it, he took out his list of cold cases from his desk drawer. This was his routine every morning. He was like clockwork. Stop at the coffee shop located in the basement of the building; say hello to Norm, the shop's owner, buy the *Boston Herald*; take the elevator up two flights; sit down at his desk and read the paper. Once finished with the *Herald's* Jumble, he would knot his tie, the ends of which, when he arrived every morning, dangled loosely around his shirt collar. He would then take out his dog-eared cold case list and just stare at it. There were thirteen cases on the list. Some had been on the list for five years; one had been on the list for what felt like eternity. They included bank robberies, child kidnappings and abductions across state lines, threats sent by United States mail to several of the local cantankerous federal judges, and one art robbery.

In the seventeen years since the robbery, McGrath had traveled across the country as well as to Europe, South America, and Asia to follow leads concerning the Gardner theft. His failure to solve the case and return the artwork to the museum where it belonged was not due to a lack of effort. The problem had been, and continued to be, that when either McGrath or one of his fellow agents followed up on a lead, astonishingly, nothing ever panned out. Having that happen for seventeen years was too much for him to take.

In one capacity or another, agents from all fifty-six FBI offices scattered throughout the country, had been involved in the investigation. McGrath's coffee stained passports were a testament to his leaving no stone unturned when a potential lead came in. They were stamped with many foreign destinations including Japan, Ireland, Spain, France, Mexico and Italy. McGrath had no clue how many American cities and towns he had landed in. He had received hundreds of leads by mail, all of which he reviewed and pursued until they were inevitably proven of no significance. Shortly after the robbery, when there were very few leads and the investigation started to stall, the Bureau established a hotline specifically for any information that could lead to the recovery of the stolen art. McGrath handled each one of those calls or referred them to the appropriate field office and pursued any he thought had promise.

He had interviewed hundreds of people, including murderers, con-men, egomaniacs, lunatics, convicted felons and their widows, art collectors, art recovery experts, known art thieves, and bank robbers; all to no avail. Seventeen years after the robbery, McGrath was no closer to solving the robbery than he was when he walked into the museum through the Palace Road entrance on a miserable, rainy morning in March 1990. Calls still came in through the Bureau's 800 number, but as had been the case for seventeen long years, nothing. It was as if the paintings had vanished from the face of the earth. He was stuck in neutral with his cold cases getting colder and colder by the minute and had basically thrown in the towel. As he tossed the list on his desk, he got up and walked slowly towards the men's room. Again, part of his morning routine.

When he returned after a meeting downstairs, he picked up the list and placed it back in his desk drawer. Looking up at the clock, he was pleasantly surprised that he had only forty-five minutes before lunch. He was very happy about that. Since his job was a bore and he was going to retire soon anyway, he didn't have a lot of spring in his walk or much fire in his belly to work the cold cases, including the Gardner robbery.

Each morning when he arrived at work, instead of sitting down focusing on and dissecting each of the investigatory leads developed by him and countless other agents over the years in the attempt to determine if anyone had missed or overlooked something, he was focused on what he was going to have for lunch. It was in fact, the highlight of his day.

He always knew what he was going to have to drink at lunch, two pints of Guinness, but never knew what daily special was going to surprise him. Today he hoped bangers and mash was on the menu. He couldn't wait to walk across City Hall Plaza and down into the North End to his favorite watering hole, the Chart House. On occasion, he would stop for a brief moment on the way to watch the seasoned shuckers in their white aprons at the nearby Union Oyster House, shucking oysters and littlenecks with incredible rapid, surgical precision. Tony, the bartender at the Chart House, as was always the case, would take care of him, placing the dark-colored stout on the bar before McGrath's sizable backside even touched the bar stool.

Tony, with his Irish brogue, always had a smile and a quick joke and didn't give a rat's ass that McGrath was a failure as a cop. As long as he paid his tab, he was all right to the barkeep. To McGrath, sitting at the dimly lit, dark mahogany wood and copper bar, dented and pitted from endless bottles and glasses placed upon it since it opened in 1957, was without a doubt a lot better than sitting at your desk with that

constant thought in your head that as a crime
solver, you were a miserable failure.

Many an afternoon, as he sat at the bar
ruminating, he would, as many of Hibernian
descent often do, reflect upon the past and
whether he was in fact, a failure. From the day
he buried his mother, some eight years before
his father passed, he tormented himself by
questioning his success or failure as a father,
husband and cop. His greatest question: had he
made his parents proud. He didn't want to
know the answer, but knew, in his heart, what it
was.

Edward "Teddy" McGrath was the second child
born to Patrick and Helen McGrath. His older
brother Tom was born two years before. They
grew up in Patrick's childhood home, a three-
decker located on W. 3rd Street in South Boston.
The house was left to Pat by Ted's grandparents,
Patrick McGrath and Mary Lee, both born in the
small village of Rosmuc located in the heart of
the Connemara Gaeltacht, County Galway,
Ireland.

Patrick and Helen were fluent in the ancient
language of the Irish and during summer
vacations had sent both boys to live with Helen's
sister, Margaret in Ireland, to learn to read and
speak Irish. As a young boy, Ted's Dad worked
at Sydney Factor's Market on the corner of F and
3rd Street, where he first met Jimmy "The

Tooth" Kelly who would become one of the most feared murderers in Southie's history. Patrick and his wife Helen had a very strong work ethic and instilled that value in their two sons. The boys learned at a young age that the world owed them nothing and that hard work and perseverance were the keys to success; with a dash of luck thrown in to help!

Patrick and Helen had met in grammar school and became childhood sweethearts. They married shortly after graduating from South Boston High School. Patrick, following in his father's footsteps, became a union longshoreman, working the docks of South Boston. With hands of steel, a vice-like grip and an intimidating physical presence, no one in South Boston dared cross him, including Jimmy "The Tooth".

Wanting better for his boys, he held a second job driving rigs for Teamsters Local 25. As soon as Ted was old enough to understand what his Dad did for work, he realized that Patrick and his union brothers considered union books, Badges of Honor. Like her husband, in order to supplement the family's income, Helen worked as a cleaning lady at the Suffolk County courthouse in Boston. Mopping the marble floors at Pemberton Place, while justice was being dispensed, she would admire the stylishly dressed lawyers in their fine suits, silk ties and monogrammed, cuff-linked shirts. As she watched them in the courtrooms and elegant, stately corridors with their clients, she hoped that one day her boys would become successful lawyers.

Chapter Seventeen: "The Intern"

As McGrath was walking toward the elevator anticipating lunch, he bumped into agent Fred Massano, the coordinator of the summer internship program at the Boston Bureau. Every summer, from May through the end of August, for the past ten years, the Boston office had offered second year law students the opportunity to work as unpaid legal interns. They were assigned to various agents for the summer to perform basic research.

"Hey Mac," Massano called out, "the interns are all meeting in the library in fifteen minutes. Yours is from Georgetown and I hear she's a real whippersnapper." Massano teased him because he knew that McGrath hated to deal with the summer interns. He referred to them as those smart-ass, wet-behind-the-ears, pain-in-the-ass, know-it-alls. When Massano's words finally registered with the neurons in McGrath's brain, he lost all facial expression and glared at his colleague. With the Chart House now out of the

question, he would have to get a two day old
baloney sandwich from Norm downstairs, smear
it with yellow mustard in order to make it
halfway palatable and eat it with the interns in
the library. His head started to throb. He was not
pleased! For the past ten years, McGrath had a
way of dealing with, or more precisely a way of
not dealing with, the intern assigned to him. He
would have each one of them spend the six to
eight weeks organizing the twelve bankers'
boxes that contained all of the evidence and
investigatory material from the Gardner theft. In
fact, the Gardner files were probably the most
organized files of any investigation within the
Bureau. His interns had serialized the
documents, tabbed all sub-files and created a
master file with a table of contents that read like
a history of the investigation.

Not once or twice, but every summer he was
assigned a law student. As was also the case for
the past ten summers, before organizing the files
again, his lucky intern would have to blow the
dust from the boxes stacked almost to the ceiling
in an archive room located in the basement of
the building. As an inside joke, on the first day
they arrived at the Bureau, McGrath always
provided each of his interns with a fully charged
flashlight. As he walked into the Bureau's library
located on the sixth floor, Massano greeted him.
"Would Katharine Savage please come
forward?" This was how each intern met their

agent for the first time. All sixty students would be seated in the library and when their name was called they would come to the front where they would be formally introduced to their summer mentor. It reminded him of a cattle auction.

McGrath hated the way the Bureau handled this and he found it to be very awkward. He didn't want an intern anyway and to be subjected to this routine every summer was punishment beyond belief. As he stood there thinking to himself what kind of nitwit the powers-that-be were going to stick him with this year, he noticed a brunette who appeared to be in her late twenties approaching the podium at the front of the library.

She was older than the other interns that had been assigned to him in prior years. In addition to how attractive she was, with her freckled nose and green eyes, he also noticed that she walked with a determined stride. She was someone with a purpose. Sticking out her hand to Massano, she introduced herself as Katie Savage and told him she was a second year student at Georgetown Law. McGrath noticed that she was very direct in her speech; "a no-nonsense kid," he thought to himself. Massano then turned to McGrath and introduced him to Savage who shook his hand with a firm grip. A small, cute smile came across her face. "It's a pleasure meeting you agent

McGrath. I look forward to working with you this summer." He forced a brief smile and welcomed her with his usual lack of warmth. He told her to gather the packet of materials that each of the interns had received that morning and directed her to meet him at his office on the second floor. "It's cubicle 214, directly across from the men's room."

Savage seemed pleased and very eager to start, much to the chagrin of the soon-to-be-retired agent. As she walked away, he thought to himself, "Here we go again, another 'smart ass, know-it-all' this summer." He threw the remnants of his crusty baloney sandwich in the wastebasket, wiped some mustard from his mouth with his sleeve and walked out the door of the library. Once she arrived at his desk, McGrath, tongue in cheek, started to explain to Katharine that she would be working on the most important case in the Bureau's Boston office, the robbery of the Isabella Stewart Gardner museum. He had his orientation speech down to a science.

Memorized since the time he had met with his first intern, it rolled off his tongue, with utter ease- it was always the same. He told them a little bit about the case, the investigation and how the Bureau needed their help in organizing the Gardner files. Organized files, as he always pointed out, clearing his throat as he did so, "were critical to every investigation." Of course, he failed to tell any of them, including Savage, one important fact: the files were already the best organized, serialized, compartmentalized, collated and coordinated files in the entire building.

When it really came down to it, it was just another way of him telling his summer interns to leave him alone while they were here, without him having to say, "Why don't you go play in traffic?" While giving his rote speech to Savage, he noticed that she sat straight back in her chair, writing down everything he said on her legal pad in her lap. She was focused on his every word, seemingly not wanting to miss one syllable. A very brief, transient thought of self-disgust momentarily filtered through the overweight agent's conscience. He thought to himself, "This kid really believes what I'm telling her about how important this case is to the Bureau and how equally important her work this summer will be to me." Although she seemed excited and eager and a little more mature than his prior interns, McGrath nevertheless, gave her the same assignment he had given all of his prior interns for the summer: organizing the dust coated Gardner robbery files. As she got up to leave and started to walk away, he called out her name and when she turned around, tossed her the traditional

McGrath summer flashlight, "You might need this."

Chapter Eighteen: "The Gardner Files"

Savage walked into the dimly lit storage room in the basement trying to get her bearings. She thought to herself, "McGrath really meant what he said about the flashlight." Everywhere she looked there were banker's boxes stacked on top of navy grey shelves. McGrath mentioned to her that the Gardner files were located at the far left-hand corner of the room. As she walked through the stacks, the dusty, yellow beam of light bounced off the boxes stacked to the ceiling. She walked to the back of the room and then, saw the name on the side of a box "GARDNER". She couldn't believe they had been sitting here in this dark, chilly space for years. When the robbery took place, she figured she was in grammar school. They were numbered one through twelve. She picked up box number one, placed the flashlight on top of it, walked back towards the door, and dropped it on a small table that had a light dangling above it. Catching her breath, she brushed the dust off her blouse and opened the box. She could see that the files were in good order. Each had a table of contents that listed the contents and numerically identified where a particular document was tabbed.

After looking through it she was somewhat befuddled why McGrath had given her the task of organizing the files when, to her thinking, they looked like they were already in great shape. As she continued to go through more of the boxes, she found that just like box #1, every box seemed to be impeccably organized, clearly not requiring any additional input from her. On Friday morning, after having gone through more boxes and coming to the identical conclusion that all were in tremendous shape, she decided to stop by to see McGrath to ask him if she could do something other than organize the files. As she stepped around the corner of McGrath's cubicle, there he was busy working on the day's Jumble, remnants of his morning cruller down the front of his shirt and on his desk. Looking up at her from behind his finger smudged reading glasses, he said, "Good morning Katharine, how are you making out with those Gardner files?"

"That's what I want to talk with you about. I've now gone through five of the boxes and it appears to me that they are already extremely well organized. From what I've seen of the five, I'm confident that the rest of them are going to be in the same shape. Is there something else I could do on the Gardner case?" Although obviously perturbed by the request, he had to think fast in order to come up with some cock and bull story. "I'm sorry, Katharine. Every summer, my intern organizes those files. I have them do it to make sure that when we need the files, that is, once we make an arrest, we will be in a great position to know where exactly every piece of paper is. It may not seem important or glamorous to you, but it really is." Disappointed, Savage replied, "Alright, if it's that important, then I'll just continue to go through them." As she walked away, McGrath, relieved, thought to himself, "Well I just took care of her for a while." He then went back to the Jumble puzzle.

Days later, flustered and frankly annoyed with McGrath, Savage was almost ready to leave for the night when she just stopped going through the box she was working on. It was box #12. She had had enough! "I can't spend the entire summer doing this no-mind, fool's errand." She walked over to box #1and opened it. The first document she removed appeared to be a chronological summary of what the Bureau had done since the day of the robbery. It was twenty-two pages long. Sitting on the concrete floor, her back up against the bottom of a shelf, she noticed that there were reference numbers for each file.

"Wow, he was right, someone really must have spent some time organizing these files!" Gardner

1-subset-A appeared to be a list of the names and addresses of all persons FBI agents had interviewed about the robbery. It was very detailed and consisted of eight pages. Along with the name and address, it contained a summary of information provided by the party of interest, along with an opinion by an agent whether that individual continued to be a potential target.

There were one hundred and twenty six names on the list. None of them, as Savage saw from what appeared to be a hand-written note from McGrath, had ever received a formal target letter from federal prosecutors. Such a letter would have put the person on notice that he or she was a party of interest and in short order, would be indicted for the robbery unless they cooperated. Despite the lack of the target letters, it soon became apparent to the second-year law student that countless FBI agents, including McGrath, had spent hundreds if not thousands of hours on the investigation. She could clearly see from the list that starting on the day of the robbery, the FBI immediately went to work on their databases. They had identified potential suspects, some of whom had been arrested or questioned for any crime involving art or antiques in the prior ten years, others having been accused of more heinous crimes, including murder. Savage also noticed that the four names at the top of the list had been highlighted.

Someone had also written the numbers 1-4 in red pen next to each name. Having grown up in New York, she was not familiar with any of the names on the list. Had she been a local kid, she would most surely have recognized the first name listed. Suspect number one was a notorious art thief from the Boston suburb of Quincy, Kyle Condon. Savage started to read the summary on Condon. She soon understood why his name was at the top of the Bureau's list.

Chapter Nineteen: "The Legend"

Condon was first charged with art theft in 1966 for a robbery at the Frist museum in Weymouth, Massachusetts, a bedroom community next door to his hometown of Quincy. Not only a thief, he also had a propensity for violence: during the pursuit following the robbery, he shot and wounded a State Police corporal. After doing some time for the Frist heist, he found himself once again in handcuffs when he was arrested for walking out of the Wheaton Estate, located in Monmouth, Maine, with several valuable paintings. The paintings just happened to be the work of the famous American artist, Andrew Wyeth.

Always a cunning soul and forever receptive to making deals with prosecutors, Condon entered a guilty plea, but was spared imprisonment when he provided authorities with information that resulted in the return of a Rembrandt that had been stolen from the Museum of Fine Arts in Boston. Although very bright and talented as a musician, Condon had a propensity for the dark side, an unfortunate trait that ultimately found him standing before a Superior Court jury in Dedham, Massachusetts for the alleged murders of two young women. As noted in the summary, although he was a prime suspect in the Gardner robbery, there was one major problem with that hypothesis: on March 18, 1990, Condon was sitting behind bars, confined to a prison in Illinois.

Although incarcerated on the day of the robbery, the Bureau was nevertheless, very confident that Condon was capable of having been the mastermind of the robbery from the inside of a prison. Even behind bars, law enforcement was keenly aware that he could have conspired with his cohorts to pull off the robbery on his behalf. Condon, however, as Savage read in the summary, always maintained that he was not involved and had no knowledge of the robbers' identities.

The Bureau may have given up on Condon, but Katharine learned that they were very interested

in one of his cronies, a wannabe by the name of
Willie Lewis, also known as suspect number two
on the list. Before Savage started to read the
skinny on Lewis, she looked down at her watch
and realized it was 5:20 PM. She was supposed
to meet a couple of the other interns at the
Blarney Stone down on Cambridge Street.

She put the papers down on the table, shut off
the light and walked out the door. She would
read about Lewis in the morning. She couldn't
wait to tell her fellow interns the case she had
been assigned to work on. As she would later
learn, one of the interns already at the Blarney
Stone, a pint of Guinness in hand, was Matt
Donovan, an older third-year night law student
at Suffolk Law School, located on Tremont
Street, some two blocks from the FBI office.
Unlike Savage, Donovan had been assigned to
work on two rather boring health care fraud
cases. He nevertheless still thought of himself as
the "big man on campus" with the ladies.

While Savage was walking over to the Blarney,
Donovan was complaining to a couple of interns
at the bar about the two cases he had been
assigned to for the summer. As was his usual
practice, he had strategically picked a bar stool
that would allow him to do two things: carry on
a conversation and check out all the talent that
walked through the front door. That's when he
first noticed her. A brown haired woman, hair

pulled back, with beautiful green eyes, entering the bar through the swinging door, small beads of perspiration glistening above her lipsticked mouth. He thought she was absolutely stunning. Her eyes panned the room and then, all of a sudden, she started to walk over to several women who were seated at a table. He noticed she walked with a determined stride, almost a strut, her arms bronzed from the summer sun. He recognized the two women at the table. They were summer interns from the Bureau! While walking over to the table, she passed the corner of the bar where he was seated. Their eyes met, for ever so brief a moment, hers' darting quickly away.

Chapter Twenty: " The Wannabe"

The next morning, Katharine sat down at the table with her iced coffee and yellow, lined legal pad in hand. She took a sip from her coffee, picked up the file and started to read about Mr. Willie Lewis. Lewis was from the Boston suburb of Brockton. He was no stranger to the law and had a long criminal record. The Bureau first had contact with him when they raided his art and antique business and residence, based on a confidential informant's tip to local police: he was in possession of an historic, Colonial-era

document that had been taken from the
Commonwealth's Archives, located across the
street from the John F. Kennedy Presidential
Library in Dorchester. Based upon the
informant's information, state police and the FBI,
search warrants in hand, conducted a joint,
coordinated raid at his home and place of
business in the early morning hours.

Although the missing document was not found
on the property during the search, evidence was
found that would eventually lead to its
discovery. The search would get Lewis in hot
water for other reasons. Several firearms that he
had no license to carry were found on the
premises and having already been convicted of a
crime, he now faced substantial federal time
under the newly established Federal Sentencing
Guidelines, enacted by Congress in the 1980s.

Savage, turning the page, looked down at a
handwritten note that read, "We now have
Lewis where we want him. This places us in a
great position of putting the heat on Lewis [and
Condon] to obtain information from him [them]
about several art robberies, including the
Gardner." There was no indication who had
written the note. There was more in the file
about Lewis. In August 1997, while awaiting
trial on the firearm possession case, Lewis made
an unsolicited, gratuitous call to the Boston FBI
office and spoke with McGrath. He boasted that

he could broker the return of the paintings stolen from the Gardner museum. Lewis professed to have critical information and details concerning the robbery and would be willing to share them with McGrath. Lewis explained that there was, of course, a *quid pro quo*. In exchange for the information, he wanted the five million- dollar reward offered by the museum and wanted his firearm case dropped.

Lewis explained that he had several tidbits about the heist: a window that was not alarmed, located near the entrance to the museum, was left purposely open and unlocked by a museum employee a week before the robbery. Lewis explained that it would have been used by the thieves, if necessary, as a second entrance if they were unable to get by the guards; the Gardner also used special bolts to secure every painting to the wall behind it making it extremely difficult to remove them; the robbers, were, in fact, only able to remove several of the bolts and damaged them in the process, becoming so frustrated two of the paintings were cut with a pocket knife and ripped from their frames.

The two paintings were by Rembrandt and both had been damaged. The day after Lewis had spoken to him on the phone, McGrath, while sitting at his desk, had opened the morning newspaper. Much to his amazement an article about the two cons, along with a photograph of

Condon was on page two! Although sitting in a prison in Pennsylvania, Condon, just like his buddy Lewis, had boasted that the two could facilitate the return of the Gardner paintings. There was, as always a catch. He would not provide any assistance to the government until all charges pending against Lewis were dropped. He likewise demanded an agreement in writing from the museum's Board of Trustees, promising that upon the return of the paintings, the Five Million Dollar reward would be given to him and Lewis. Condon also demanded one more thing from the Feds: he must be released from prison immediately even though three years remained on his fifteen year federal sentence. Savage read another one of McGrath's hand written notes. "Monday August 18 1997, 11:43 AM: received telephone call from Lewis. He and Condon will provide photos taken of several paintings...with paint chips from outer edges of Rembrandt's 'The Storm on the Sea of Galilee'...previous demands remain the same...conversation lasted about one minute... ETM." What Savage didn't see in the file was what McGrath did with the information after he hung up the phone with Lewis.

Chapter Twenty-One: "The Boss and The Hatchet Man" FBI Headquarters, Boston, August 18, 1997

Ending his conversation with Lewis and hanging up the receiver while scribbling his notes, McGrath got up from his chair, walked over to the Special Agent in Charge's office and peeked in from the doorway. Seeing his boss at his desk, stacks of paper to his left and right, he asked if he had a minute. McGrath walked in and closed the door behind him. He began to outline to Leary the conversation that had just taken place with Lewis, referring to his notes as he spoke. When he finished, Leary turned in his chair, picked up the phone, dialed a number and then, as McGrath sat there, heard his boss say over the secure land line, "Good morning, Mary, this is Special Agent Leary from the Bureau. Is the United States Attorney available?" A few moments went by and then McGrath heard his SAC say "Good morning, Sir, there are some new developments in the Gardner museum case. If your schedule permits, the lead agent on the case and I would like to meet with you at your office this afternoon to brief you. We are not able at this time to determine the validity of representations that have been made to this office concerning the stolen paintings, but we feel they are important enough to warrant a meeting with you. Thank you, Sir. I appreciate that. We will be there at 2:00 PM."

At ten minutes to 2:00, his long time trusted Executive Assistant, Mary Campo, escorted Leary and McGrath into United States Attorney James Morrissey's conference room. Both took seats at the massive, cherry wood table. A very short time after they arrived, the glass doors to the room swung open and Morrissey, along with his First Assistant and the Assistant United States Attorney assigned to the case, walked into the room. Pleasantries and introductions having been made, the group got down to business. Morrissey looked across the table to Leary and nodded, signaling to the SAC that he could begin. Leary started to give a summary of the nature of the recent contacts made by Condon and Lewis with the Bureau and then turned the meeting over to McGrath for more specifics. Morrissey's First Assistant took notes as each of the agents spoke. McGrath explained that according to Condon and Lewis, a local newspaper reporter had been provided with photos and paint chips from what they claimed to be two of the Rembrandts taken from the Gardner. The paper claimed that the paint chips had already been examined by an art expert from New York. McGrath held up a small vial explaining to the group that the paint chips in question were in the small glass container. He then picked up a piece of paper from the desk and turned on the projector to display the art expert's letter on a screen located at the front of the room.

As had been promised by the two convicted felons, the Bureau received the expert's report that morning along with the other items. McGrath started to read from the report. "Various paint chips from an alleged Rembrandt painting were received for study to determine whether they were from the Gardner museum paintings stolen in March 1990. Solid particulate was examined at moderate magnification using a light-focused microscope in my attempt to determine whether they came from different color areas of subject painting. Three very small representatives of light brown, brown and dark brown particulate were chosen for sampling. Small portions of each were removed with a very fine xenon needle and dispersed into individual pigment particles using an alcohol-based solution. This process was required in order for the samples to be examined under magnification. It is my opinion, based upon what I observed, all three samples are very similar in pigment composition and particle size, although there appeared to be a slight variation in shades between the three samples. Lead white was also observed adhered to some of the brown particulate, which, in my opinion, is consistent with product commonly used by Dutch masters in the 17th century. All in all, the paint layers, in my opinion, are typical of Rembrandt. I feel that it would be very unlikely that anyone today would be familiar enough with Rembrandt's materials and methods to produce these paint layers. Furthermore, it would be almost impossible to find the same types of chalk and lead white today that were used in the 1600s. It should also be noted that burnt sienna is unusual today, being a mixture of very finely divided and coarser particles. I feel that it is very likely these chips came from a Rembrandt."

Finished reading, McGrath looked up at the group and recommended that he contact the professor to ask him some questions concerning his opinion and how he arrived at it. He also suggested that the photographs and paint chips be provided to the museum to allow their own experts to review the report and material. He then expressed his opinion about Lewis and Condon: "We all know that on occasion we have to rely upon the help of LSOS to solve cases, particularly in cold-cases such as the Gardner. I think we should give these two what they're looking for if they can pull off what they say they can. I don't see a down side and, anyway, Condon's sentence is almost over and Lewis's case is of little or no significance to us or to your office."

An unexpected heated debate ensued between the prosecutors and the two agents, especially between McGrath and Morrissey, the United States Attorney. He made it quite clear from the get-go that he didn't see any difference between negotiating with Condon and Lewis and common thugs who take hostages. "I am not going to negotiate with these two. I appreciate the stakes are high and we are talking about priceless works of art, but we are setting a dangerous precedent here that we damn better stay away from," Morrissey pointedly explained, tapping his index finger on the conference room table all the while.

"With all due respect, Sir," Leary interjected, "if Condon and Lewis are really on the up-and-up, and the chips are from the Rembrandt and the photographs are indeed authentic, shouldn't we take a chance and negotiate with them?" Morrissey, appearing contemplative and annoyed, glanced over to his First Assistant, Frank Cullen, who nodded ever so slightly in the affirmative. He then sternly retorted, "We will not cut a deal behind closed doors. The negotiations need to be transparent and there will not be any consideration until we obtain solid, concrete evidence that these two individuals have provided *bona fide* information and are in fact able to produce the paintings. Do I make myself clear, gentlemen?" That's when McGrath, who had remained silent since giving the initial briefing jumped in.

"Sir, again with all due respect," his tone of voice firm, " I have devoted the last seven years to this case and could fly around the world three times with the amount of frequent-flyer points I have accumulated in running down every God damn lead. I don't particularly appreciate what I perceive to be your reluctance to deal with Condon and Lewis. They may have something here and what I'm hearing is that you don't want to deal with them to try to get paintings back. The Gardner is the largest robbery of art in United States history. I just don't get it," his voice escalating in volume. Leary, feeling very uncomfortable, squirmed in his chair. Morrissey appeared beside himself.

McGrath's tone of voice and demeanor was not expected nor anticipated by the group. When he attempted to respond, McGrath, exploded across the table at him and yelled, at the top of his lungs, "I'm not finished yet! I'm getting this awful feeling, in my stomach, that maybe you don't want to solve this fucking case. Well I'll tell you something right here and now," the obvious frustration of the last seven years escaping from deep within, "I will continue working this case if it kills me. With you or without you!" McGrath got up abruptly from his chair and pushed the glass doors open and walked out. The three people left seated in the room were both stunned, speechless.

The United States Attorney, after regaining his composure, turned to Leary and said, "Speak with McGrath to see what prompted his unanticipated tirade and have the New York FBI office arrange a meeting with the art expert in order to obtain additional facts about why he thinks the paint chips are from the Rembrandt. Arrangements should also be made for the paint chips to be sent over to the Gardner museum conservators so they can run their own analysis on them. Please speak with both Condon and Lewis to inform them what steps are going to be taken and advise them, in no uncertain terms, if they want to cooperate, what the ground rules will be." Morrissey emphasized to Leary as he glanced towards his First Assistant, that these two convicted felons would embarrass neither him nor his office.

"I am quite dubious that anything will come from their offer and relay my feelings to McGrath. Frank, we also need to draft a press release for distribution to the media. Take care of that for us, okay?" The three stood, shook hands and the meeting was over. As Morrissey and Cullen walked back into the inner office, the United States Attorney closed the door and said, with a concerned expression on his face, "You and I both know that opening this Pandora 's Box could be a real quagmire for the Bureau and for us. I'm concerned about McGrath. Place a call and have someone keep an eye on him from the 'Stable'. He could be trouble. We're going to have to keep him on a very short leash. I'm starting to get a bad feeling about where this is headed!" Cullen, hatchet man that he was, nodded and then responded, "Not a problem Boss, I'll take care of it."

Chapter Twenty-Two: "The Shady Antique Dealer"

Turning to suspect number three on the Gardner list, Savage started to read the summary on Allan Whitcomb, also written by McGrath. She learned that Whitcomb was a native of Massachusetts and that after a run-in with the law he had settled in San Francisco, in 1983. He then moved to Carmel-By-the Sea, a very quaint, high-end, ritzy town on California's rocky coast, where he opened an art boutique.

In the late 1970s, he pleaded no contest when the FBI field office in Providence, Rhode Island, got wind of his scheme to try to buy a painting from an art dealer on College Hill with a bum check. Unfortunately for Whitcomb, the shop's owner turned out to be an undercover FBI agent. The scheme having gone south, Whitcomb found himself standing before judge Jeremiah Blackwood in the federal court in Providence. Blackwood, having a reputation for being lenient on non-violent, white-collar criminals, didn't put him in jail but, rather, imposed a large fine and placed him on supervised probation. As a condition of his probation, he was banned from conducting any business either directly or indirectly in the six New England states that involved the sale or purchase of art. Whitcomb had grown up in the Humarock section of Scituate, Massachusetts, and was an art dealer who had a particular interest in paintings, prints, drawings and sketches of horses, jockeys and racetracks. His favorite artist of that genre was Edgar Degas. It was clear from McGrath's notes that Allan Whitcomb and his brother Michael, along with their Dad, Paul, were well connected in Boston and had access to police officers and police uniforms. They were in good standing with the Boston police since the patriarch owned a police supply store in the South End and had a slew of police officers as clients.

Michael owned a marina, in the shadow of the federal courthouse on Boston Harbor. In addition to being a marina, the small, weather shingled building built on pilings had a small bar, a restaurant and a back deck that looked out on the water. Because of its location and scenery, FBI agents and Boston police officers spent many off hours there, drinking beers and checking out the after-work talent from nearby financial district offices.

Continuing to read about Allan Whitcomb, Savage wasn't surprised to read that McGrath had traveled to Carmel to interview him He

appeared at his place of business in Carmel on
March 27, 1990. He must have had his spiral
notebook with him on the trip because his
handwritten notes were stapled to the summary.
Turning in her chair, she grabbed Condon's and
Lewis's files and flipped quickly to the back of
each one. As she expected, both files also
contained McGrath's original handwritten notes.

"When I entered Whitcomb's art boutique
located on Main Street," McGrath had written,
"He asked if we could talk inside his office away
from his employees. I had no problem with his
request. Whitcomb first explained that based
upon his record and his interest in paintings of
the nineteenth and twentieth century masters,
particularly Degas, he wasn't surprised that he
had been contacted by me. He admitted that he
was in Boston on the 18th of March, having
arrived there from San Francisco on the 16th. He
decided to come to Boston just to get away from
the grind and constant demands of owning a
business. He made the March trip to Boston to
have some fun. When he arrived in Boston, he
said he took the Red Line to Park Street and then
walked over to Sam Simeone's shoe and leather
business located on Boylston Street in the Back
Bay. Simeone is a former college room mate.
That evening, they went to a Mexican restaurant
in Cambridge before returning to Dorchester,
where they spent the evening. The following
day, Saturday, March 17th, St. Patrick's Day, he

visited his brother, Michael at his marina and had a few drinks at the bar along with another close friend, Marshall MacDonald. He told me that he walked around fashionable Newbury Street and Charles Street, where he decided to get a haircut. Later in the day he again met up with MacDonald. The two had dinner at a local Chinese restaurant not far from MacDonald's apartment in Dorchester. He spent the rest of the night at MacDonald's, staying up until 1:00 AM. He spent Sunday watching an NBA basketball game, had dinner and went to bed. He flew back to San Francisco on Monday morning. At the end of the conversation, I was surprised when Whitcomb developed somewhat of an attitude, becoming almost cocky. This change in attitude was abrupt and arose when I brought up the subject of his arrest in Rhode Island years before. He said he didn't trust the FBI but felt comfortable talking with me since I was from the Boston office and not Providence."

"Whitcomb explained that he learned of the robbery when he arrived back in Carmel. He recalled reading in the *San Francisco Examiner* that five paintings by Degas were stolen. He had discussed the robbery with other friends and family members in passing and thought that someone had stolen the items from the Gardner. He was particularly upset about how the robbers had viciously cut several of the paintings from their frames. He agreed to take a lie detector test."

Putting down McGrath's note, Savage wondered whether Whitcomb had ever taken a polygraph test. She located the polygraph examiner's report that was attached to a long strip of paper that resembled an electrocardiogram tracing. It was the hard-copy printout of Whitcomb's physiological responses to questions posed to him by the examiner, recording his blood pressure, pulse and breathing pattern. He denied any involvement, and based upon his "body responses" to each question the examiner at the time was of the opinion that he was not being deceptive. Savage noted that the report was actually a copy of the original and when she examined it a little closer, it appeared to her that the examiner's opinion noted by the letters "NADO" or "No Apparent Deception Observed" had been typed over. The font was clearly different than what was on the rest of the page. She jotted a note on her legal pad, "Where is Whitcomb's original polygraph report?" Continuing with her review, one of McGrath's handwritten notes fascinated her.

In the early 1980s, Whitcomb had owned an art shop in the South End of Boston, having closed it when the Feds in Rhode Island arrested him. She looked for a customer list from the store in the file, but couldn't find one. She also sifted through the box to see if there were any documents that showed what art and antique dealers in the Boston area Whitcomb had done business with. She scribbled another note on her yellow legal pad, "Any customer lists/ credit card receipts from Whitcomb's shop, any subpoenas... wasn't Lewis also in the art business...did they know each other...did they conduct business... did they hang out with others at bars or clubs in Boston?"

Chapter Twenty-Three: "A Can-Do Attitude"

Savage knew McGrath had no clue about her background. He was aware that she was a law student at Georgetown, but had no idea that she had spent time working as a law clerk in the Bronx District Attorneys' office in New York City. While there, she was assigned to the homicide section of the office and had worked closely with a seasoned prosecutor on several notable homicide cases that had gone to trial. She was actively involved in preparing trial subpoenas, the preparation of trial exhibits, as well as the coordination of government witnesses, including two forensic specialists, both of whom had provided expert opinions at trial connecting the defendants' DNA to each crime scene. Both cases ended in guilty verdicts and both defendants received mandatory life sentences.

McGrath also didn't know much about his intern's personal life and, really didn't care to know. Savage was a first generation Polish-American who grew up in Glen Cove, New York, located on the fashionable North Shore of Long Island. Her parents had immigrated to the United States in the 1950s and settled in the mostly blue-collar town that also had its share of wealthy estates, including one that had been the home of J.P. Morgan, the wealthy railroad baron. When her father arrived in Glen Cove, he became a grounds keeper at a local estate owned by a wealthy tax lawyer who, each morning, was chauffeured to Wall Street. Every morning, when the limousine drove out of the driveway through the black, iron gate on its way to the Long Island Expressway, the chauffeur or the tax lawyer, if either one cared to look, would have seen the small, quiet man on his hands and knees, pulling crabgrass from the estate's massive lawn. It wasn't a glamorous job but it was good enough to put food on the table for his wife, Marisa, and their only child, Katharine, who had been born at the local hospital located just down the street from where the Savages now lived on Dosoris Lane.

Both of her parents were of strong stock, extremely hard workers and well liked by their employers, just like McGrath's. Marisa spent ten hours a day running a sewing machine at the local tailor shop. She was a talented seamstress who was always keenly focused on detail while stitching fine raw silk that would ultimately be transformed into expensive suits and ties worn by the local gentry. She loved to read mystery novels, always trying to anticipate what was going to happen next. Her husband, Edward, on the other hand, didn't read much except for the local newspaper and the weekly *Penny Saver*, clipping coupons from it now and then to help with the family's budget.

Katharine had inherited her parents' good qualities: hard work, loyalty, grace, honesty, ingenuity and an unending curiosity. As a child, she was very inquisitive. She had attended the nearby Catholic grammar school and then went on to its high school and then went on to College. Her LSAT scores were good enough for her to earn a scholarship to Georgetown University Law School where she now was in her second year. She had a full-time job during the day in Washington and attended the evening division of the law school. She is obsessive-compulsive, incredibly organized and has never suffered fools gladly. She was raised by her parents to understand that it is not who is right or wrong but, rather, what is right and what is wrong; a rule she has practiced her entire adult life both professionally and personally. Given an assignment or task to accomplish, she was always "can-do" and relentless as a bulldog!

Chapter Twenty-Four: "No Luck At All"

Suspect number four on the list was a wild-eyed, bad-boy from Roslindale, Massachusetts, William "Slick" Feldman. In 1966, at the age of twenty-six, Feldman was accused of the murder and armed robbery of a Railway Express Agency clerk at South Station in Boston, Massachusetts. He, along with a co-defendant from Charlestown, Massachusetts, was tried and found guilty by a unanimous jury. Both were sentenced to life terms for trying to steal a piddling $20,000.00.

After serving sixteen long years of his life sentence, "Slick" hit the jackpot when the proverbial "Bluebird" flew into his cell at Walpole State Prison. With the help of two young, aggressive public defenders and a lengthy evidentiary hearing that strongly suggested Feldman was an innocent man, a Suffolk Superior court judge had the unusual testicular fortitude to grant his motion for a new trial. Based on newly discovered evidence, the District Attorney ultimately realized he could not prove the case against Feldman, and so, dismissed the case. Feldman was released from prison and into the awaiting arms of his family. Before too long however, Willy would be back to his old bag of tricks.

After reading through the file, Katharine learned that "Slick's" luck would unfortunately run out in a cold, lonely, one-room apartment in Randolph, Massachusetts eerily, almost one year to the day after the Gardner heist. It was clear from the agent's summary, that when he was released, Feldman, not surprisingly, gravitated to other bad boys he had met while doing stints at Walpole and Norfolk State prisons. Members of that "fraternity" included: Carmine Martino, Bobby Datoli, David Mercer, Kyle Condon and Willie Lewis.

Just as it was on the day of the robbery, another unusually warm day delighted the winter worn of Boston. Carmine Martino wasn't soaking up rays however. He was in his windowless office at his shop in Dorchester on the phone with the Randolph police department. He had made the call to ask the desk Sergeant to send a patrolman over to Feldman's apartment to conduct a well-being check on his friend. "I'm concerned about my good buddy because he always comes by the shop to shoot the shit but I haven't seen him or heard from him in two days. Thanks. I appreciate your help. Yeah, you can call me back on this number if you have any info."

The FBI agent's summary identified Officer Brad MacDonald of the Randolph PD as the Officer dispatched to the location. "After getting no response, I had to kick the door in. I found the subject on the living room floor, stone cold dead from what appeared to be an apparent heroin overdose. A cloudy syringe still protruded from a vein in his left arm. I radioed dispatch to have them contact the Medical Examiner's office." Savage was astounded to read the last sentence of the FBI agent's summary: "Although the Randolph police advised they received a well-being call from Martino at 11:20 AM, reliable sources have confirmed that Martino was seen at Feldman's apartment earlier that morning and it is believed that by some unknown manner or ploy, effectuated the victim's demise by a drug overdose."

Chapter Twenty-Five
Panama City Beach, Florida, March 27, 1990

As usual, the morning paper landed in the bushes of Tommy Szanszlo's condominium, the invariable resting place of the local paperboy's errant toss. Walking out in his coral pink robe and slippers with eyes half open, the first cigarette of the day in his mouth, he reached down into the bushes and muttered some swear words under his breath, picked up the paper and shuffled back into the house. Trying to pry his eyes open and jump-start the engine, he started to drink his coffee and read the newspaper. "Same old crap," he thought to himself. "Fight between two females leaves one dead"; "Diver spots white shark"; "Car-jacker shoots Pompano man" and, last–but–not–least, "Armed men rob Southwest Dade County McDonald's".

"How low can you go...robbing a fucking McDonald's," he whispered to himself. Turning the pages, a blurb in the National News section caught his eye. Originally from Boston, he was always interested in reading about what was going on up in Bean Town. It read: "Boston, Massachusetts. During the early morning hours of March 18, 1990, just hours after the festivities of St. Patrick's Day had concluded, two males, allegedly dressed as Boston police officers, entered the Isabella Stewart Gardner museum on false pretenses and robbed the museum of thirteen priceless works of art with an estimated value of Three Hundred Million-Dollars. The items taken included a painting by Vermeer, five sketches by Degas of jockeys and racehorses, two Rembrandts, a Chinese vase dating back to the Shang Dynasty and a gold finial from one of Napoleon's regiments." He again read the words "...five sketches by Degas".

Putting the paper down, he shook his head. This time the words came out of his mouth: "The only son of a bitch I know in Boston who would have the balls to pull this off is Allan Whitcomb!" Allan was a kid he had grown up with in a seaside town south of Boston back in the 60's. He knew Allan was an art dealer who had a unique interest in paintings of horses, jockeys and racetracks, particularly those of light pastel watercolors. He also knew the Whitcomb brothers along with their Dad, Paul, were well known in Boston and knew police officers and had access to police uniforms, walkie-talkies, badges, scanners and handcuffs. The family was well connected with the Boston police since Paul owned a police supply store and his son, Michael knew many members of law enforcement who hung out at the harbor marina bar he owned. The three had gonads the size of Mount Everest! Tommy picked up the paper and became almost gleeful when he read the last sentence of the article: "The museum is offering a one million-dollar reward for information leading to the arrest of the perpetrators and the recovery of the art work." His eyes sparkled as he got up to call his sister, Mary, a divorce lawyer in Brockton, Massachusetts.

Chapter Twenty-Six: "College Kids, An Empty Keg and The Man In The Car"

Savage removed another file from a box that read "Emmanuel College Students, March 18, 1990". Since March 17, 1990, was St. Patrick's Day, most of the nearby college students were having parties in their dormitory rooms or in off-campus housing. Once word got out about the robbery, several students who had been on Palace Road that early morning contacted the Boston police. They, in turn, referred them to the FBI. She started to read the statements taken from the students by various agents. Joseph Falvey, an Emmanuel College sophomore, arrived at 24 Palace Road at approximately midnight on March 18th to attend a keg party. He arrived there with several friends. Learning that they had run out of beer, he stayed for only about ten minutes and left. Along with his friends, he started to walk up Palace Road towards the Gardner museum.

While walking along and horsing around a bit, Falvey heard one of his friends complain that a man in a parked car on Palace Road, on the museum side of the street, was staring at him. Falvey explained that he was about six feet away from the vehicle and despite the fact that the car's windows were somewhat foggy, he was still able to make out the silhouettes of two men and was also able to make out the features of the one sitting in the driver's seat. He described the small, two-door vehicle as being white or beige and possibly several years old. He described the driver's skin complexion as dark olive. He explained that he later learned from another friend that the two men he observed were police officers. He remembered looking at his watch as he left Palace Road; it was 12:25 AM.

Keri Jardin, who had been with Falvey that night, explained that she also saw the vehicle and the two men sitting in it. She didn't believe the car was running but remembered the brake lights were illuminated. She told the agent who interviewed her that she was spooked by the man in the driver's seat, who she described as a white male possibly in his early thirties with coarse, dark, black hair. He had a thick, dark mustache and was olive-skinned. She described the vehicle as a two-door that was light tan, cream-colored or possibly white.

Another friend, Jason Pratt, who was giving Jardin piggy-back rides while walking down Palace Road, noticed the two men sitting in the car when still another Emmanuel student out that night, Nancy Hellmann, whispered to him that one of them was staring at her. Pratt later told the authorities that he got a real good look at the driver. He described him as being a white male whose eyes appeared to be widely spaced apart, almost having the appearance of being of

Asian descent. He described the vehicle as being either a Dodge or Plymouth hatchback, blue or steel grey and probably of a 1985-1988 vintage.

FBI Headquarters, Boston, 2007

As Savage continued to review the files, she could not believe how massive the Gardner investigation had become and how many potential suspects and theories there were. It was clear to her that agents from across the country had tracked down every lead and had spoken to anyone and everyone who had any information concerning the robbery. Everyone, from card readers, psychics and mind readers had an opinion about the robbery. Theories were endless, running the gauntlet from the surreal to the supernatural. After going through so many documents, Savage understood the magnitude of the crime was directly proportionate to the number of "whodunit" crackpots who, in time, would eventually come out of the woodwork. Despite that, she was amazed how the Bureau had handled anyone who professed to have information about the robbery or the location of the paintings.

She could tell from reading the documents that the agents acted with professionalism and spent endless hours listening to stories and theories and followed up any lead they believed had merit. She also appreciated the fact that, as was true with any investigation, particularly one the size of the Gardner robbery, agents, including Ted McGrath, at some point, must stop to assess where the case stood. Simple questions like who remain the strongest suspects, what theories still hold the most promise, what are the strongest leads, and what, most importantly, should be done next to solve the crime.

Savage was not aware McGrath had made that assessment. However, his thoughts about where the case stood would not be found in any file. On the one hand, while marveling at the breadth of the investigation, she could not understand why the robbery had not been solved given the resources and manpower that had been expended by so many over the past seventeen years. It was as if the paintings, Chinese vase and finial had vanished into thin air.

Chapter Twenty-Seven: "Regret and Remorse"

As she peered down into Box #6, she could see a file labeled "Jack Casey March 22, 1990". She picked it up and opened it. McGrath had written the summary. Casey, who lived with his wife Linda in Portland, Maine, called the Maine State Police on the morning of March 21, 1990. While reading the *Portland Press* at the breakfast table with his wife, he almost fell off his chair when he saw an article in the New England News Briefs section of the paper. "Two men dressed in police uniforms robbed the Isabella Stewart Gardner museum during the early morning hours of March 18, 1990, the day after St. Patrick's Day." He had never mentioned anything to Linda about the two men he had observed at the museum while he waited for her before they left the building on March 11, 1990. "Oh my God, I can't believe it, they robbed the museum!" Startled, Linda quickly looked up from her crossword. She was stunned by her husband's sudden outburst." As Jack started to read the article she was astonished to hear what he recounted to her about their visit to the museum while in Boston just a week earlier. She sat at the table spellbound by her husband's story, also incredulous that he had never mentioned it to her before. They both were numb. Neither one of them could believe that someone would steal priceless works of art. Linda actually felt sick to her stomach. Her beloved "The Storm on the Sea of Galilee" and "The Concert," as reported in the article, had been ripped from the walls of the museum, the "Storm" cut violently from its frame. "How could this have happened?" she asked her husband, who just shook his head in disgust.

Casey was not only upset with the news about the robbery but also disgusted with himself for not having told the museum guards what he saw on the 11th. He wanted to contact the authorities to tell them about the two men dressed in raincoats and hats that he found to be so suspicious that day. After collecting their thoughts, they decided to call the Maine State Police. Detective Zarella of the Maine State Police interviewed the Casey's at their home and then provided their information to McGrath. Before heading to Maine, McGrath had prepared a photo array of suspects he had obtained through an initial analysis of the Bureau's database of known art thieves. Sitting in the Casey's cozy den in their home in Portland, McGrath listened intently to what Casey had to say. He recalled in detail, what he had seen while waiting for his wife before they left the museum to return to their hotel. When McGrath asked him to describe the two men, he described how they were dressed and how one of them was stooped over as if he had a back problem. Casey then mentioned that the older of the two had a very distinguishing facial feature: a rather prominent nose. McGrath then pulled out the photo array with twelve photographs on the cardboard sheet. He placed it on the coffee table in front of Casey and asked him if he recognized anyone. Focusing on the collage of photographs and taking his time, Casey stopped, looked up and then down again and pointed to photograph # 11. He said, "I think this guy was at the museum on March 11, 1990. However, I can't be sure of it. The only problem I have is that the person in the photo looks younger than the man that I saw that day."

McGrath turned to him and said with a smile, "He is, that photograph is a year old. The agent then turned and pulled out a piece of paper from his brief case. He handed it to Casey. It was the Boston Police Department's sketch of the two robbers. Casey looked at it and pointed to suspect #2 and then looked back up at McGrath and said, "It looks like the guy I saw but, again, I really can't be sure."

Chapter Twenty-Eight
FBI Headquarters, Boston, Monday, March 25, 1990, 8:20 AM

On March 25, 1990, the Gardner's ostensible victim/security guard Alexander Morris walked into the FBI building located at Government Center and was handed a pass. He was directed to pin it to his shirt collar. The receptionist then called McGrath to let him know that Morris was there for his 9:00 AM appointment. A few moments later, McGrath walked into the glass-enclosed, secure waiting area, shook hands with Morris and then brought him to a room on the fourth floor. The former museum guard was there to undergo a polygraph examination. Before taking the test, McGrath first asked him if he had any questions or concerns.

"I am very concerned about the robbery because I told about twelve people over the past six months about the lack of security at the museum," he answered. "When we smoked pot to kill time, someone would always bring up the lack of security. The more we smoked and drank, the more we talked about how the security really sucked. Some of my buddies used to brag about how they could rob the place and get away with it. I figured it was just the pot or booze talking. After the robbery, it definitely crossed my mind that one or more of them might have really understood how second or third rate the security was and took advantage of it. I had very strong feelings after the robbery about being responsible in part. After giving it some thought, I believed that one of the robbers in fact, had the same facial features as a guard I had worked with who was fired two weeks before for showing up drunk for his shift. I admit I can't be absolutely sure that it was the same person. I wasn't familiar with the guards who worked the night shift because, as I explained to you on the day of the robbery, it was not my usual shift and I only worked part-time. Although the museum had strict rules and regulations, the guards who worked the 11:00 PM to 7:00 AM shift routinely broke those rules."

"We played games while working to fight off the boredom. We tried to avoid tripping all of the motion detector alarms while doing our rounds. It was a challenge, but one that we were very good at. It was a game of cat and mouse! It was really a lot of fun." McGrath couldn't believe what he was hearing. "One time we had a Halloween party that all the overnight guards threw that included about twenty to twenty-five people." McGrath thought to himself, "What we have here is a major league museum with a fucking bush league security crew." He found it simply unbelievable!

FBI Headquarters, Boston, Late June 2007

Savage started to feel uneasy about going through the files. She thought it best to be honest with her mentor and tell him what she had been doing and to apologize. Listening to her, he twirled his eyeglasses in his hand. He didn't seem too pleased. Placing his glasses on the desk as Savage felt her heart beating, he looked at her and said, "Well, did you solve the case?" She felt relieved and then responded, "Not yet." Looking down at her notes, Katharine had some questions for him. Before she could start, McGrath spoke. He explained to her that the Gardner case was what prosecutors referred to as a "cold case," one that had remained unsolved for a long period of time despite tremendous efforts to solve it. Her eyes seemed to widen as he continued. "The best way to approach a cold case is to have a fresh set of eyes go through the entire file; to basically have someone totally unfamiliar with the case, take a retrospective look-see at it. To find out what had been done in the past to determine what, if anything, might be done to now jump-start the case." She edged forward in her seat.

"I would like you to do just that in the Gardner case for the remainder of the summer. Any grand jury materials in the file, which are clearly marked as such, are absolutely off limits and are not available to you. However, everything else will be. I want you to be that second set of eyes. Forget about organizing the files. I want you to carefully review all documents and physical evidence with a goal of trying to bring new life into an otherwise dead case. Give me suggestions on what might be done to breathe new life into it." Pleased with herself, she grabbed her yellow legal pad, stood up and before leaving, glanced at all the colored pins on McGrath's cubicle. "What do all those pins represent?" He looked at the world map, looked back at her and in a defeated tone, said, "Each pin represents a location in the world where either I or another agent has traveled in connection with the Gardner robbery. All those places and not one nibble, never mind any bites!"

He gave her the key to the archive room and then, almost as an afterthought, pulled a flashlight from his desk, tossed it to her as he quipped, "You might need this." She caught it mid-air and then placed it back on his desk. "Don't you remember, you already gave me one? It's already come in handy." McGrath's immediate thought: "The kid is as sharp as a tack and maybe, just maybe, might find something in the twelve boxes that could jump start this dead battery of a case." Despite that brief notion, he realized what he hadn't told her during their first meeting. It really didn't matter what she found, the time period to prosecute anyone involved in the heist, known as the statute of limitations, had come and gone eleven years before in 1995. "Oh well," he thought to himself, "Why spoil her day, she's excited about her project. At least it will keep her out of my hair for a while." As Savage left his desk, he looked at his watch, noticed it was time for lunch, put on his scally cap and headed out the door for the Chart House. His hope that he wouldn't have to deal with Katharine for a few days or weeks was short-lived.

The following afternoon, once again sitting across the desk from McGrath, Savage was curious about what documents he had obtained relevant to Allan Whitcomb's potential criminal culpability. "Hundreds if not thousands of documents have been collected through subpoenas. All of them are located in the evidence room, a secure, locked location on the fourth floor." When he asked her for specifics, she explained, "I'm looking for any documents that might identify passengers who may have sat next to Whitcomb on his flight east or his flight back to San Francisco on the 19th of March. Also, were any customer lists or credit card receipts from Whitcomb's antique shop ever received from him or his credit card companies? Are there any lists of people or businesses Whitcomb may have conducted business with?" Not recalling whether the exact items had been requested, McGrath picked up the phone and called the agent who was responsible for the evidence room. "Hi Phil I'm sending my intern up to you so she can take a look at the evidence boxes in the Gardner museum case. Thanks I appreciate that." Placing the receiver down, McGrath, for the second time in two days, again hoped that he would not have to deal with Ms. Savage for a couple of more days or if he was lucky, for the rest of the summer. She, on the other hand, had a different plan. She was going to show him that she could win his favor and with some luck of her own, help figure out who stole the paintings, the finial and the Chinese Ku. McGrath, who felt satisfied, turned back to the day's Jumble puzzle. As she walked away from his cubicle, he cried out, "Don't forget your security pass and that flash-light!"

Getting off the elevator on the fourth floor, agent Curcio greeted her at the door to the evidence room and then brought her over to a row of shelves that contained boxes full of plastic evidence bags and what appeared to be documents. He pointed to boxes located high on top of the last shelf in the rear of the room. "Those are the Gardner evidence files. They contain evidence from the scene and documents that were produced pursuant to federal subpoenas. If you need any help just let me know." Savage moved the sliding ladder that was attached to the steel shelving, climbed up and grabbed one of the boxes. She carried it down and then placed it on a table. When she opened the top of the box and looked into it, she became mesmerized. It contained clear plastic bags that held evidence obtained from the Gardner museum.

Chapter Twenty-Nine: "A Mere Coincidence?"

As had been the case throughout the investigation, the agents had been extremely thorough. They had, in fact, obtained copies of the airline tickets for Whitcomb's flights to and from Boston in March 1990. He had purchased one round trip ticket on Northwest Airlines. On his flight to Boston, according to the flight itinerary and passenger lists provided by the airline, Whitcomb sat in seat 12A. On his return flight to San Francisco, he sat in seat 14C. The two Boeing 737s had three seats on each side of the aisle and with the help of the lists the agents were able to identify the passengers who sat next to Whitcomb. The passenger on the flight from San Francisco was a college student attending Boston University. She was returning to school after Spring Break.

When interviewed, she surprisingly was able to remember the gentleman from San Francisco who, she recalled, was very talkative. In fact, she told the FBI agent that she remembered him because he talked incessantly when all she wanted to do was to sleep. She explained that he went on and on about his art business and French paintings. She recalled that he seemed to have an inflated ego and was annoying and cocky. At one point during the flight, she actually pretended to fall asleep with the hope that he would stop talking to her. She couldn't recall anything else about the man other than, as she told the agent, he reminded her of an actor she had once seen on television re-runs, but couldn't remember his name or the show he played in. The passenger who sat next to the white male seated in seat number 14C on the return flight from Boston, by chance, also recalled Whitcomb when shown his photograph.

He told the agent that the man was probably middle-aged and was very quiet. He really didn't say much of anything during the almost six hour flight. He remembered the gentleman not for anything he said but how he acted during the flight. He seemed to be very nervous and kept moving around in his seat, so much so that he moved to a seat in the back of the plane to get as far away from Whitcomb as possible. He, too, just like the passenger in seat 12B, also remembered the man because he thought he had the facial characteristics of an actor in a 1970s sitcom. Placing the documents back into the box, she started to write questions to herself on her legal pad. While going through the documents and finding what appeared to be inconsistencies, she needed to get her thoughts on paper. "Four people have now identified Whitcomb and all of them have said that he looks like an actor on television. All four can't be wrong about that. It's not a coincidence they all have said the same thing about his facial appearance. What doesn't make sense is that Fager and Casey place

Whitcomb or someone who looks likes him, at the museum one week before the robbery on the 11th and possibly on the 18th. How can that be? Whitcomb has what looks like airtight, rock-solid alibis for both days."

Chapter Thirty: "Brown Bag Lunch with the SAC"

It was the practice of Special Agent in Charge Leary to meet with small groups of summer interns every Friday at 12:00 in the main conference room. He referred to it as a "brown bag lunch with the Special Agent-in-Charge". It was an opportunity for the students to meet him, and more importantly, each other. The SAC wanted to make sure they learned some things while working at the Bureau and, at the same time, had some fun. Topics discussed were generally of little consequence and usually included a history of the Bureau, the types of cases handled by the agency, and individual war stories from agents concerning particularly interesting cases that may have had some notoriety. As Savage sat at the long conference room table waiting for the SAC, she started to talk with several of the other interns. One of them was Matt Donovan, who was at the Blarney Stone when Savage walked in to meet friends several weeks earlier. He mentioned that he saw her there with two other interns that he recognized. Just as she finished introducing herself, Agent in Charge Leary walked into the room. He spoke for about twenty-five minutes and then, as was his custom, when lunch was over, he welcomed questions.

A student from Harvard Law School asked about what the Bureau was doing about identifying terrorist cells in the Boston area. Another student, from New England School of Law, questioned whether the Bureau, since the events of September 11th, was sharing information with the CIA and, if so, how had inter-agency communication been improved. The last question was from Savage. "Do you have any thoughts why the Gardner museum robbery has not been solved, given it happened almost twenty years ago? Is it still a priority? What steps, if any, was the Bureau taking to try to solve the case?" Leary was not pleased. You could tell by the look on his face. Trying to be professional, he looked at Savage and responded with the standard, bureaucratic, canned answer: "The robbery and the recovery of the paintings continue to be a priority. It has been very frustrating to me personally, and to the Bureau as an institution, that we have not solved the case."

Leary then thanked all the students for coming. Before he left, he walked over to Savage and shook her hand. "Hello Katharine where are you attending law school and which agent are you working with this summer?" She replied, "agent McGrath." The chief nodded, realizing now why the questions were asked. The law student, over the past few weeks, had seen McGrath in action firsthand and knew what his priorities were and were not. Solving the robbery didn't seem to be one of them. "Well I hope you enjoy the summer and I'm sure you will learn some things from agent McGrath."

Chapter Thirty-One: "The Print"
FBI Headquarters, Boston, March 25, 1990, 3:30 PM

As McGrath walked Morris to the elevator after he completed his polygraph examination, he bumped into agent Maher, who asked him to stop by her office when he had a chance. Maher's office, located in the basement of the building, had the appearance of a laboratory. Cameras, microscopes and all types of chemicals and reagents were neatly stored on shelves in the small, cramped room. When McGrath walked in he could see that she was looking into a microscope. She heard him enter and said,

"You might want to take a look at this. This is a photograph of a print I lifted from the doorknob on the inner side of the cryptic door leading into the Dutch Room. I digitally enhanced it to obtain greater detail." McGrath sat down in the chair and squinted into the eyepiece of the scope as he turned the wheel to focus in on the print. He could see what appeared to be a small fingerprint with some displaced dust scattered around it.

As he continued to look, he mentioned to Maher that he could see the print and that it didn't appear to him to be anything unusual. Maher then asked him to look a little closer. That's when he saw it. He could make out what appeared to be a white granular powder interspersed with the grey dusting material used to lift the latent image. Maher asked him, "Do you see the white grainy stuff?" McGrath responded that he could and asked the analyst what it was. "It's the powder from the inside of a surgical glove. The stuff that makes it easy to put them on and take off. Whoever turned that door knob to enter the Dutch Room during the robbery was wearing at least one surgical glove and it had a hole in it." McGrath, looking up at her, appeared confused. Picking up on his quizzical look, Maher responded, "OK, what do we have? We have a discernible print that appears to be from a male subject, which is consistent with the guards' stories. We also now know that whoever grabbed the door knob was wearing at least one glove and that it had a hole in it. When he touched it, unbeknownst to him, it left a powdery residue. Because of where the print was found, I'm almost positive that the subject is left-handed. If he was right-handed, the print would have been located at 7:00 rather than at 5:00 where it was found. We also know that anytime someone puts on that type of glove, his or her hands always sweat. So, in this case, whoever this poor bastard is, he had the unlucky fortune of not only leaving a print of his left index finger he also left sweat mixed in with the white powder. By doing so, he also left his DNA." McGrath finally appreciated the significance of Maher's finding.

Chapter Thirty-Two: "A Solid Alibi or Not?"

Savage was still perplexed about Whitcomb's alibi. She wanted to find the questions put to his alibi witness during his polygraph examination. The alibi witness told the agent when interviewed, that Whitcomb had spent the night of the robbery with him, having never left his sight except when they went to bed. Savage also wanted to read the original written opinion of the polygraph examiner to check out two things:

one, if she thought the witness was being truthful or deceptive, and two, whether the original report could have been tampered with, the way Whitcomb's appeared to have been. After searching through the file, she finally found the piece of paper that listed the questions.

The examiner had asked the alibi witness whether Whitcomb was with him the entire night of March 18th and, the day after, when, according to him, he gave him a ride to the airport for his return trip to San Francisco. After analyzing the tracings on the polygraph tape, the examiner formed the opinion that the subject showed absolutely no deception and was being truthful. Savage's head started to spin. What bothered her and what she couldn't understand was the fact that Jack Casey, although not really sure, believed Whitcomb could have been one of the two suspicious men at the museum on the 11th of March.

"Could Casey have been mistaken about the identification or possibly the date," she thought to herself. Casey, however, had provided McGrath with the receipt for their stay at the Ritz. It was dated March 12, 1990 and referenced that the $260 bill was for the evening of the 11th. Continuing to look through the file, with a new awareness of why McGrath had become so frustrated over the last seventeen years, Savage came across two other documents that really started to make her head whirl. A local FBI agent in San Francisco confirmed what Whitcomb had told McGrath. He indeed had a solid alibi for the 11th. He was in San Francisco attending an antique show and was more than willing and able to make the three people he attended the show with available for McGrath to interview. The second document was a memo to the file dated May 21, 1990 from McGrath.

"Despite promising evidence to the contrary, at this point in time, based upon the results of polygraph examinations and solid alibis, Whitcomb is no longer a person of interest nor is he a suspect in connection with the Gardner museum robbery." Placing the memo back into the file, Savage was frazzled. She wanted to go back to her apartment to take a hot bath before going over to the Blarney Stone. Before heading out for the night, she made a note to herself on her legal pad, "Did they close the book on Whitcomb too soon? Is it a mere coincidence that he arrived in Boston two days before the robbery and left the day after? How reliable are polygraph tests? How solid are his alibi witnesses in California? Was the antique show at a hotel and if so, are there security tapes available to put him there? Of the thirteen items stolen from the museum, twelve were paintings or sketches. The only other things taken were an obscure, antique Chinese vase and the

Napoleonic eagle. The only reason those two items would have been grabbed was for their monetary value (vase) or sentimental value (eagle). Somebody had to know that the vase was a valuable antique worth significant money. Maybe the vase and the finial were calling cards of either one or both of the thieves. Maybe the two items were taken as an afterthought, possibly as souvenirs, after finishing ripping the paintings on the laundry list from the walls and securing them at the guard's desk?"

Chapter Thirty-Three: "Clues From The Hard Drive" FBI Headquarters, Boston, March 27, 1990

McGrath was with the Director of Security, Lyle Harrison, to go over forensic analysis of the hard drive from the guard's security desk computer. "I wanted to show you what a more thorough scan disclosed. As you know, an initial review showed that motion detectors sounded 133 times throughout the building between 1:24 AM, when the robbers were believed to have first been let into the Palace Road entrance and 2:37 AM, when the outside door closed as they walked out into the quiet and still air of Boston's early morning. McGrath interrupted, "before we get into what else the hard drive tells us, can we again go over what type of electronic security was in place at the time of the robbery."

"Monitor #1 shows four images that are fixed, but each image can be zoomed in on for a closer look. The four locations monitored are the front parking lot, the back parking lot, the Palace Road driveway and carriage house and the Two Palace Road entrance. Monitor #2 shows live, real-time shots within the museum as well as the identical four locations as Monitor #1. The third monitor provides fixed images from cameras #1 and #2 viewing the back parking lot. The last monitor shows the guard desk area. There are four outside cameras located at the rear of the building. The first three cover the same area as the fixed image monitors. The one additional outdoor camera is located at the garden door entrance and exit. Inside the museum we have two cameras located on the first floor. They show images on the television screens that are live shots. Those don't record, so as a result, there is no record of people coming and going." McGrath recalled there was also a camera located above the guard station that had been directed away from the front of the guard desk and up toward the ceiling. He then asked Harrison about the VCR located in the assistant director of security's office.

"The only cameras recording," Harrison responded, "were the four fixed from Monitor

#1 and the one at the watch desk." Any questions on security," Harrison asked. "No, I'm all set," McGrath replied. "Okay, pull up your chair so you can see the computer screen to follow along with me."

"This is a breakdown of every single motion detector alarm that was triggered the night of the robbery. It also identifies and cross-references each and every time the Palace Road door opened and closed. The time frame is 12:34 AM through 2:37 AM when the employee entrance door last closed. As you already know, 133 alarms sounded throughout the building between 1:24 AM, when the robbers were believed first let into the Palace Road entrance and 2:37 AM, when they exited and the outside door closed behind them. All alarms that sounded during that stretch of time were confined to the first and second floors. I believe the two knew exactly what they were looking for because it is clear from the data on the hard drive; they entered no other area of the museum, other than the rooms where the art was taken. It also appears they knew how to get where they wanted to go, in the shortest amount of time. Just for the hell of it, I went back to approximately an hour before the two apparently were let in by security guard Fager." McGrath, now very much interested to see where Harrison was going with this, moved his chair closer to the desk. He could see the hour and minutes listed, as well as a graphic that read "Palace Road Door Openings and Closings". The graphics, in red, yellow and blue bar type columns, were very easy to follow and to understand.

"Look here," as Harrison pointed to the screen. At 12:11 Fager begins his first patrol. The guard that Morris would ultimately relieve, Elliot Neufeldt, who, by the way had worked a double shift; signed off on the computer at 11:37 PM. Morris arrived about ten minutes later at 11:47 PM. It's interesting that Neufeldt, although having signed off at 11:37 PM, at least according to this, didn't exit the building until eleven minutes later at 11:48." As soon as Harrison said that, McGrath recalled Morris telling him when being questioned the day of the heist, that one of the two robbers reminded him of the guard that he had just relieved. "You can see here at about 12:46 AM, Fager is on the fourth floor and then walks down the fourth floor back stairs, into the Long Gallery and then arrives on the third floor. He walks into the Tapestry Room, the Little Salon, then into the Italian Room at approximately ten minutes to one. Shortly thereafter, he comes down to the second floor and then the first when he passes by the main entrance, walks over to the Garden back door, opens it and exits the building. He enters the Carriage House, goes up to the second floor, I assume to check out the issue of the fire alarm sounding and then re-enters the building through the Garden door entrance, at a little after 1:00 AM." McGrath, who was sitting there very quietly, not saying a word, was impressed with the presentation but unimpressed with the information. He wondered where Harrison was going with it.

Chapter Thirty-Four
FBI Headquarters, Boston

After speaking with McGrath and with what she perceived to be his reluctant approval, Savage obtained Whitcomb's telephone records from March 1, 1990 through June 30, 1990. There were approximately 127 phone calls made from his home phone and the business phone in Carmel. Going through the records was very tedious and time consuming and, without entering each individual number into a database, Savage had absolutely no way of knowing the identity of the person the call was placed to nor its location. The only thing she could establish from the records was the date and time of each call, the number and the area code. Since the majority of the calls were made from home, Savage decided to start with the calls made from the antiques shop and run those through the Bureau's computer.

They numbered about 35. McGrath had arranged for her to use a computer at a vacant desk on the other side of the office. The Bureau had installed very sophisticated software that could provide a tremendous amount of information when a telephone number is entered into the system. If the number came from a commercial business, because the computers were networked to all fifty Secretaries of States' offices, the date of incorporation would be provided, as well as the names and all addresses of the Directors and Officers. It would also identify the nature and type of business that was allegedly being conducted at each address. The first numbers she typed in were those placed to area code 617 for Boston, Massachusetts. There were about twenty-two of them.

As Savage sat at her desk, she slowly and methodically entered each business phone number into the computer, making sure she typed in the correct number and then waited a few seconds for the information to appear on her screen. Going through the data, she found that most of the calls were to local businesses located in and around Boston. Most of them were very short in duration and were made to other art and antique dealers. Coming to the last few pages of billings she typed in the number 617-123-4567. She sat back in her chair took a sip from her Dunkin' Donuts coffee and waited patiently for the screen to light up. When it did, she sat up and looked closely at it.

On May 21, 1990, Whitcomb placed a call to an automobile transport business located at 1227 Broadway in Somerville, right outside Boston's city limits. She found it curious that Whitcomb had made a call to that location. "He sells antiques, why would he be calling an auto transport business from his shop?" She shifted her weight in the chair and then moved the cursor across the screen to the icon that would bring her to the corporate database at the Massachusetts Secretary of State's office. She clicked the mouse and then, once again, sat back in her chair. The screen flickered. Acme Auto Transport was located at that address. The President of the corporation was one Maurice Leonard who lived in Chestnut Hill at 110 Morning Glory Lane.

Savage minimized the corporation web site and clicked the icon that would bring her to a law enforcement database that would provide all kinds of personal information about Leonard. Each and every address he lived at for the last twenty years would be listed, including the names and ages of any and all household members who also may have lived with him at each location. Financial information including any existing debts, mortgages or liens would also be provided. The last piece of information the database contained was a list of Leonard's neighbors for each address. She typed in the address and then hit the enter button. Sixteen names were listed and, as she perused the list, no name popped out at her, that is, until she got to 180 Morning Glory Lane. Her eyes widened when she saw the name: Whitcomb.

Paul Whitcomb and his wife, Ellen, had lived at that address since September 1952. It listed his occupation as an owner of a police supply store located in Boston's South End. He had owned the business there since the early 1960s and it had been at the same location since that time. She scrolled down the page to where Whitcomb's residential addresses were listed. She was not particularly surprised to see the names. Both Allan Whitcomb and Michael Whitcomb were listed as occupants of the family home in Chestnut Hill. It appeared that the two, along with their two sisters, Arlene and Alicia, had lived there until they married. She hit the print key on the computer to print the documents that she planned on showing to her summer mentor. She was excited.

The following day, as she sat across from him, McGrath, with his reading glasses precariously placed at the end of his nose, scanned the documents that Savage had just handed to him. As she watched him flip through each page, he grunted. He was not easily impressed but given this find, maybe there was something to it. Finished looking at all the material, he took his glasses off, looked up at Katharine and said, "Pretty good. What do you think the next step should be?" She thought for a moment and then responded, "I think we should find out who he spoke to and why." McGrath pulled his chair closer to the desk, cleared his voice and said, "Here's the problem. The phone call was made sixteen years ago. We had the records back then but we didn't have the support staff or the analysts to do at that time what you just did," McGrath explained. "Well, we should at least determine whether the place still exists and I'm sure if the owner, Mr. Leonard, is still alive, we could put him in the grand jury and ask him under oath why Whitcomb called him and what he asked him to do. We could also have him produce any and all documents he has that memorialize any business transactions between him and Whitcomb."

"We could also ask him what his relationship with Allan Whitcomb was." While she spoke, McGrath fiddled with his glasses, subconsciously twirling them in his right hand. He did this any time a person with a suggestion he didn't like confronted him. Although he didn't like it, he knew the kid was right and he also knew that if he decided to throw Leonard into the grand jury, Savage couldn't know about it nor could she be told what if anything came from it. "Thanks, Ms. Savage; I'll give it some thought. Again, good work." As Katharine walked away, making sure she was gone, he turned in his chair, picked up the phone and started to dial the number for the Assistant United States Attorney assigned to the Gardner robbery. He was going to ask her to draft two grand jury subpoenas, one for a person and one, for the production of documents from that person's business.

Chapter Thirty-Five: "The Mystery From The Blue Room"

Harrison continued going over the motion detector data with McGrath. "The next piece of data I find to be very interesting. At 1:02 AM, the Palace Road door opens. Not the outside door, but the inside one. Within the same identified minute, that is, still at the 1:02 AM reading, the inside door alarm continues to sound. It continues to be triggered until the computer clicked digitally to 1:03 AM." McGrath once again was not impressed and then politely asked a question that basically translated into "So what?" That's when Harrison's response got the seasoned agent's attention.

"You can see that the outside door is then opened and still within the 1:03 AM time slot, the inside door is opened. It has been the belief of all investigators involved in the case, including you, that Fager let the robbers into the museum at 1:24 AM. I believe there could be an alternative explanation. Someone opened the Palace Road inside door and held it open for close to a minute. The outside door was also kept open! Within that two minute stretch the outside door closed and the inside door opened." Finally, the kid from Southie started to understand where Harrison was headed.

"It is undisputed that at 1:24 AM, Fager buzzed the two robbers into the security desk or at least that's what Fager has claimed. Here, you can see it right here on the bar graph. At 1:24 AM, the outside door opens and before the computer's clock clicked to 1:25 AM, the inside door opened and then shut." McGrath pushed his chair away from the desk and rubbed his ruddy face. After a long pause, he said, "Let me get this straight. You think it's possible that this Fager character not only let the two nitwits into the museum at 1:24 AM, but also could have let other people in twenty minutes earlier when he held the doors open for almost two minutes. During those two minutes he could have handed the 'Portrait by Manet' out the door to anyone standing at the door and they would have been off to the races!"

"That's very interesting that you mention that, Ted. Fager triggered the main entrance motion detector at 12:51 AM. The motion detector is located right above the entrance to the museum and is designed to pick up any movement in the corridor leading into the museum's courtyard. It would obviously pick up anyone walking in that hallway or by it, where it meets the courtyard. By the way, the main entrance corridor is the only way to get into the Blue Room. Here's the crazy thing about what this data is telling me. The main entrance alarm went off only once that night and that was when we believe, Fager tripped it at 12:51 AM while he was doing his rounds. It never tripped again the entire night. One of the robbers had to trigger that alarm when he entered the Blue Room to grab the Manet portrait."

Repeating himself, to make sure McGrath understood what he was implying, "The alarm never sounded after Fager tripped it. I don't know how to explain it and when I confronted Fager and told him what I had discovered, he had absolutely no explanation for it." McGrath looked at Harrison and said, "You're right. I asked that asshole if he had any explanation about the alarm outside the Blue Room sounding only once that night. He looked at me with that stupid expression of his and told me that, upon reflection, he never did get to pulse the first floor alarms to turn them off. Fager told me that was when, at least according to him, the robbers first pressed the doorbell. If he didn't pulse the first floor, that motion detector outside the Blue Room should have been tripped and it wasn't. Fager's explanation to me was that the robbers themselves must have known something about how to manipulate the computer security system. I just don't buy that. Anyway, they certainly weren't concerned about tripping the alarms up on the second floor. Why would they have cared about the one in the Blue Room? It doesn't make any sense."

Chapter Thirty-Six

When he got back to his office after being briefed by Harrison, his head was spinning and he had a throbbing headache. He sat at his desk scratching his head, thinking how crazy it was for the museum to have allowed two pot-smoking college students to protect millions of dollars' worth of art. The age-old adage "You get what you pay for" kept playing over and over in his head.

He continued to believe that the robbers, no matter how many in number, had to have been helped by someone from the inside who knew the museum like the back of his hand. Two things cemented that belief as far as he was concerned. Number one was the basement. You either had to know the layout or you were brought there by someone who did. It was too small, dark and cramped to have someone unfamiliar with it navigate it with only a flash-light. Number two was the fact that the robbers somehow knew the shortest route to the Dutch Room: up the back stairs, past the laboratory, through one wooden door, a secret panel that held "The Storm of the Sea of Galilee" on the other side and then on into the gallery.

McGrath recalled that the hidden panel had been swung open and pushed out into the room. The three chairs that rested on the other side had been pushed out by about three feet. There was no doubt in his mind that the thieves entered the Dutch room through that private entrance and that someone had told them of its existence or else, brought them there that night. He continued to scratch his head. Looking over his notes in his notebook, he recalled that Morris had told him that he thought one of the robbers reminded him of the guard he had relieved for that shift. "Do we know for sure whether that guard actually left the building when he said he did?" McGrath thought to himself. Morris also told him that he never did actually see Fager being brought down into the basement that early morning.

The only thing Morris could confirm was that he saw his partner being led away by one of the robbers in the opposite direction from where he stood. There were all types of loose ends and questions to be answered. The seasoned agent realized that he had his work cut out for him. His immediate plan was to hook Fager up to a polygraph. Taking the copy of the motion alarms analysis out of his pocket, he started to peruse it. At 12:34 AM, Fager, listed as the operator of the security computer, edited the database. McGrath wrote a note to himself to ask the guard about that notation. Shortly thereafter, at 12:39 AM, the alarm in the Dutch Room went off and then ten minutes later at 12:49 AM, the 4th floor lab doors opened and then closed within that time sequence.

"That time interval," McGrath thought to himself, "certainly would have been enough time for someone to have opened the door to the roof let people in and then close it. It really doesn't seem to be a coincidence that at the exact time Fager is in the Dutch Room, the door to the laboratory on the roof opens and closes. McGrath continued to think about possible scenarios. He appreciated the fact that one of the two guards wouldn't have had to let anyone in from the roof. All someone had to do was leave the door unlocked. He knew that it could have been as easy as that because of what Harrison had showed him before he left to go back to the office. As the two were walking through the outside courtyard on the way to the parking lot adjacent to the greenhouse, Harrison stopped and said, "Oh, I almost forgot. I want to show you something." They walked over to the rear fire escape that led up to the fourth floor and to the door that Mrs. Gardner used on occasion to get some air when she had difficulty sleeping at night. While climbing up the escape, McGrath looked up at the iron grates and asked, "Are you sure this thing is safe? It looks a little rusty." He had a concerned look on his face but with Harrison's assurance, he began the climb. McGrath didn't like heights and with each step, the stairs swayed a bit, giving him pause to wonder whether they would ever make it to the roof before the whole thing collapsed. Fortunately both made it to the rooftop and after McGrath caught his breath Harrison showed him the entrance to the room. Of modest size, it was Isabella's bedroom and was now used as an office by the museum's Director, Madeleine Karp. What McGrath couldn't get over was what Harrison told him as they stood there. "For the past six years I have asked that locks be placed at the bottom of the fire escape and at the top here as one enters the roof. As you can see, the request has fallen on deaf ears and so, anyone, just as we did, could have walked up the fire escape unimpeded and into the museum through an unlocked door that early morning."

Chapter Thirty-Seven: "The Grand Jury And The Transport" Boston's Federal Courthouse, July 27, 2007

Grand Jury Room Number 3 is one of five such rooms in the John Joseph Moakley Federal Courthouse located on the Fan Pier in South Boston. The ten-story, red brick building sits at the foot of Boston Harbor. Unfortunately, none of the five-jury rooms has windows, making them feel like square boxes. In retrospect, the architects may have been omniscient in keeping the rooms windowless. On any given day, 26 grand jurors, who may sit for up to eighteen months in those rooms, hear evidence presented by Assistant United States attorneys. During those long sessions, less than 100 yards away in the middle of the shipping lane of Boston Harbor, terrorist attack vulnerable LNG tankers, loaded to the gills with liquid natural gas, float by every week on their way to the Port of Chelsea. On this July morning, sunlight filtered through a single skylight located directly above the jurors' heads.

Finishing their coffee and muffins provided by the United States Marshal's Service, they all settled into their seats and awaited the arrival of Assistant United States Attorney Amy Fowler, a forty-something, no-nonsense, seasoned federal prosecutor who had over twelve years of trial experience with the Massachusetts United States Attorney's office.

Although vertically challenged, her aggressive, in your-face personality made up for any of her physical shortcomings. She was a formidable opponent and made it very clear to friend and foe alike, that if you crossed her, she would bury you. It was well known throughout the office and by the local defense bar that Fowler, on more than one occasion, had ripped a defense attorney or their client a new sphincter muscle if she thought they weren't being straight with her. She arrived at the office after being recognized by the United States Department of Justice as a student scholar in her third year at Harvard Law School. Once hired by the United States Attorney, Fowler was assigned to the Major Crimes Unit or MCU. She then did a short stint in the Organized Crime Strike Force Unit and then returned to the MCU as the assistant chief. She was a favorite of United States Attorney Morrissey's, who thought she possessed exceptional talent as a prosecutor.

On the first day of the grand jurors' service, Fowler had presented a summary of the Gardner museum robbery as well as the current status of the case: dead in the water. She explained that it happened in 1990 but emphasized that new evidence had been discovered recently that needed their review and consideration. Using a power point presentation, the first slide appeared on the white screen: "In Re: The Isabella Stewart Gardner Robbery of Priceless Works of Art". The grand jury room is a small, thickly carpeted nondescript space that consists of three theater-like rows of chairs that gives it the feel of a private screening room with exceptional acoustics.

The jurors face the lone witness stand located front and center; the jury foreperson and his or her assistant, also a juror, sits at a table to the witness's left. The foreperson takes count each morning to determine whether a quorum of sixteen exists and at the end of the day collects the jurors' notebooks, none of which can leave the room. Federal prosecutors sit at a table located to the right of the witness. It is usually crammed with boxes of evidence, every piece already pre-marked as an exhibit to be placed in front of an often quivering, stammering witness. A certified court reporter sits directly across from the witness and records every word said, none of which can be disclosed. The proceedings are, in fact, secret. The witness, however, is not prohibited from telling third parties what was asked and what, if anything, was said. No one else in that room can disclose whether a grand jury has in fact been convened and under no circumstances can they breach the secrecy of the proceedings.

The day's proceedings commenced when Assistant United States Attorney Fowler introduced herself to Leonard. She advised him of his important constitutional and procedural rights: "Sir, you have certain rights and obligations sitting before this grand jury. First, you have the right not to incriminate yourself pursuant to the Fifth Amendment to the United States Constitution. That is, if I ask you a question and you believe the answer may subject you to criminal prosecution, you do not have to answer it. Secondly, although you do not have a right to have your attorney present in this room, you may speak with him or her at any time after a question is posed to you and before you answer it. You must answer it unless, again, it would incriminate you. Lastly, as I indicated to you in the beginning, you have certain obligations throughout this process. You must tell the truth! If it is determined that you have not been completely honest and truthful, you could face criminal charges for perjury, for which, if you were to be found guilty, you could face five years in federal prison. Do you understand, Sir?" Leonard responded that he understood.

As the questioning began, Fowler first focused on Leonard's relationship with Paul Whitcomb. Both he and Whitcomb, who he explained was now deceased, were members of the same church and were so, for many years. He lived four houses down from the elder Whitcomb and his wife, Ellen. Neither he nor his wife had ever socialized with them but knew their four children since they were teenagers. He also knew that the family, when the children were young, lived somewhere on the South Shore. "I operated my motor transport business out of the Somerville address for many years and had never conducted any business with any of the Whitcomb's except on this one occasion, in May of 1990. Being meticulous about keeping my records in good order, I brought the one and only document that my attorney and I believe to be responsive to the subpoena *duces tecum* that was handed to me at my home by an FBI agent. It's an invoice to Paul Whitcomb dated May 24, 1990 for services rendered."

Leonard explained that Paul Whitcomb had approached him after religious services in early May and asked him if he could arrange to have a vehicle transported to the San Francisco, California area on the 21st of the month. "I told him that I could and although I thought it somewhat unusual, I really didn't give it much thought and agreed to help out. The fee was $400 and the vehicle, as a personal courtesy, was loaded on the truck where it was garaged, rather than brought to my shop in Somerville. At the time, I took out a piece of paper and wrote down the name and the address where the vehicle could be picked up." Handing the piece of paper to AUSA Fowler, she noticed that the note that had been written almost twenty years before was pretty much dog-eared after so many years. It was still, nonetheless readable.

She read it out loud to the jurors. "180 Morning Glory Lane, Chestnut Hill, Massachusetts, Michael Whitcomb. Is that correct Mr. Leonard?" He nodded in the affirmative. "Where was the vehicle being delivered and to whom," she inquired. "7568 Bay View Road, Carmel-by-the Sea, California," he responded. "And who did you understand lived at that address? By the way," Fowler asked before Leonard answered, "Sir, don't all vehicles have to be delivered to a specified contact person and to no one else?" "That is correct. The contact person for this vehicle was Allan Whitcomb." "What type of truck did you use," she asked. "It was a standard auto transport carrier that could hold up to six vehicles." "Was this the only vehicle placed on the truck?" "No, the truck was at full capacity, fully loaded with six vehicles. Since the Whitcomb vehicle was going to be the last one taken off, it was the first in line at the top of the carrier, directly behind the cab. The other five vehicles were going to Cleveland, Chicago, Fort Worth, Galveston and Tucson, then my driver was going to head up the coast on Interstate 5 to Carmel." "Were you paid for the service?" "Yes, Paul Whitcomb paid me in cash the day after the vehicle arrived in California."

"Do you remember anything else about this transaction," Fowler asked. Leonard, looking contemplative for a moment, responded, "Yes I do. My drivers always drive the vehicles onto the transport, it's really for insurance purposes, we don't want anybody getting hurt or to have a vehicle fall off the carrier when it's being driven on. In this instance, much to my dismay, I distinctly remember Michael Whitcomb demanding in no uncertain terms that he drive the vehicle onto the carrier and not my driver. I didn't want him to do it but he was quite firm, so I acquiesced. He drove the vehicle on and then locked all the doors and put the keys in his pocket. He told me that his brother, Allan, also had a set of keys to the vehicle and would provide it to the driver when the vehicle arrived in San Francisco." Fowler turned and looking at the jurors, politely asked Mr. Leonard to step outside for a moment.

As the door closed behind him, making sure it had closed completely, Fowler, as was her customary practice, asked the jurors if they had any questions for the witness. Juror #12, a middle-aged black male who worked for the Postal Service said he had one. Fowler had to first screen all questions to make sure they were appropriate. She listened as the juror spoke. She agreed that it was an appropriate question and, in fact, was one that she herself should have asked.

Leonard walked back into the room and sat down at the witness desk. AUSA Fowler explained to him that one of the jurors had a question. He didn't seem to mind at all. "Sir, does the invoice identify the year, make and model of the Whitcomb vehicle?" Looking at it as Fowler handed it to him, "No it does not." But then said, "I don't need the invoice. I clearly remember the vehicle. Because this involved a member of my church and he was a neighbor, I personally met my driver at Michael Whitcomb's house in Chestnut Hill the morning the vehicle was picked up. I went there to make sure everything went smoothly. It was either a 1988 or 1989 Plymouth Lancer hatchback and it had metallic, beige white paint." Juror #12, hearing the response, immediately asked, without getting Attorney Fowler's approval, "Why are you so confident about the make and color of the vehicle? You transport hundreds of autos a year, why do you remember this particular one?"

Looking directly at the juror, Leonard replied, "It was the first, last and only time that someone other than one of my drivers ever drove a vehicle onto one of my trucks. Sitting before you today, I can still see Michael Whitcomb driving that light colored hatchback up the ramp and on to the top of the carrier. He brought it to rest right behind the cab and then climbed down the ladder on the side of the truck. My heart was pounding. By the way, it was also the only time in twenty five years that the owner of a vehicle kept the keys rather than handing them to my driver."

Chapter Thirty-Eight: "The Brother"
Boston-FBI, March 27, 1990, 12:45 PM

Savage continued to wonder whether anyone had questioned Michael Whitcomb about his possible involvement in the robbery. Before sitting down with McGrath, she planned to do some research without his knowledge, on Michael, herself. She purposely arrived early at the office one morning. She turned on her computer and entered the Bureau's database, known as Law Enforcement Concepts. The first thing she had to do was to obtain his social security number and date of birth. She typed in his address, and as usual, waited for the screen to flash. In a matter of seconds, Michael Whitcomb's personal information was in front of her.

He was born in the Humarock section of Scituate, Massachusetts, and not to be outdone by his sibling, he too was a convicted felon; having tried to outsmart a health insurance company by submitting bogus claims; not once, but twice. He was caught on both occasions. Just like his younger brother, Michael, never did any time for his crimes. He was placed on probation and ordered to pay a large fine. Looking at all of his information, Savage saw that he owned a marina in Boston. She was now ready to put his social security number into the Isabella Stewart Gardner museum robbery database to see what, if anything, he had told the FBI. She was able to do this with ease due to the fact that eight months before, computer experts from FBI Headquarters in Washington had taken every single document in the twelve banker boxes and scanned into the Bureau's computer system. His name came up on the screen several seconds after she typed in his social security number. She was amazed at what she found! Other than his name, there was absolutely no reference in the Whitcomb file concerning Michael. She couldn't believe it. Hitting the backspace key on her computer, she scrolled back to the section of the file where photographs of all persons interviewed were located. She found photos of the two guards, of Casey and his wife, of Lewis and Condon, and of Allan Whitcomb. When she saw the photo of Whitcomb she heard herself say out loud, "Oh my God, Whitcomb really is a dead ringer for suspect #2!" She grabbed the sketch of the two suspects drawn at the time by a Boston police sketch artist from the bottom of her legal pad, and compared it to the photograph of Whitcomb. She couldn't believe the resemblance. The facial characteristics were remarkably similar, including a small cleft on his chin, and a rather unique, protuberant nose. She, however, could not find any photograph of Michael in the photomontage. She thought to herself, "How could that be?" She decided to broach the subject of Michael's missing photo with McGrath.

Chapter Thirty-Nine
Boston's North End, July 28, 2007, 9:30 PM

Katharine and Matt were sitting at a table at Mike's Pastries on Hanover Street, some three blocks where "The Clam" DePasquale held his daily audience, while she vented her frustration about the Gardner case. Although he didn't know the specifics of the case she was working on, he appreciated the fact that it was causing Katharine some heartburn. As the two sat in the muggy air of a hot summer night in Boston, he was letting her blow off some steam.

"I can't figure out why the robbery has never been solved. On the one hand, McGrath and other agents have worked their tails off without any success. Not just for two or three years, but for almost twenty. Despite that, nothing has turned up. Based upon what I have seen in the files, the Bureau wrote off Allan Whitcomb way too soon and for no agent to have even spoken to Michael Whitcomb in seventeen years is simply unbelievable!" Matt sipped his espresso, patiently listening. "There seem to be an awful lot of inconsistencies in the case, but I just can't figure it out or put all the pieces together. I remember when my family and I would go up to the lake in the Pocono's for a couple of weeks each summer and my Mom and Dad worked on the puzzle with me before we went to bed. I used to get really frustrated when I got stuck trying to put the pieces together, but I never gave up. Well, let me tell you, I'm stumped with this Gardner case. I'm trying to help solve the puzzle when I have this feeling that I'm not sure I've been given all the pieces. It's making my head spin." Out of breath, Katharine looked across the table and shook her head. Clearly exasperated and on a roll, she continued.

"One of the things that is also getting me down is when the agent I'm working with on the case treats me like I'm a second grader. I realize I don't have much life experience but I work hard and am very determined. One of these days if that grouchy old bastard talks to me like I'm a two-year-old or patronizes me, I'm going to tell him to stick it!"

"Why don't you come with me tomorrow to look through receipts and canceled checks from the shop the guy in California owned for several years in the early 1980s. His name is Allan Whitcomb and his shop was called 'Unique Treasures and Antiques'. Those records were subpoenaed right after the robbery and I don't know if anyone has ever even looked at them!" Matt, sensing that Katharine was tired of talking and needed some sleep, asked for the check. They emptied what remained in their tiny espresso cups and finished the last remaining morsels of the chocolate walnut bourbon cake they had shared. As they started to walk up Hanover Street towards Katharine's studio apartment on Joy Street in the Beacon Hill section of the city, Katharine's mind continued to race. Matt assured her that things would work out for the best and that after a good night's sleep, she would feel better in the morning. He kissed her on the cheek and gave her a look of reassurance. "I'll see you at 8:00 in front of Two Center Plaza and I'll bring the coffee," Matt said to her. "Thanks, I need the help and encouragement."

Chapter Forty: "French Connection?"
FBI Headquarters, Boston, July 29, 2007

Katharine and Matt unlocked the door to the office and turned the lights on. They seemed to be the only two people in the building. It was

8:30 on a Sunday morning and it was a beautiful summer day in Boston. Instead of being at the Bureau going through documents, the two should have been walking on a sandy beach somewhere on Cape Cod. They were there to go through the credit card receipts and canceled checks of Allan Whitcomb's antique business. Katharine found the box that contained all of the documents that referred to Whitcomb.

Instead of looking at the documents in the Bureau's database, Savage wanted to go through the hard copies of each canceled check and store receipt. Opening the top of the box and looking through it, she came across two envelopes labeled, Whitcomb/Unique Treasures and Antiques Documents #1 and #2. As she unclasped the first envelope and opened it, Matt could see the disappointment on her face. I can't believe it. They are in complete disarray! The first thing we're going to have to do is to put them in chronological order by date. Why don't you take the second envelope and organize that one while I do the same with the first." She then turned the envelope upside down and with a thud, all of the papers fell out onto the table. "This is going to be a lot of fun," she said sarcastically. Matt picked up the other envelope and started to walk over to a table on the other side of the room. As he began to walk over to the table, he stopped and asked, "By the way what names and businesses am I supposed to be looking for?" Katharine responded, "I gave you the list with the names the other day. Tape it on the table so you can refer to it as you go through the documents."

"I'm sorry I forgot about the list. I may have been thinking about something else at the time," he said with a smirk. Stopping what she was doing, Savage looked up at him with a darting glare that relayed to him what she was thinking without having to say a word. "You jerk, don't you realize that you have zero chance with me. Focus on what we need to do this morning." Getting the message, Matt figured he'd better start organizing the files because right now, he was going nowhere with Ms. Savage! The two organized the batches of documents and spent the next several hours looking at each piece of paper, with no results. Matt had gone out to get some iced coffees to give both of them a little energy boost. They continued to go through the documents, when Katharine heard Matt call out, "I think I may have found something."

Katharine walked over to him and asked, "What is it?" "It's probably nothing, but here's a check made payable to a business that's on the list." Handing it to Katharine, he could hear her gasp softly as she saw the name on the canceled check, Timeless Treasures. Matt could see the look on her face and before he could even ask her what they had found, she said, "I can't believe it. Willie Lewis owned Timeless Treasures and he's selling antiques to Allan Whitcomb?" The date of the check was April 11, 1981. When she saw what Whitcomb had written on the Memo line located at the lower left corner of the check, she could actually feel her pulse quicken. He had written, "For paintings." "Allan Whitcomb purchased paintings from Willie Lewis in 1981," Savage said. "Who is Lewis?" Matt inquired. "He's a known art thief and convicted felon. He was one of Kyle Condon's minions. Back in 1997, they offered to broker the return of the paintings. The powers to be didn't think the offer was legit, so nothing ever came from it. In fact, the United States Attorney's office ultimately proved that their representations were bullshit. I wonder if McGrath or anyone else knows today that Whitcomb and Lewis appear to have done business together."

Katharine was excited about what they had discovered and, much to Matt's chagrin, wanted to finish going through the remaining documents. She asked Matt to make a copy of the check. Picking up a VISA credit card receipt dated September 13, 1989, Katharine could barely read the name on the slip. It appeared to be 'Paula Cohen Beauvais'. Thinking the person might be of French origin or possibly married to a French national, Katharine walked over to the copier and made a copy of the receipt. She had decided to look for any French names on the credit card receipts because of the attempted theft of the flag and the theft of the Napoleonic eagle.

Katharine wondered if there might be a relationship between Whitcomb and one of his customers. She figured that a patriotic French national with some money, may have taken some extreme steps to have the finial, as well as the flag, rightfully returned to the citizens of France, notwithstanding the museum's consistent refusal to do so for over fifty years. Taking the other items from the museum, Savage believed, may have been "payback" or "rent owed" for the museum's snub to the French for half a century. When the two had finished going through every single piece of paper, the sun was setting and they were both exhausted, but happy. As a result of their hard work they had found six canceled checks all made payable to Timeless Treasures and four credit card receipts from Paula Cohen Beauvais. She tucked the copies underneath the pages of her yellow legal pad and turned off the lights. As soon as she had a chance she was going to type Beauvais' name into Law Enforcement Concepts, press the enter button to see what, if anything, popped up!

Chapter Forty-One: Federal Courthouse, Boston, August 2, 2007

It was 11:47 in the morning when Attorney Fowler's telephone rang. Looking down at the caller-id, she could see it was a blocked number. The only people who knew her number and whose numbers would always come up blocked were agents calling from one of the federal agencies she represented. She picked up the receiver and said, "Good morning, Amy Fowler." She recognized McGrath's raspy voice immediately. He started to explain the reason for his call. It concerned the Gardner robbery. Grabbing her diary and a pen, she was ready to jot down what he told her. She also was somewhat dumbfounded by the call, the second in as many weeks. Before calling her to request the two subpoenas in connection with Maurice Leonard's grand jury appearance, she could not remember when he had last called. Frankly, she was surprised to hear that he was actually still working the case.

"Hi Amy, do you have a minute?" "Sure, go ahead Ted, what's up?" "Unbeknownst to me, my summer intern and another intern were in the office this past Sunday looking through canceled checks and credit card receipts from the antique shop owned by a guy we looked at concerning the Gardner robbery, Allan Whitcomb. We went after him hot and heavy as a person of interest, in fact, he was a *bona fide* suspect, until we realized he had several solid alibis and after he passed a polygraph. Once that happened, I was instructed to draft a memo to the file by the SAC at the time, Charlie Quintal, officially closing him out as a suspect. At the beginning of the summer, I assigned my intern, Katharine Savage, to the Gardner case and asked her to organize the files. Well that lasted about two weeks and then I sat down with her and asked her to approach it as a cold case. I really didn't think she would, but she seems to have taken me at my word. She and the other intern discovered some interesting things while going through the documents. I have to admit, I don't know if anyone had looked through those things before they did. I don't feel comfortable discussing what they found over the phone, so could I come by and show you the documents?"

"Absolutely, I have an arraignment at 1:00 PM in front of Judge Slattery. I should be finished by 1:30. Do you want to come by at 2:00?" "See you then. Why don't I fax over to you the pertinent documents so that you can take a quick look at them before heading downstairs to the arraignment?" "That would be great," Fowler said. When the door to the United States Attorney's office swung open, McGrath could see AUSA Fowler. She was running a few minutes late but he didn't mind. He enjoyed watching people coming in and out of the office and bumping into AUSAs he had worked with over the years.

He also enjoyed flirting a bit with the cute receptionist sitting at her desk, answering the phone and handing out security badges to visitors. She was securely situated behind two inches of bulletproof glass and made sure that she collected all of the passes from visitors when they left the office. Seeing Fowler, he got up and walked over to her. She shook his hand and then both walked down the long office hallway lined with the portraits and photographs of former United States Attorneys spanning some two hundred years. The two walked into Fowler's office overlooking Boston Harbor.

He sat down and when she excused herself to take a call, he marveled at the number of agency awards that covered the office walls, along with the many patches from federal law enforcement agencies she had worked with over the years: FBI, Secret Service, HHS, Postal, U.S. Marshal Service, ATF, DEA and many state and local police departments. Placing the receiver back into its cradle, she picked up the papers that he had faxed over to her. He held copies in his hand. "This is interesting," as she started to read them. "Before now, did we know that there was a relationship between Whitcomb and Lewis?" McGrath responded that he was unaware of any relationship between the two before Savage brought it to his attention. "You know we should probably put Lewis's ass in the grand jury to see what he would say. But, that would no doubt be a total waste of time, since whatever he did say, I wouldn't believe, just another "Lying Sack"! McGrath jumped in. "I have been of the belief since day one that there has to be a common thread between all of the suspects we've taken a cold, hard look at, including Kyle Condon, Willie Lewis, William Feldman, Allan Whitcomb, Carmine Martino, Bobby Datoli and David Mercer. I've never been able to determine if all or just some of them were somehow connected. My summer intern at this inauspicious moment, my retirement, has discovered the first possible link in the chain. I bet if we dig deeper into the histories of these characters and scratch the surface a little bit more, we would eventually find that common thread."

"I know you are retiring in a few weeks. The timing is terrible because there just might be something to this. I certainly appreciate the fact that you are anxious to retire and that you can't wait to get away from our horrible New England winters by escaping to sunny Florida. I would never ask you to stick around but would you be willing to do a couple of things for me before you leave? Again, there just might be something to this. What I heard from Maurice Leonard in the grand jury about the Whitcomb brothers was, as you know, a revelation. Now we also know at least one of the Whitcomb boys did business with Lewis. Could you, for my benefit, so I can get up to speed, draft a summary of what you believe to be the critical, salient points of the investigation, with any suggestions as to what we might next do? Would you also be willing to speak with Ms. Savage about the possibility of her staying on for three months or so to work with me in this office on the investigation? She would be a direct report to me."

"I will start on the summary in the morning when I can speak with Ms. Savage. But as to any suggestions as to what might be done next, I don't have a clue," McGrath replied.

Two Hours' Earlier

Fowler hadn't given the head's-up to McGrath that Savage had just finished briefing her about a possible French connection between Michael Whitcomb and Ms. Cohen-Beauvais. "After seeing her name on credit card receipts from Allan Whitcomb's antique shop, I entered Beauvais' name in the Bureau's Law Enforcement Concepts database. She was born in 1948, divorced after a marriage of twelve years and currently works as a pharmaceutical sales representative for Merck. She has no criminal record and from the addresses listed, it appears she re-married in 1978 to Francois Charles Beauvais, who apparently owns homes in Paris and in Boca Raton, Florida. When I scrolled further down the page listing her various addresses over the years, one place where she lived with her parents into her late teens caught my attention. She, like Whitcomb, had grown up in the small seaside community of Humarock which is located about thirty miles south of Boston." Fowler smiled since she realized Katharine was unaware that her girls and she lived ten minutes up the road.

"Given the fact that both she and Whitcomb grew up in the same town, I wanted to see if, by chance, there might be a connection since both were born around the same time. There was only one way to find out. On a Monday morning several weeks ago, another intern and I drove down to the south shore, through cities and towns I had never heard of, Quincy, Weymouth, Hingham, Cohasset. We went to the Scituate High School to locate the class yearbook for the graduating class of 1965."

"Once in the library, we were brought to the section of stacks that contained all of the yearbooks dating back as far as 1957. We found the 1965 book and turned to the section that contained that year's senior portraits. It was a small class. We found Allan Whitcomb's rather awkward appearing picture and on page 21 the senior portrait of Paula Marcia Cohen. Allan Whitcomb and Paula Cohen, now Beauvais attended the same high school! While flipping through the pages we came across photographs of the senior prom for the class of 1965. Again in black and white, on page 48, there was Allan Whitcomb and the young and innocent-appearing Paula Cohen dancing the night away, arm-in-arm, at the senior prom at Scituate High!"

"This is terrific work Katharine. I really am impressed with your drive and initiative. I'd like you to continue to go through the files, page by page, to make sure some important item or fact has not been overlooked. Based upon what we now know about the possible relationship between Whitcomb and Beauvais. In the mean time, I am going to have an agent do a background check on Paula's husband, Francois Charles Beauvais."

Federal Courthouse, Boston, August 14, 2007
"The Paint Chips Memo"

Savage knew Fowler was right. The only way to be absolutely sure that nothing had been missed or overlooked in the twelve bankers' boxes was to look at each and every piece of paper; clearly not a glamorous assignment but nevertheless, as she now understood, an essential one in a cold case. She was up to the task and was actually quite pleased that Fowler had enough confidence to have given her such an important assignment, just as McGrath had done when she first arrived at the Bureau. The War Room was no bigger than a shoebox but at least she had all the boxes there in one place and it had a good size table that allowed her to spread papers out while she looked through them.

Culling through the remaining boxes, she came across a memo to the file from Agent McGrath that concerned Lewis and Condon. She was under the impression that nothing had ever come from their proposal to the United States Attorney to broker the return of the paintings. Once museum archivists examined the paint chips, they were of the opinion that they were consistent with paint used by the great Dutch masters, including Rembrandt and Vermeer. However, Lewis pitched to the feds that the paint chips were from the "Storm on the Sea of Galilee". Since the museum still possessed the frame, along with the wooden stretch that held what remained of the "Storm's" canvas, museum archivists were able to compare it to the paint provided by Lewis. It was the unanimous opinion by the museum's experts that, although the chips may have in fact been from a Rembrandt, they did not come from "The Storm on the Sea of Galilee".

One line in McGrath's memo however, was particularly interesting: "Although the museum experts all believed the paint chips were not from "The Storm," they all were of the opinion that the burnt orange chips in the vial were made from the shells of a certain species of beetle found in Holland. Those chips were very much consistent with the paint used by Vermeer in "The Concert". While Katharine was looking through the files, AUSA Fowler had left a voice mail message for SAC Leary asking him, when he got a chance, to find out when prints from the Gardner robbery had last been run. She also asked him to fax over to her the names of all the people whose fingerprints had been processed to date in connection with the heist. She next spoke with the agent who had taken the case over from McGrath who had retired a week before, Bryan Mullen.

Chapter Forty-Two" The Rookie"

Mullen had graduated from the Academy in 2006 and was definitely a rookie and at the bottom of the pecking order. He, not surprisingly, was handed Teddy McGrath's dog-eared cold case list just as the grey haired agent, scally cap in place, walked out the door for the last time. Fowler had asked Mullen to do some digging on a French national by the name of Francois Charles Beauvais and his wife, Paula Cohen-Beauvais. He had inherited Ted McGrath's cubicle on the second floor. The multicolored pins were still stuck to the walls, as was the color montage of the thirteen items stolen from the museum. Mullen looked down at the two names provided to him by AUSA Fowler.

He was in the NCIC Interstate Identification Index, part of the Criminal Justice Information System or CJIS database. Typing in the name Francois Charles Beauvais, he hit the enter button. In a flash, the screen light up and there, in black and white, was everything anybody ever wanted to know about Monsieur Beauvais. "He is a white male born October 3, 1940 in Paris; 5'7" in height and weighs 175 pounds. His hair and eyes are brown and he has a home in Boca Raton, Florida. He owns a Cadillac Escalade with the license plate FCB-KCB and has a tattoo, of unknown coloration and configuration, on his upper right arm." Mullen could see that Beauvais' record was minimal. In 1976, in Miami's Dade County, he was charged with Knowingly Receiving Stolen Property. The notation on the court docket read "Dismissed in Furtherance of Justice". It was a clerk's fancy way of saying the government didn't have enough evidence to convict him. Other than that one case, it appeared that Beauvais was a law-abiding senior citizen enjoying time both in sunny Florida and in beautiful Paris. Mullen then typed Beauvais' social security number into the Law Enforcement Concepts database. He could see from the addresses in Boca and in Paris that the guy was loaded. He could also tell by the size of his yacht, which for tax purposes was conveniently registered in Delaware. It was a massive, 185 foot ocean-crossing vessel named "Some Like It Hot," and was owned by his French software company that had a posh address on the elegant Champs Elysees. It looked like Beauvais was the President and CEO of the corporation as well as the owner of substantial shares of its stock In any event, it was clear to Mullen that Beauvais was a man of wealth and substantial means and appeared to be someone with an appetite for the finer things in life.

As he continued to go through the database, Mullen also learned that Paula Beauvais had no criminal record. As he waited for the background copies to be printed, Mullen jotted a note to himself. "Check with the Coast Guard and the local Boston marinas to see if 'Some Like It Hot' was in local waters in March 1990 including the Cape and the islands. Do some research to see what makes this French flag so important that the robbers spent a significant amount of time trying to remove it from its bolted, iron frame."

Federal Courthouse, Boston, Several Days' Later: "The Waterloo Banner"

AUSA Fowler's Administrative Assistant, Suzan Kelly, walked into her office and handed her several pages faxed to her by SAC Leary. It was the list of names of everyone whose fingerprints had been run and also a short note from him, indicating the prints that had last been put through AFIS in 1999. The list had at least thirty names on it including Allan Whitcomb, Willie Lewis, Kyle Condon and a slew from Boston's criminal Athenaeum. Fowler got up and walked down the corridor to the War Room. She sat down at the table and tossed the list to her intern.

"These are the people the Bureau has run fingerprints on from the lifts at the museum."

Katharine scanned the list and then looked up and said, "I don't see Michael Whitcomb's name on it. Is there some reason his prints were not run? They should have already been in AFIS because he has felony convictions!" "You're right. I don't know the answer to that, but in the morning, I'll have Mullen run a background check on Michael." Several hours later, AUSA Fowler received another fax, this time from Mullen. He confirmed that Michael Whitcomb's prints had never been run through the Bureau's AFIS, since he was never considered a suspect in connection with the robbery. Fowler whispered to herself, "I wonder if anyone ever spoke to Michael after the robbery to see if he, like his brother had an alibi for the 18th of March." She got up from her chair and walked over to the War Room where Savage continued to go through the boxes.

"Katharine, could you do me a favor? Could you pull out the file on Michael Whitcomb and bring it down to my office when you get a chance?" As Fowler left the room, Savage started to go through the index to see what box had Michael Whitcomb's file. After going down the list, she realized there was a small problem with Fowler's request. There was no file on Michael Whitcomb. His brother Allan's file was referenced in the index, but there was no Michael. She then grabbed Allan's file to see if there was anything that referenced Michael. She couldn't find anything until she came to a small, letter size envelope that was sealed.

Opening it, she removed a single piece of paper that had been folded in half and then stapled. She removed the staple and unfolded the paper. The top read "Memo to the File" and was dated May 16, 1990. It was written by Ted McGrath's former boss, Special Agent in Charge, Charlie Quintal. Savage couldn't believe what she read. "An anonymous note addressed to this office was received this date 15.05.90. It was postmarked Boston. It was typewritten and stated the following: "Allan and Michael Whitcomb = ISGM robbery. The evidence is there...find it!"

Savage picked up the envelope. Someone had hand-written the words: "Confidential For SAC's eyes only!" on the front of it. She got up and hurriedly walked out of the room towards AUSA Fowler's office. As she did so, agent Mullen had just finished his self-imposed homework assignment concerning the Napoleonic flag. His memo to the file read: "This was no ordinary military banner and I can appreciate why someone, particularly a Frenchman wanted it back. Several local archives referenced the banner as far back as the Curley Administration in Boston. In 1947, shortly after the end of the War, his Honor, once a recipient of Isabella's good charm and fortune, while speaking at a French rally in Boston, reportedly declared in no uncertain terms that the flag should be returned to the people of France since it "was the standard carried by the old guard at the historic battle of Waterloo." According to the report, the Mayor paused purposely for a brief moment and then, with his usual blustery blarney declared, "If that cannot be arranged, I will take it back personally, I could use a long vacation right about now." The banner had a great deal of sentimental, but more importantly, military significance to the French government as well as to the people of France.

It was an embroidered banner from the early 19th century. It was sewn on blue, white and red silk cloth with gold thread that displayed cedar in a wreath, an eagle, bees and a crown. From its formal design, in the style of the First Empire, there was no question that it was designed for Napoleon. It was acquired by Isabella in 1880 during one of her many visits to New York City. She placed it in the Short Gallery, encased in an iron frame, close to the ceiling and to the left of the door leading to the Tapestry Room. Mullen was particularly interested in a possible French connection involving the flag and the robbery for several reasons. When he sat down and analyzed when and where the motion detectors had been triggered the night of the robbery, it appeared one of the robbers left the Dutch Room where they first entered, walked through the Italian Room and then into the Little Salon/Short Gallery area. "It appears, based upon the time and effort expended in the Short Gallery that the crooks most definitely, had their minds set on grabbing the flag, since, by my count, one of them spent over thirty minutes trying to pry it from the iron frame's grasp. Because of the difficulty in removing the screws, I believe they gave up and finally settled on the next best thing, the finial."

It was Mullen's belief, although he realized he was new to the case, that three items, not necessarily in any order of priority were most definitely on the top of the thieves' shopping list: the "Storm," "The Concert" and the French banner. With Quintal's note in hand, Fowler wanted to provide the information to her direct supervisor, AUSA James London, chief of the Major Crimes Unit. Once Fowler had briefed him, London said, "This is very peculiar. How could the Bureau after having been given this apparently reliable source information shortly after the robbery have never even interviewed this fucking guy? I'm going to have to run this up the flagpole and in all likelihood; it will end up in the lap of the First Assistant. From what I just read and heard I don't have a fucking clue where this is headed. However, I don't have a warm and fuzzy feeling about it. I think this is going to create a boatload of agita for somebody! Before we do anything, I would like you to find

out as much as you can about this Whitcomb
guy, and then we can sit down again and figure
out a game plan. By the way, aren't you
scheduled to be in the grand jury in a couple of
days anyway with that rock star wannabe
museum guard, Fager? Were the two guards or
any other asshole that the Bureau looked at back
in 1990, ever put in the grand jury and cross-
examined under oath? We should maintain
status quo and you should go forward with the
grand jury. Who knows, maybe if you jam Fager
hard enough, he'll talk. At this point, I guess we
have nothing to lose."

Chapter Forty-Three: "The Polygraphs"
Federal Courthouse, Boston, August 16, 2007

Savage searched the files to find Allan
Whitcomb's polygraph reports. Finally, she
pulled a copy and examined it by holding it up
to the light. It appeared to her that the font used
to type the examiner's opinion was without
question different from the rest of the page. It
also looked like someone had used whiteout on
one particular section of the document that read:
"NADO or No Apparent Deception Observed".
She then picked up the original and looked at
that. When she focused on the bottom left-hand

corner where the certified examiner's opinion was located, she couldn't believe her eyes. It read: "Results are Inconclusive." Picking up both versions and placing them next to each other on the table in front of her, she could see that none of the examiner's opinion appeared on the copy. It was gone! At the same time, across town, agent Mullen was scrolling down his computer screen looking at documents that had been scanned by the analysts from Washington. He came across a letter written in 1994. The letter was anonymous and addressed to the Gardner museum. He began to read it.

The unknown author boasted that he or she had information concerning the robbery and the whereabouts of several of the more valuable pieces including the Vermeer. The writer stated that he or she had no interest in obtaining a sentence reduction for an incarcerated individual, nor were they seeking anything in return from the Bureau or the United States Attorney. They simply wanted the reward money, nothing more, and nothing less. Mullen noticed that some of the language seemed encrypted, with specific instructions to be followed by the museum or law enforcement if they were interested in the writer's proposal. If interested, a certain combination of numbers should be published in the *Wall Street Journal's* business section; specifically the section listing the foreign exchange rate. The anonymous writer requested that the exchange rate figure for the Italian lira be intentionally misplaced by one decimal point. If the intended misprint appeared, the writer would understand that the museum had interest in continuing the dialogue.

Mullen read that when the museum received the letter, they immediately turned it over to the Bureau who in turn, forwarded it to its forensic laboratory in Quantico, Virginia. McGrath had requested a physical analysis as well as a psychological profiling of the anonymous author.

Chapter Forty-Four
Federal Courthouse, Boston, August 17, 2007

George Moore, the coordinator of the grand jury for the United States' Marshals Service had the responsibility of checking off the jurors' names as they arrived each morning. Today, he thought they'd shown up earlier than usual. Maybe it was the coffee and bagel spread that was set up in the adjoining room. Fowler, when informed by Moore what time the jurors had arrived, knew that it had nothing to do with the goodies or the fine weather, rather, it had everything to do with today's witness, former Gardner museum guard Jay Fager. The now almost forty year old who had settled in the Seattle area, still had that shaggy dog look to him. His youthful black hair was now peppered with streaks of grey.

It also looked like he probably still played the steel guitar in a rock band but, as the jurors would soon hear, his musical talent was confined to Saturday night gigs at local chicken wire-shielded, beer soaked, roadhouses. There was absolute silence in the room as Fager sat quietly at the witness stand. The jurors were anxious to hear what he had to say. Several of the female jurors whispered to each other that they thought he was handsome with his streaks of grey. "Am I going to need an attorney?" was his first question. "I can't advise you one way or another on that," Fowler said. "If you tell the truth during the entire proceedings, then you cannot be prosecuted for perjury. On the other hand, you do not have to answer any question that might or could possibly expose you to criminal prosecution. Do you understand?"

"Yeah, I do. I want a court-appointed lawyer. I climb and cut trees for a living and I don't make much money, so I can't afford to hire my own. I won't answer any questions without a lawyer." With that, Fager got up and walked out the door and took a seat in the waiting area directly outside the room, right next to George Moore.

"Fager won't testify without an attorney and he tells me he can't afford one," Fowler explained to London a few minutes later in his office. "As we both know, the court can only appoint a lawyer for him on Fifth Amendment issues, not as counsel for the entire process. He has something to tell us but he's afraid because he thinks we can charge him with a crime. I explained that the time period when we could have prosecuted him, if he was involved in the robbery, is long past. He didn't really seem to understand that. He's concerned about what could happen to him now, not seventeen years ago."

London replied, "Well, I suppose we could give him blanket immunity if he's willing to tell us everything he knows about the robbery. But, it will take Washington a couple of days to even read our request for immunity and then a couple more to have the Deputy Attorney General sign off on it. That's probably the way we should go. I think that will be our best shot. Have the victim witness advocate book three more days for Fager at the Boston Harbor hotel. The hell with it, we'll call his bluff. Once we give him immunity, the bum will answer your questions, whether he likes it or not."

Chapter Forty-Five
Hingham, Massachusetts
August 21, 2007

As usual, Fowler was running late. She had every intention of making the 5:15 PM commuter boat to Hingham, where her two daughters were home waiting for her to make dinner. There always seemed to be something else to do or telephone calls to return before she could turn off her office lights and go home. It used to be that during the summer months, work in the pipeline would slow down. With recent budget cuts, that was no longer the case. Now there was more work for fewer people. Fowler really didn't need the assignment of the cold Gardner museum case, but being the hard-hitting prosecutor she was, she never complained and approached it with the same intensity and vigor as she brought to the bank robbery case she had been assigned just a week before.

She was lucky enough to catch the 5:45 PM ferry out of Rowe's Wharf and during the 45-minute trip down to the Hingham Shipyard, she planned on just closing her eyes and listening to her music. She settled into her seat at the bow of the boat, put her earphones on and started to decompress. James Taylor's "The Secret of Life" filtered softly into her brain. Her quiet time was short lived, and soon she felt her cell phone vibrating. It was Washington. The immunity request had been approved and faxed to her a few minutes ago. Now she couldn't relax. Her mind raced with thoughts of what Fager might tell the grand jurors in the morning. She put the phone and the I-Pod back into her pocket and took out her laptop. She began banging the keys as she drafted questions she was going to pose to her prize witness in the morning.

Grand Jury Room Number Three
Federal Courthouse, Boston, August 22, 2007,
10:00 AM

"Mr. Fager, I place before you a four page document that I have marked as government's Exhibit 1 for purposes of this grand jury. I would ask you to turn to the last page. Is that your signature, sir? Did you read the document before you signed it and if so, do you understand its terms and conditions?" Fager responded in the affirmative to both questions. "Did you sign it freely and voluntarily and under no duress?" "That is correct, I did." "What is your understanding as to what your obligations are pursuant to that agreement?" "It is my understanding that if I answer your questions truthfully, even if one or more of them could incriminate me, I am, nevertheless, required to answer it. I cannot refuse to answer a question based upon my Fifth Amendment privilege against self-incrimination." "What, if anything, have you received from my office in exchange for answering all questions put to you," Fowler asked. "Again, if I answer all of the questions truthfully and honestly, I have been informed by you that I cannot be prosecuted for what I say. I also understand the time period has elapsed for your office to prosecute me for things that may have occurred in 1990, but I could still be prosecuted for not telling the truth to this grand jury. I have been given immunity." "Do you wish to proceed, Mr. Fager?" "Yes, I do."

Chapter Forty-Six
FBI's Forensic Laboratory, Quantico, Virginia, June 9, 1994

Just a little over a year before, on April 25, 1993, the FBI opened its $130 million state-of the art crime laboratory on the grounds of the Quantico Marine Corps Base, a short distance from the FBI Academy where McGrath had graduated years before. The state of the art facility is used to analyze evidence from anywhere in the United

States as well as from places across the globe. It provides free analysis of everything from blood, tissue, and bones, to bomb fragments for local, state and federal law-enforcement agencies. Its 650-plus employees include experts in document examination, genetic analysis and on-site crime scene investigation. The Bureau started psychological profiling in the 1960's in an attempt to understand violent criminal behavior.

One unit, the FSPG or Forensic Sociopat1hic Profiling Group, assists law enforcement agencies in crime scene investigations. Based upon evidence obtained, members of the FSPG present specific profiling suggestions to aid local police in identifying possible suspect types. Although primarily used in the pursuit of serial killers, the FSPG has analyzed documents in poison pen letter writing cases, including the anonymous letter to the Gardner. Agent Oliver Jones, a twenty-year veteran of the Bureau's profiling section, was given the task of analyzing the letter received by the Gardner from the anonymous author. After reviewing it, he had sent a hard copy of his findings to McGrath in Boston. Jones' report read as follows: "The letter was simply addressed to the Gardner museum. Although the writer in the body referred to the *Wall Street Journal*, the envelope was postmarked Boston, suggesting that whoever sent it might be from the Boston area. The text was well written and the grammar and vocabulary were consistent with the writing level of someone with a college education."

He found it interesting that money was mentioned only once in the letter, which suggested to him that, it might be an indication that the author was more concerned with his or her criminal exposure than any reward. Trying to interpret what was said and not said, Jones further opined, "If the letter was sent by the people who stole the paintings, they had finally come to their senses and realized that, although of significant value, the paintings were worthless or of little value unless they could be marketed and ultimately sold. By sending a letter to the museum with what was really a penny ante demand in exchange for the return of the art, it is obvious to me that the thieves recognized that their last chance to cash in on the robbery was to have the museum itself take the paintings back in exchange for the reward money."

"Unfortunately for them, because of the tremendous value and notoriety of the priceless works, with the passage of time, their spoils had transformed from the precious, gold wine goblet of Midas, to the chaffy lead of Macbeth's poison'd chalice."

Chapter Forty-Seven "The Sleuth And The Fire Extinguisher" Thirteen Years' Later

Agent Mullen held the same report in his hand that McGrath had read back in 1994. He could see that agent Jones was very firm in his opinion about the person who wrote it. "The author, although in all likelihood having graduated from college, has a belief that he or she is smarter than anyone else including federal law enforcement officers, who continue to work the case. The tone of the letter exudes an attitude of intellectual arrogance bordering on pathological narcissism from someone who is in fact of average or below average intelligence. The author's illusion of superior intelligence coupled with his amplified self-worth should be exploited in the likely event he contacts the museum again. Whoever from the museum is going to deal with the writer should purposely act as if they are beneath his superior intellectual level and play along with his egocentric, overly confident personality. It is my firm belief that if done properly, this "chess match" approach will ultimately lead to a blunder and his or her ultimate incarceration."

Putting Jones's report back into the file, Mullen continued to review McGrath's summary. Flipping through the pages, he came to a section McGrath had identified as "Extinguisher". Reading on, Mullen learned that it referred to a particular fire extinguisher that the now retired agent and Harrison had examined in the Short Gallery right below where Napoleon's banner hung, back in 1990. For some reason, the two were curious about the security pin located at the top of the unit that controlled access to the valve that allowed release of fire retardant material.

They both wondered how the pin had become partially dislodged from the safety mechanism. Other than the short reference to the pin and a note about a yellow tag that the two had found on the floor directly below the extinguisher, there was nothing else in McGrath's summary. Mullen walked over to his computer and clicked the desktop icon that read "Gardner Prints." He wanted to see if anyone had checked for prints on the fire extinguisher. It was clear to him what Harrison and McGrath thought at the time, that maybe one of the robbers had grabbed it and used it to break the glass in the two frames holding the Degas' just four feet away. Mullen believed that perhaps in the process of doing so the pin had partially dislodged from the safety valve. As he waited for the screen to tell him if the extinguisher had been checked for prints, he thought, "If one of the robbers grabbed it to smash the glass, maybe the fool left some prints."

When the screen flashed, his question was answered: the fire extinguisher had not been dusted for fingerprints. He picked up the phone to call the Bureau's new fingerprint specialist, Robert Franci and the museum's newly appointed Director of Security, Anthony Fenore, who had recently been with the Department of Homeland Security. Mullen wanted to bring Franci to the museum to dust for latent prints on the fire extinguisher. Fenore had been with the Transportation Security Administration at the T.F. Green Airport in Warwick, Rhode Island for four years. Based upon his impressive resume, the museum hired him as their new director of security. When he came on board, his first priority was to conduct a thorough analysis of the museum's security. What he found was shocking. The alarm system was outdated. No one knew for sure how many security guards were actually employed, never mind who was working during a particular shift. There was no master list or electronic monitoring with security badges to monitor who and when people entered and exited the building. There was still only one outside alarm at the guard desk, despite the fact that the security desk configuration had been revamped after the robbery. The fire escape that led up to the roof and to the 4th floor room where the alarm had triggered the night of the robbery still had no lock or electronic pad code. As Harrison had explained to McGrath as the two stood on the roof back in 1990, anyone could still get up to the roof by climbing the fire escape and enter the building with ease. After outlining his recommendations, the trustees were eager to implement them and, before too long, a new security system appeared, finally approaching 21st century technology.

Fenore walked with Mullen and Franci up the stairs near the courtyard into the Short Gallery. The first-generation fire extinguisher was still there. Looking at the safety card, it had been serviced on a regular basis since the robbery and was still in good working order. The three saw what Harrison and McGrath had seen and described seventeen years before: the safety pin was still sticking halfway out of the safety mechanism. Mullen, when he glanced to the left, could see where the sketches by Degas had once been on display. While Franci dusted the fire extinguisher for prints, Fenore was showing Mullen the exquisite pencil sketch by Michelangelo that was four feet from where the missing sketches had been ripped from their frames. Turning to Fenore, Mullen asked, "Weren't the two frames that held Degas' sketches on the wall in pieces when the police arrived, as he pointed towards an area of the dark wood?"

"They were not completely smashed but the glass from them was shattered. Although some of it remained in the frames, most of it was found in shards on the floor directly below where the prints had been. In fact, I believe right about here," as he pointed to an area on the brick floor. "Other than the fire extinguisher, is there anything else in the area that could have been used to break the glass?" Mullen asked. "Not that I can think of," Fenore replied. As soon as the last syllable came across the director of security's lips, he and Mullen heard Franci say, "Guys, come over here for a second." Franci had finished using his magical dust on the front of the fire extinguisher and was about to do the same on the back of the cylinder, when he called Mullen and Fenore over.

"I was just about to dust the sides of this thing when I noticed something on the right side of it. Here, take a look." Mullen got on his knees and, with the aid of a flashlight that he always carried with him, peered towards the back of the extinguisher, closest to the dark paneled, mahogany wall. Since the unit dated back many years, unlike newer models, this one had a wooden mallet clipped to the right side of the canister to be used in case of a fire to tap the security pin out in a hurry if someone was having difficulty removing it with their hands. "Anthony, take a look at this," Mullen said, as he continued to shine the beam of light to the side of the cylinder. "Did you know this mallet was here?" Mullen queried. "Never knew it was there and never thought to look until ten seconds ago," Fenore replied. Mullen and Fenore stepped away to allow Franci to continue with his work. When he was finished dusting for prints, he pulled a pair of surgical gloves out of his pocket. He put them on and delicately plucked the small wooden mallet from behind the extinguisher and dropped it into an evidence bag. "There are no prints of any value that I can see on the fire extinguisher. I'm going to check for prints on this thing," as he held up the plastic evidence bag that contained the mallet. Under the microscope I will be able to figure out, at least preliminarily, whether there are any latent prints on it. It certainly would have been a handy tool for the guy who grabbed the five Degas sketches particularly if he knew it was there before he got here. He wouldn't even have had to touch the frames. Grab the mallet, smash the glass with it and then snatch the prints. That would have taken about three seconds. He could have snapped it back into its holder on this side of the cylinder," as Franci pointed to the right side of the cylinder, "out of view from anyone and everyone who walked by it for the next 100 years. No one would have known it was there until they had some reason to use it or look for fingerprints like we just did."

Chapter Forty-Eight: "The Droplet Of Blood"
FBI Headquarters, Boston, Four Days' Later

Mullen was sitting at his desk eating his lunch, reading the *Boston Herald* when the phone rang. It was agent Robert Franci downstairs in his laboratory, still located in the bowels of the building. "Mullen, I've looked at that mallet. If you have a couple of minutes why don't you come on down and I'll show you what I found."

"I'll be right down," Mullen responded, tossing the last bit of his pastrami sandwich into his mouth. Just as McGrath had walked into the lab and found agent Maher looking into the microscope searching for fingerprints from the door knob from the inside of the secret door to the Dutch Room, so it was when Mullen walked in some seventeen years later. Franci was peering into the microscope and, hearing the door open, looked up and greeted the rookie agent.

"I've spent some time looking at this thing. The fire extinguisher that it came from must be an antique, you sure it still works?" he said jokingly. Then he became serious. "This is what I can tell you. There are several prints on the mallet but they are not good enough to use. There is no question that at some point in time, somebody, maybe one of the robbers or someone else for that matter, grabbed it for whatever reason. It could have been someone eighty years ago for all we know. In any event, the prints are bad so they can't help us."

"When I was looking for prints, I found something that is very interesting. I want to show you something under the microscope." Franci stood up to let Mullen sit down to look into the scope. "Try to focus in about an inch above where it starts to turn down towards the head of the mallet." As Mullen tried to focus in on the area of the mallet Franci had located, he could hear him say, "It looks like there is some brownish, black material within the wooden fibers, but it is very small." "Good. You found it. Do you know what it is?" "Not a clue, maybe it's the remnants of the stain they used when it was made."

"Pretty good guess. It is a stain but it's not from when it was made. It's blood. The material in the wooden fiber of this little hammer is a droplet of blood and if I were a betting man, it was probably unwittingly donated by someone who had the brilliant idea of using the handy little gavel to break some glass in some picture frames back in 1990." Mullen, now looking up from the microscope turned to Franci who quipped, "Hammers, sharp glass and human skin usually equal blood. I bet whoever used this trusty little hammer the night of the robbery didn't even realize that he had cut himself. I've already requested a forensic blood analyst from Quantico to come on up to take a look, and to do whatever they need to do to transform this little crusty, old blood stain from its petrified state into a shining gem of evidence."

Chapter Forty-Nine: "An Incredible Tale"

Fowler was standing to the left of the witness table in grand jury room No.3. There was a quorum and all of the jurors were in their seats. Fager was seated at the witness table directly in front of the court-certified stenographer who swore him in. "Do you swear to tell the truth and nothing but the truth so help you God?" "I do," Fager responded in a very serious tone. Almost in sync with his response, a thunderclap sounded and rain started to pound the skylight directly over the jurors' heads. "Mr. Fager, I believe you have something to tell this jury about the Isabella Stewart Gardner museum robbery?" "I do," he responded. "I want to get this off my chest. I've been carrying this around like the chains of Jacob Marley for almost twenty years. Back in early January 1990 I was pretty heavy into pot and unfortunately graduated to cocaine. Most nights when I was working at the museum I would show up with a good buzz on. Why not? It was such a freaking bore just walking around in the dark. Other than having a buzz and trying to outsmart the alarms by crazy stunts, most of us would go nuts during those eight hours if we weren't high. They paid us crap money and so we really didn't have much allegiance to the museum or to our bosses. We were college kids! They really didn't treat us very well but we could have cared less. My focus at that point in my life was to get high and to play in my band. It didn't really work out the way I wanted it to. Instead of being just a pothead, I started dealing to support my growing love affair with the nose candy."

"The shit hit the fan when my supplier came to me one week looking for his money. Like a complete dope, the money I got from the people I sold to started to go up my nose, and not into his pocket. When the man came knocking for his money, it was all gone and that's when I had to basically go into hiding. He luckily didn't know where I lived and he had no clue that I worked at the museum. I used to meet him at various locations around town to pick up the drugs. I didn't let him know where I lived but he did know where I was going to school so I stopped going to classes. I was in big trouble and I needed some help. I mentioned my situation to a couple of the guards at the museum to see if they could lend me any money, but they both said they were broke. If I didn't come up with the money, and it was a couple of thousand bucks, my supplier told me in no uncertain terms that he was going to have a couple of his boys from Dorchester break my legs or worse."

"Here I was a college student with leg breakers after me. I was scared shitless." Fowler and the jurors were spellbound. "Our band used to play at an after-hours bar in the South End on Canard Street. It was a weird place with all kinds of city people, both young and old. There were straight people, gays and believe it or not, guys who liked to dress up as women. All we knew was that they all liked to mingle and listen to some music after the bars closed at 2:00 AM. We got paid in cash and would smoke a couple of bones while we played and just enjoyed watching people."

"One night when I was packing up the equipment, this dude approached me and from out of the blue asked me if I worked at the Gardner museum. I had no idea why he wanted to know. Anyway, I told him that I did. He asked me if he could talk to me outside and since he didn't look like a psychopath, the two of us walked out together. He told me that he had a proposition for me. He said he had a nephew who also worked at the museum and when I asked who it was, he told me it didn't matter. He was very glib. In a matter of fact tone, he said that he knew that I had a drug problem and that

I owed money to the wrong people, who, in his words, were very capable of hurting me very badly. He said he could help and when I asked him how, he said he had the ability to call the wolves off. All I needed to tell him was how much I owed and he would take care of it."

"I didn't give a flying fuck what he wanted in return as long as he could get the leg breakers off my tail. I would have sold him my first-born for him to get me out of that jam. He put his hand on my shoulder while we continued to walk and said that the only thing I would have to do some night was to let two guys dressed in police uniforms into the museum through the Palace Road entrance. If I agreed to do that, he would take care of my problem. I knew right then and there what I was going to do but I told him I would need some time to think about it. He asked me if the band was playing next Saturday night and when I told him that we were, he said he would be there and I could tell him what my decision was. He turned to me and said in a rather frightening tone that he really wanted to hear from me before then."

"The last thing he said really scared the shit out of me. Again, in a very threatening tone, he told me to really think hard about it because if my answer was no, although the leg breakers didn't know where I lived, he did. He then took a dime out of his pocket and stuck it in my face and said in a very menacing tone, 'Do you know what I can do with this? I can ruin your fucking life! Do you understand? Don't think too long about it'. He then tossed me the dime and told me to use it to call him and nobody else, especially the police. He handed me a piece of paper with a number on it and then walked off into the night."

Chapter Fifty: Grand Jury Room Number Three, Federal Courthouse, Boston, August 22, 2007, 2:00 PM

The jurors were on the edge of their seats anxiously waiting to hear more of what Fager had to say. He continued with his amazing story. "I knew what I had to do. So two days later I called the guy, who, by the way, never gave me his name, and told him I was in. We agreed to meet at a local bar down the street from my apartment. We sat at a table way in the back, where nobody could hear us. It was early in the day so the place was empty except for the bartender and a couple of drunks. He gave me instructions and told me what was going to go down."

"He explained that I had to make sure that they gave me the 11:00 to 7:00 overnight shift on the 17th. He told me that at about 1:00 in the morning on March 18th his nephew would open the inside door on Palace Road and then the outside door. I was to make sure that whoever I was working with that night be as far away from the guard desk as possible doing his rounds. The nephew would hand off Manet's portrait that he'd grab from the Blue Room to a driver who would be in a white van parked on Palace Road leaving the empty frame on a chair in the director of security's office. They would take me into the basement and secure me with duct tape and handcuffs to wait for the police."

"I think Morris told the FBI agent, I think his name was McGrath, he saw me being escorted down the corridor in the opposite direction from him. Well, that's true, but I wasn't brought down until later. In fact, I think Morris told someone that he had heard footsteps near him on several occasions that night. He was right. The first time was when one of the robbers went down there to see if he was alright and the next time was when they brought me downstairs to tape me up and secure me to a pole in a different area of the basement. Morris was absolutely right when he told McGrath that when he was in the basement and everything was quiet, there was some noise directly above him that sounded like there were more than two people, as he said, 'working upstairs'. Well, there was me, the nephew, and the two cops."

"Oh yeah, I almost forgot. The guard that I was supposed to work with that night purposely called in sick. That's how I ended up working with Morris. There are a couple of other things you should also know. The guys dressed up as cops weren't wearing walkie-talkies. The things on their belts looked like police issued radios, but they were really portable police scanners. They somehow knew what frequency the Boston police were using that night. They listened to the chatter on the scanners, and knew that they were in the clear because they never heard dispatch request any cruiser to head to the museum for reports of suspicious activity, a break-in or any robbery." What Fager next relayed to the jury was a bombshell.

"I don't have any firsthand knowledge how they knew what frequency BPD was going to use that night, but I had heard through the grapevine that at least one or a couple of real Boston cops were in on the robbery. They were allegedly friends with a City of Boston building inspector who had the Fenway as his sector." What he said next caused the jaw of everyone in the room to drop. "By the way when I radioed Morris to have him come down to the security desk, he told the FBI and Boston police that he was doing his rounds at the time. That's bullshit. He was sound asleep in the fourth floor bedroom. The radio call woke him up! I'm ashamed of what I did but I had to do it to save my skin." When he finished telling his astonishing story, Fowler asked him the question everyone in the room wanted to know the answer to: "Who was the nephew?" "It was Eliot Neufeldt, the guard that Morris had supposedly just relieved!"

The AUSA then placed eight photographs in front of the now confessed accessory to the largest theft of art in United States history and asked, "Have you ever seen any of the people depicted in these photographs before?" Dead silence. You could hear a pin drop as Fager reviewed the photos. "Yes, I have," as he picked up one of them. "This is the guy who approached me that night at the club and offered to help me get out of a jam I was in. He's the same guy who told me what I had to do. I will never forget his face and those piercing eyes! He scared the living shit out of me." As he turned the photo to look at the back of it, someone had written a name in pencil. The jurors were on the edge of their seats.

"Whose name appears on the back of the photograph," Fowler asked. "David Mercer," Fager responded. "Mercer, at the time, explained to me that the van would have the words 'security' in yellow letters printed on the driver and passenger side doors and yellow flashers on its roof. I got the drift that the nephew had had a run in with the assistant director of security, so he placed the empty frame on a chair in his office. When I asked him about that he just said that it was his nephew's way of saying 'fuck you'. Once the painting had been handed off, the nephew was going to come back in and hide in an area just under the stairwell to the second floor."

"It's the same set of stairs Morris walked down when I radioed him. He went on and explained to me that, at about 1:20 AM, two men dressed as police officers, would arrive at the employee entrance and when they rang the doorbell, I was to let them in. He told me that when the other guard eventually showed up at the desk, I was supposed to act shocked and put on a dog and pony show, like I was stunned. The last thing he told me was that when the other guard arrived at the security desk, his nephew would head on upstairs to the conservation laboratory where he would wait for the two guys dressed as police officers. The kid was there to show them the most direct way into the Dutch Room, through the secret paneled door that had 'The Storm' hanging on the other side." Listening to this incredible story, Fowler glanced at the mesmerized jurors who were scribbling notes as fast as they could.

"The only thing he wanted me to do was to let the two guys in and then help them and his nephew put the paintings in white plastic tubes without damaging them. He explained that once that was taken care of, they would take me down into the basement and secure me with duct tape and handcuffs to wait for the police."

Chapter Fifty-One: "The Forensic Expert" FBI Headquarters, Boston, August 28, 2007

When Mullen arrived at his desk early the next morning, still astonished by what Fowler had told him yesterday about Fager's testimony, he hit his voice mail button to listen to his messages. The first message was from agent Franci. He sounded excited. The forensic expert from the lab in Quantico was able to obtain enough of the dried blood from the wooden mallet to run it through the Bureau's DNA Analyzer and then the database to check for any matches. The expert had traveled to Boston in order to brief Franci and Mullen. He went on to say that he didn't want to provide any more information over the phone and that if he were available he should meet them at 8:30 in the morning in the laboratory. Mullen looked at his watch. It was 8:15 AM.

When he walked into the lab, Mullen could see that the 'guy' from Quantico was actually a 'girl', agent Lynn Cramer, who had a particular academic interest in genetic/antibody analysis of long forgotten blood, tissue and bone. She held a PhD. in forensic science from Yale University School of Pathology and had completed several fellowships in archaeological forensics at the National Institutes of Health in Bethesda, Maryland. After introductions, she started to brief them.

"The material on the mallet is indeed blood. It is type O, which is very common. About 45% of Americans have that blood type. It is from a male and, in my opinion, has been on that piece of wood for quite some time. I extracted the DNA and analyzed it for the presence of a set of specific DNA regions or what we call markers. When I performed an antibody analysis of the blood, I found something unusual. The antibodies showed that the individual who left his blood on the mallet had suffered from a chronic, familial, inherited hemolytic anemia that is normally confined to populations from countries bordering the Mediterranean Sea. It is called Thalassemia or Mediterranean Anemia, a rather rare blood disorder." Mullen, listening to all this scientific garble, started to feel a headache coming on. "That finding limits the number of people in our database population that we need to be looking for," she said, tongue in cheek.

"Whoever this guy is, his ancestors were from a country that borders the Mediterranean Sea. Let's see, that narrows it down to: Italy, France, Spain, Turkey, Slovenia, Croatia, Bosnia/Herzegovina, Montenegro, Albania, Greece, Syria, Lebanon, Israel, Egypt, Libya, Tunisia, Algeria, Morocco and, oh yes, last but not least the tiny Principality of Monaco." Catching her breath, she smiled at the two agents.

"Just last night, I had my colleague at Quantico start to do the genetic portion of the analysis to see if there were any matches. It will take several days and hopefully, something will show up. Obviously, the only way there will be a match is if someone has for some reason already provided his DNA. As we say in the jargon of forensic science, we can obtain DNA either the easy way or the hard way. Getting it the easy way would generally be from a sample a defendant gives to law enforcement pursuant to a court order or blood warrant. The latter method of obtaining one's genetic material, on the other hand," as she once again smiled at the two male agents, "would be when it's taken during a post-mortem examination while a pathologist dices and slices the corpse lying in the supine position while frigid water churns underneath." As Cramer finished, she turned around and looked over at the two agents and took a bite from her bagel. It appeared to her that the two were about to lose their breakfasts. Looking back at her, they both thought that she actually appeared to be enjoying the whole thing!

Chapter Fifty-Two: " The Dead Speak"
FBI's Forensic Laboratory Quantico, Virginia,

As Cramer had represented to Franci and Mullen, her colleague had processed the blood found on the mallet and was now in the lab waiting to see if there was a match. The computer screen on Dr. Thomas Fischer's granite counter flashed, signifying that there had been a hit on the blood. Doctor Fischer, a long time forensic scientist with the Bureau, was pleased that there was a genetic match from the blood found on the mallet. It was from a thirty-four year old white male from Malden, Massachusetts, named Bobby Datoli.

In the vernacular of the forensic scientist, Datoli had not donated his genetic material; the Chief Medical Examiner of the Commonwealth of Massachusetts had taken it from him on the day after Veteran's Day, 1997. Datoli's badly decomposed body was found hog-tied in the trunk of a car parked at Manchester International Airport. His head had been almost completely severed from the rest of his body and he had many puncture wounds, the apparent result of being stabbed multiple times on his torso, hands and forearms. The latter wounds suggested there had been a brief, defensive struggle that ended, unfortunately, in his untimely demise. Fischer walked over to the computer terminal on his desk and typed Datoli's name into the Law Enforcement Concepts database. When his record appeared on the screen, Fischer could see that he was no stranger to the law. Based upon his Board of Probation record, Fischer counted seventeen separate encounters with the criminal justice system. It consisted mostly of misdemeanors: assault and battery, larceny under $250 and check cashing fraud. One entry, though, was a felony arrest. In 1982, Datoli and a co-defendant, tried to slip out of the Museum of Fine Arts in Boston, located just down the street from the Gardner, with a valuable painting.

The two had brazenly tried to pull off the heist in broad daylight. But for the watchful eye of a guard perusing the security monitors, they might have gotten away with it. Since the two were grabbed before they were able to exit the museum, they were charged with attempted robbery in the Roxbury District Court. Standing before a judge, they both admitted that the prosecutor had enough evidence to find them guilty. By doing so, they were placed on probation for a term of eighteen months. The judge ordered they be barred from all museums in the Commonwealth, an order that probation would have to monitor for compliance.

There was one tiny problem with making it a part of the plea bargain: it was impossible to either enforce or monitor. As a consequence, it turned out to be a promise that ultimately would be broken! Fischer wanted to see who Datoli's co-defendant was so he typed in the docket number from the Roxbury District Court. When the screen flashed he looked at the caption on the complaint. He read it out loud, "COMMONWEALTH v. ROBERT F. DATOLI and DAVID MERCER".

Chapter Fifty-Three: "The Wise Guys From Dorchester"

When Mullen read Fischer's report he wanted to learn as much as he could about Datoli's co-defendant, David Mercer. He discovered that Mercer was a tough kid from Avon, Massachusetts, who had been a terrific athlete in high school. For some reason, the burly kid with the charming smile started to hang around with the wrong crowd at some point in his early twenties, and eventually crossed over the line to become a vicious criminal and suspected killer. At the age of thirty-six, Mercer had been found guilty in October, 2001 by a federal jury of conspiracy, attempted robbery and related firearms offenses for his role in a 1999 scheme to rob an armored car facility in a town not too far from where he lived at the time.

A judge in the United States District Court in Boston sentenced him to a prison term, of 46 years. One of Mercer's co-conspirators in that botched robbery, Carmine Martino, who had been sentenced to a similarly lengthy stint for his part in the attempted robbery, died in prison. Mullen learned that Martino was one of the robbers who went to prison for his role in the infamous 1968 Brink's robbery in Boston. He was also charged in 1992 with running a million-dollar cocaine ring in cities and towns south of Boston, all from an auto shop located in Dorchester, where his crew had planned the 1999 armored car facility heist. Mullen was startled by what he next read about Martino. An FBI informant provided information that Martino and, other Italian brothers in organized crime, was involved in or at least possessed information about the Isabella Stewart Gardner museum robbery. The rat fingered him as the mastermind behind it. Now, the rookie agent possessed something much better than a confidential informant's word. He had hard, concrete evidence that both Datoli and Mercer appeared to have also been active participants in the Gardner robbery.

Chapter Fifty-Four: "The Letter And The Mysterious Notes" Federal Courthouse, Boston, August 27, 2007

After speaking with Mullen, Savage wanted to locate the original envelope that contained the anonymous letter to the museum. She wanted to show it to Fowler to suggest that they run a genetic test on the flap of it. Whoever sent it back in 1994 might not have appreciated at the time, that some of his or her DNA may have been left on the flap when they sealed it! There was no question in her mind, that with the incredible technological advancement in forensic medicine and science, the Bureau could definitely lift some genetic material from the envelope. It took her several days to locate it because for some reason, it was not in the correct evidence bag. With the help of agent Curcio, they found it in another evidence bag marked "saliva". When she broached the subject of having it analyzed for DNA, it took Fowler about three seconds to pick up the phone and dial Mullen's number at the Bureau. Savage heard her say that she wanted him to come by and pick it up in the morning and forward it to Quantico for analysis. She would leave the envelope on her chair in her office in a manila envelope, since she had a 9:00 hearing in the morning. She ended the conversation by asking him to let her know first thing if Quantico came up with any positive findings and if she was not available, to give the information, good or bad, to Ms. Savage.

Home from work and exhausted after a hectic day, Savage stood on the stairs of her apartment on Joy Street fumbling for her keys. With a laptop slung over her shoulder and a bag of Chinese food held precariously in her left hand, she was having some difficulty finding them. As the door opened, she noticed a folded piece of white paper fall to the cobbled stoop. Flipping the light on as she walked into the tiny cluttered apartment and dropping the items in her arms on the counter, she walked back to the doorway, bent down and picked up the piece of paper. Figuring it was a note from one of the other interns she unfolded it as she walked back to the lighted counter. While she poured a glass of Pinot Noir, she read what was on the typewritten note. "Follow the Paper Trail...Do Not Get Discouraged... Find the Pieces of the Puzzle that Should be There But are Not...STRIKE FORCE..........Deve-se estudar para aprender". Stunned, she walked over to the overstuffed chair and plopped down with the note still in her hand. She sat there in silence and stared at the words as she took a long sip from her glass of wine.

Boston's Federal Courthouse, the Next Morning

Katharine told no one about the note. She was sitting at the table in the War Room when the telephone rang. It was agent Mullen. "I tried to reach Fowler but got her voice mail, so I called you. I received word back from the people at Quantico concerning the envelope. Just as with the blood sample, the analysis of the envelope also took a couple of days and agent Fischer performed it for us this time as well. The bad news is that unfortunately, there was no identifiable DNA material on the flap. The good news is that Fischer, who tells me he is always thinking outside the box, didn't end his examination of the envelope there. He told me while sitting there with the envelope in his hand; a light went off in his head. He realized that there was one other place he could check for DNA evidence on the envelope other than the flap. Although whoever had sent the letter apparently didn't lick it to seal it, maybe they did the next best thing with it: licking the postage stamp, official issue of the United States Postal Service."

"He told me it was a more difficult task than analyzing the flap since he needed to remove the stamp from the envelope without destroying any DNA that might be there. With some dexterity and patience and some steam, Fischer was able to remove the stamp from the envelope in order to swab the adhesive back of it, hopefully picking up DNA from the sender's saliva. He lucked out! He told me he was able to obtain a very good sample. That was the good news; now, the bad. When he entered the DNA into the Bureau's database, there were no positive hits. He ended the conversation by telling me that the only way we're going to be able to determine who this DNA belongs to is to identify who we feel are still viable suspects."

"After compiling a list, he told us that we had to obtain their hair, saliva or blood to compare with what he has down in Virginia. He said it was going to be a long shot, but there are no alternatives. Why don't I take a ride over so we can make a list of who we might want to get samples from and figure out a game plan on how we can obtain them? We can then present it to Fowler to see if she agrees. It seems to me that the Whitcomb brothers as well as Condon, Lewis, and Mercer would be on the list since I don't believe we have any genetic material from them. Datoli and Martino shouldn't be on the list because their DNA was already in the database. If it were their DNA there would have been a hit. So they're excluded. As for the others, we're going to have to figure out a way to get samples for Fischer.

Mullen, who was not aware of Savage's work in the Bronx District Attorney's office the prior summer, was surprised to hear what she had to say in response. "It seems to me that all we need to do is to place surveillance on them for a couple of days or so to see where they drink and get their hair cut. A haphazardly tossed cigarette butt or several strands of hair quickly lifted from a barber's floor would do the trick. It would take an undercover agent five seconds to pick up the cigarette butt and a quick "excuse me I just dropped something" for another agent to snatch several strands of hair off the floor. It could be done very easily and without anyone of them knowing what had just taken place. Why don't you come on by around 4:00 PM when we can run it by Amy?" "I'll see you then," Mullen said as he hung up the phone.

Fowler, Mullen and Savage were seated at the table in the War Room, putting their heads together trying to devise a plan to obtain DNA material from the people they believed may have been involved, either directly or indirectly with the robbery and the mailing of the anonymous letter. Fowler spoke first. "I think the surveillance suggestion is a good one. The only problem is, do we know if all these characters drink or smoke? If they don't, we're out of luck going down that road. The haircut idea I think is a good one and would be our fall-back position. I'm just afraid that someone in the barber shop or salon might see what was going on and ask why we are picking up strands of hair off the floor from their last customer."

"The last thing I want to do is to spook any one of these guys. At this stage, we don't want to tip them off that we are looking at them as suspects. If they get wind that we are looking at them, the paintings could be lost forever." Mullen piped in, "I don't think that's going to be a problem. I have already spoken to my chief and he has agreed, at least for the moment, to provide several additional agents to do the surveillance here in Boston. They're extraordinarily good in undercover work. In fact, the two agents are probably the best in the business according to my SAC. He wants me to speak with the San Francisco field office to see if they would agree to assign a couple of agents to tail Allan Whitcomb in Carmel. I will make that call in the morning but I don't think we'll have any problem with that request. If our agents keep their eyes on Whitcomb's shop and if he smokes and has an occasional cocktail after work, they should be able to get a sample from him."

"If, on the other hand, he is living an altar boy's life, which I highly doubt, the agents will have to go trolling for his silvery locks wherever he gets his haircut," Mullen said. Fowler interjected, "Whitcomb shouldn't have any clue that we are looking at him now, seventeen years after the heist. It should be relatively easy for the agents to remain undercover and not spook him. As for his brother Michael, he should also have absolutely no inkling that we're looking at him; so, we should be in good shape. I think we are going to have a potential problem with Mercer since he is in custody. However, we can speak with the Bureau of Prisons if need be to have them help us with a sample. Katharine, between now and then, could you please take a walk over to Suffolk Superior court, which is now located at the old federal courthouse, and make copies of the docket sheets in the two criminal cases that were brought against Michael Whitcomb."

Chapter Fifty-Five: Suffolk Superior Courthouse, Boston, Massachusetts, August 30, 2007

While going through the docket sheets at Superior Court, Savage learned that the criminal cases against Michael Whitcomb were both disposed of by way of admissions to sufficient facts, just short of a guilty plea. With the assistance of very capable counsel, he was placed on probation and ordered to pay restitution to the two corporate victims of the fraud, Allstate and the Fireman's Fund. The facts, as alleged in the indictments, involved a scheme of submitting health insurance claims for services that had never been rendered to patients by the prescribing physician. The scheme was very simple. Motorists injured in car accidents sought treatment at local neighborhood physical therapy clinics. After receiving non-invasive treatment such as heat and massage, the patients would go on their way. They weren't aware however, that the corrupt owners of the clinics were submitting bogus claims to the insurance companies demanding payment for more expensive tests. The indictments alleged that Whitcomb was partners with a Russian businessman who owned physical therapy clinics in mostly low-income cities. When the insurance companies finally developed software to track the number of claims submitted, they red-flagged clinics that were submitting excessive numbers. Whitcomb's clinics were on that list. That's how he and his partner in crime got caught. They became greedy and the scam crumbled down around them. As Savage stood at the copy machine she wondered," If the two had not gotten greedy and stayed under the radar screen, submitting just enough claims that would not have been picked up by the software, the two of them would have made a ton of money. The age-old maxim in law enforcement circles finally caught up with Whitcomb and his partner in crime: 'pigs get fat, hogs get slaughtered'."

Chapter Fifty-Six
Two Weeks' Later

Fenore had just returned from a meeting with agent Mullen at the Bureau. He was very pleased with his enthusiasm and energy but continued to be disappointed with the lack of progress in the case. As he threw his jacket on the hook behind the door where he had taped a copy of the "Storm," he noticed a package on his chair. He picked it up and saw that it was addressed to him and had a San Francisco postmark. The words "Personal and Confidential" in red ink were written across the front. It contained a videocassette. His interest was piqued since he would receive emails and letters from all kinds of people on a daily basis about the robbery but this was the first tape he had received. He placed it in the VCR he had in his office and pushed the play button. The initial grey fuzziness turned shortly to color to reveal a man, probably in his early sixties, talking to the camera. It was a question-and-answer format with someone off-camera asking questions about the Gardner robbery. The man on camera was dressed in black and wearing sunglasses, making him look like one of the Blues Brothers. He was complaining about how he had been falsely accused by the FBI of being involved in the Gardner museum robbery in 1990. Throughout the short clip, he lamented how the Bureau and its agents had tormented and hounded him for years, notwithstanding his constant denial that he was involved in it, and his solid alibis for the night in question.

Fenore was blown away by what he heard next. The strange looking character looking directly into the camera said in a very distinct Boston accent, "I want to clear my name about the Gardner museum robbery. Let me say this once. I was not involved in the robbery! I want the world to know that I am the person to deal with if a thief or robber, from any location on the planet, wishes to return any stolen art work to its rightful owner, including those taken from the Gardner museum in Boston. If anyone wants to come forward to return a painting or other stolen museum pieces, I will act as middleman and broker for the return of any works of art. No questions asked." Fenore's first reaction: "Why was he doing this?" The answer came next. As he watched and listened to the remainder of the video, he heard the mysterious man say: "My only intent is truly an altruistic one, to act as a conduit for the return of stolen art treasures of any kind to museums around the world. Why? So the public can once again enjoy what has been, sadly, taken from them. Simply put, it is the right thing to do and I am more than happy to act as the intermediary for any crook or thief, to accomplish that goal." Fenore was truly blown away!

Boston's Federal Courthouse, The Next Morning

Fowler, Savage and Mullen were, once again, all seated in the War Room. They had just finished watching the video dropped off by Fenore. Katharine was speechless. When Fowler saw the look on her face once the second short clip ended, she asked her what was wrong. "I can't believe it, the guy in the videos is Allan Whitcomb. He's sending out the word to anyone who will listen, that he is available to broker the return of any stolen pieces of art to their owners, including the Gardner. It's unbelievable. Remember, back in 1997, two convicted felons by the names of Lewis and Condon offered to broker the return of the Gardner paintings in exchange for some consideration from this office? It never went anywhere because they wanted their jail terms reduced and the U.S. Attorney wouldn't go along with it. Now we have Whitcomb, who is a person of interest in the robbery despite the fact that he was written off by the Bureau shortly after the heist seventeen years ago, trying to do the same thing. The only difference is that Whitcomb is apparently not looking for anything in return. We also now know that Whitcomb and Lewis had a business relationship."

Fowler, listening, spoke up. "I don't buy what he is saying about why he's trying to do this," she said. "He's a convicted felon, right? He's not doing this out of the goodness of his heart. He has to have an angle and we need to find out what it is in short order. Given this new development, we need to expedite trying to get DNA from the Whitcomb brothers and anybody else we think is a viable suspect. It seems very strange to me that Allan Whitcomb, although having been discounted as being involved in the robbery, is now trying to broker the return of stolen artwork, from among other places, the Gardner. Something doesn't make sense. Let's get the undercover agents in place here in Boston and in San Francisco within the next several days, so we can do a little genetic harvesting," Fowler said. "I'm confident that the four agents, two on the west coast and two on the east coast, will be in place within forty-eight hours," Mullen replied. However, as with most things involving the federal government, the group would soon find out that coordinating the surveillance operation between Boston and San Francisco took much longer than it should have.

Chapter Fifty-Seven
Carmel by the Sea, California
September 13, 2007

The streets of the beautiful village of Carmel by the Sea are lined with upscale art studios, antique boutiques, restaurants, and bars. Storefront window displays, although smaller in scale, equal the luxuriously decorated windows on Fifth Avenue in New York at Christmas time. One of the shops, "Artful Taste," with its distinctive blue awning out front, offers expensive paintings and antiques. Located at 1166 Main Street, it caters to the well heeled of Carmel and wealthy tourists in the area who come play at Pebble Beach. Four doors down from Whitcomb's shop, is the tourist attraction, Fog's Breath, a small tavern owned by a Hollywood actor. As Mullen had promised Fowler, after receiving the go ahead from their SAC two days before, two undercover FBI agents had secured a location directly across the street from the always-busy tavern. To minimize the chance of being detected, they sat quietly in a van parked at the curb a few car lengths down the street from his shop. Although the lettering on its side read "Jay's Plastering and Drywall" there was no plaster, trowels or buckets inside. What it did contain was highly sophisticated electronic and sound devices that enabled the two agents to hear every word spoken in Whitcomb's shop.

For the first several hours of surveillance, only four or five customers walked in to browse. Based upon the size of the package they walked out of the shop with, a couple appeared to have purchased a painting, but for the most part business was slow. At about 5:40 PM, however, the two agents heard someone, in what sounded like a male's voice, say that he was heading to the Breath. Several seconds later, peering through the one way glass in the van's driver's side window, they saw a white male whose hair was in a ponytail walk out of the shop.
He looked like Whitcomb but appeared older than in the RMV photo given to the agents by

Mullen. It was also difficult to confirm it was their target because he was wearing sunglasses. The two watched him enter the tavern and then they sat and waited. About twenty minutes after he entered, he appeared in the doorway and stepped down the two small steps and onto the sidewalk. They were in luck. His sunglasses were off and they were able to get a very good look at him as he placed a cigarette in his mouth and lit it. Smoking it almost down to the filter, he then flipped it into the gutter and walked back inside. Not skipping a beat, agent Robert Kline opened the passenger side door, quickly jumped out, walked over to where the cigarette butt had landed and picked it up. If anyone had been paying attention and looked closely at Kline's right hand, they might have found it curious that the young man from Jay's Plastering was wearing a surgical glove. Hopping back into his seat, Kline dropped the now secure piece of evidence into the small plastic baggy evidence bag and handed it to his partner as he grinned and said, "Like taking candy from a baby."

Boston's Waterfront, September 16, 2007

Agents Kevin Smith and David Butler had a combined twenty-four years of experience at the Bureau. They were both very adept at surveillance and undercover work. They were no nonsense guys and were clearly the type of agents their colleagues would want next to them when the proverbial hit the fan. They were more than happy letting the younger agents handle the bank robberies and hostage taking cases. Surveillance work was just fine with them. Mullen had briefed them about the case and Michael Whitcomb's potential involvement.

Their sole task was to obtain an item that contained his DNA that Quantico could use to examine and run through their genetic database. They told Mullen they understood their assignment and were happy to help out.

They then asked the rookie agent where Whitcomb hung out. When Mullen told them that he ran a marina/bar down off Atlantic Avenue, they both looked at each other and started to laugh, "I hope our bar tabs are all paid up!" The marina is located not far from the Union Oyster House where agent McGrath used to stop to watch the shuckers perform their magic on his way to the Chart House. It is also located about three blocks from the Federal Courthouse. Although the bar inside the marina is small, because of its location and terrific view of the harbor it is a favorite hangout of local members of the FBI and other law enforcement officials.

Most evenings around 5:30, regulars from the courthouse, local union contractors and the usual crowd from the FBI, including agents Butler and Smith would be gathered at the bar. When the two seasoned agents strolled into the marina the night after Mullen had briefed them, it was just like any other. Many of their colleagues were already there. When Mullen had given them Michael Whitcomb's RMV photo, they both laughed. They had seen that face many times before. He knew both their names and greeted them every night. Whitcomb was a creature of habit. He would walk around the bar to make sure everyone was behaving and having a good time. As Butler and Smith greeted and shook hands with their colleagues, they ordered a couple of beers.

Like clockwork, Whitcomb walked out from a room at the far end of the bar and scanned the room. He looked to be in his early to mid-sixties and was in good shape. Based upon what he was wearing, he obviously had an affinity for colorful, fancy clothes and from the looks of his hair he probably had it coiffed on fashionable Newbury Street. There was one other thing peculiar about Whitcomb. Everyone noticed it when they first met him. He had a rather protuberant nose. During the many hours spent belly to the bar Butler and Smith noticed that in addition to his habit of taking his walkabout, he would always stand at the far left hand corner of the bar and drink coffee all night long.

Although it was not Butler's customary practice to order a cup of coffee after having a couple of beers, he did so this night. The two agents planned to create a scene that would divert Whitcomb's attention from the bar. They could then discreetly grab his cup and replace it with Butler's. The two walked out of the bar pretending they were going to have a cigarette.

That's when they agreed on the diversion that would give Butler an opportunity to make the switch. When they walked back in, they purposely migrated towards the group of agents that stood closer to Whitcomb.

As Smith started to walk over to the men's room he intentionally dropped his beer on the floor. Whitcomb, hearing the crash, looked over and saw what had just happened. Smith could see through the corner of his eye, as he bent over to start picking up shards of glass, that Whitcomb had picked up a towel from the bar with his left hand and started to walk over to where Smith stood apologizing profusely for the mess. That's when Butler made his move. With the skill and speed of a career professional, Butler scooped Whitcomb's cup, and with the same gentle dexterity, placed his own cup on the saucer. It took about three seconds. In order to prevent any contamination, just as in Carmel, Butler wore a surgical glove on his right hand. He walked quickly over to the men's room and, taking out an evidence bag, gently dropped the cup in. As the two walked out, Smith turned to Butler and said, "Did you get a chance to see what hand he used to pick up his coffee cup?" "Yes I did. The same one he used to grab the rag and wipe the floor with, his left."

Chapter Fifty-Eight: "Stumped"
Federal Courthouse, Boston, September 23, 2007

The trio of Fowler, Mullen and Savage were once again seated at the table in the War Room. They were waiting for a conference call with agent Fischer. The coffee cup and cigarette butt had been sent down to Quantico. Fischer had left a voice mail on Mullen's phone that he wanted to go over his findings with them today at 3:00 PM. It was now 2:58 PM. When the phone rang on the conference room table, Fowler hit a button on the conference call unit and said "Good afternoon agent Fischer. This is AUSA Amy Fowler and I am here with agent Mullen, who I believe you know, and my law clerk Katharine Savage. We appreciate you taking the time to speak with us and we hope you have some good news." "Thank you, Attorney Fowler," as he also said hello to Mullen and Savage. "I do have some news for you but I don't know if it's good or bad because I am not privy to the names of any of the targets in your investigation. I will tell you that what we found is quite odd." As Fischer continued, the three in Boston anxiously listened, guarded anticipation showing on their faces, particularly Katharine's. "We created a DNA profile from the material taken from the cigarette butt and when we compared it to that found on the stamp from the anonymous letter sent to the museum in 1994, there was a perfect match. Here's where it gets complicated. The small amount we were able to recover from the coffee cup is also a dead ringer for the DNA we found on the stamp! Bryan, correct me if I'm wrong, I thought you told me that the DNA samples were collected from two different people, right?" Fowler, Savage, and Mullen, who were now looking at each other, were stunned. As Fowler pressed the mute button, she looked directly at Mullen and asked, "How could he have gotten those results?" Mullen sat there with a puzzled look on his face. With the mute now off, he answered the question.

"The samples were obtained from two separate individuals, two brothers, one living here in Boston and one out in California." "Well that solves the puzzle," Fischer responded, with excitement in his voice. "These two brothers are not only siblings. They were born on the same day, probably just minutes apart. Given the DNA results, they have to be identical twins! That explains our results. The DNA from identical twins would be the same, they would be mirror images of each other!" Fowler, sounding a little aggravated with Fischer jumped in. "Are you sure about the results of the testing? What is the error rate, or more appropriately, the accuracy rate when we're talking about DNA?"

"That's an excellent question, Amy. We want to be as accurate as possible. Since an individual's liberty is at stake, we run the genetic material through three highly calibrated, highly accurate molecular spectrophotometers. If there is any discrepancy at all between any of the three, we are required by our own written policies and standards to opine in writing that the results are inconclusive. In any case where DNA evidence is at issue, as it is in most if not all cold-cases, given the testing inconsistencies, our opinions would never meet the very high criminal standard of proof beyond a reasonable doubt."

"As to the accuracy rate, let me just say that it will never be 100% because there is always the slight possibility that the DNA match may be by mere chance. However, the probability of that happening is about 0.001%. In layman terms that's 1 in 100,000 or an accuracy rate of 99.99%." The three were flabbergasted. The conference call was over. Fowler turned to Mullen and before she could even open her mouth he shook his head and said, "It didn't occur to me to ever compare the two RMV photos of the Whitcomb brothers. I never really thought about it. "Don't worry about it. Can you call your assistant at the Bureau and have her e-mail the two digital photos to us in the next few minutes?" Fowler asked.

They had regrouped at Fowler's desk when the e-mail with an attachment arrived. She was seated in her chair with Mullen and Savage standing behind her looking over her shoulder. She double clicked the e-mail from Mullen's assistant and then clicked the attachment. Two digital photos appeared. One was from the California Registry of Motor Vehicles and the other from the same agency in Massachusetts. "Fischer was right," Fowler blurted out. Although Allan appeared older than Michael, it was obvious they were identical twins. They sat there dumbfounded. Savage couldn't help herself, "They're both dead ringers for suspect #2 in the Boston police sketch," she said, as the three turned around to look at the blow-up of the BPD sketch that was taped to the wall behind them.

"We need to get as much information on Michael Whitcomb as soon as possible and we have to figure out what his brother is up to with this new web site. I also want you to fill out the necessary paperwork to obtain all of Bobby Datoli's medical records. I want to confirm that he had that exotic disease that the blood expert talked about. This case has been around for way too long and I think it's finally starting to pick up some momentum. Bryan, we need to keep it moving. I need you to find out from the Bureau of Prisons where David Mercer is incarcerated.

Wait a minute; I can get into that database from my computer."

Fowler turned in her chair and typed in www.bop.us. "He's doing a forty-seven year stint for that attempted armored car facility heist. He's at the federal pen in the mountains of West Virginia. You need to get down there and speak with him. Given his lengthy sentence he might have an incentive to tell us about his involvement in the robbery. He should also be able to tell us who else was involved and maybe, just maybe, where the paintings are. I want you to obtain Michael Whitcomb's fingerprints from the Boston police. They should have them in connection with his two Suffolk Superior court cases. Someone needs to get the dockets for me to make it easy for Boston PD to pull his prints. Once you get them please run them through AFIS as soon as possible and let me know if there are any hits on any of the prints lifted from the Gardner. We could use some help right about now from Ted McGrath, who's probably sitting in his chair on the beach in Sanibel having a cold one. He knows more about this case than the three of us combined. Anyway, such is life; let's get moving on what we need to do!"

What the other members of the group didn't know was that Katharine had again received a typewritten note. Just like before, the small plain white piece of white paper was folded and found stuck in the doorjamb at her apartment. This time the note read: "STRIKE FORCE...USA...1990... Deve-se estudar para aprender". Savage didn't understand what the encrypted message meant but she desperately wanted to figure it out. This was the second time a reference was made about the Strike Force, so she decided to do some research to find out which Assistant United States attorneys were members of the Unit back in 1990.

Chapter Fifty-Nine Boston Police Headquarters, September 24, 2007

The brand-spanking new headquarters of the Boston police is located about three blocks west of the Gardner museum. Sergeant Eddie Lawrence escorted Mullen to the fingerprint section of the office located on the second floor. As they walked into the room, Mullen was amazed to see that there were hundreds if not thousands of binders with numbers marked on each with black magic marker. Lawrence explained that the various identifying numbers corresponded to the names of all persons whose fingerprints had been taken by Boston PD in the last forty years.

ARTFUL DECEPTION

The shelves were stacked with piles and piles of
them. The numbers had all been put into the
Department's computer but due to budget
restraints the hard-copy prints had not been
scanned into the system. "When I entered
Michael Whitcomb's name and personal
information, his identifier came up immediately.
His should be over here in box number
267468/binder 0947," Lawrence explained, as
ashes from his cigarette fell to the floor. "Since
they are organized numerically, it shouldn't take
long to find them. Here they are," as he picked
up a cardboard pouch that had the name
'Michael Whitcomb/FELON 19874567' written
on it. "Looks like all of his fingers, including his
thumb, were rolled when we arrested him for
the insurance scam." Mullen got into his vehicle
for the ten-minute ride back to his office. He had
already given the heads-up to agent Franci, who
was responsible for putting the prints into AFIS
that he was on his way. When he walked into
the basement office, he took the package out of
the file handed it to Franci and said, "It's a
complete set. Sometimes our friends in blue
down the street don't always do a full one."

Franci carefully entered the card into the
computer's scanner. The process took about two
minutes and then he turned to Mullen smiled
and said, "Michael Whitcomb's prints are now
officially part of the Automated Fingerprint
Identification System." Seeing the green light

flash on the scanner, Franci hit the search button and then sat back along with Mullen to see if there were any matches. It seemed to Mullen like it was taking forever, but it had been only about eight minutes when the screen began to flash in red. They both sat up and peered towards the screen. They couldn't believe what they saw. One of Michael Whitcomb's fingerprints matched a fingerprint that had been lifted from a doorknob at the Isabella Stewart Gardner museum by agent Maher in March 1990.

The print had been lifted from underneath the mushroom shaped portion of the brass, ornate knob of the secret door leading into the Dutch Gallery. Mullen took out his cell phone to call Fowler while Franci continued to read the analysis of the prints. He could hear Mullen from behind on the phone, "We have a match! We have a match on Michael Whitcomb's prints! One is a perfect match of a print lifted from the museum back in 1990! I'm on my way!" As Mullen headed out the door, Franci, who was still reading the report, whispered to himself, "It's a print from his left index finger."

Federal Courthouse, Boston, Massachusetts, Later that Afternoon

The three were stunned by the discovery of Michael Whitcomb's fingerprint on the doorknob leading into the Dutch gallery. Fowler, sitting at the table with a legal pad, was jotting down what they knew about the investigation at this point. "We now have solid crime scene evidence that Michael Whitcomb was involved in the actual robbery. His or his brother Allan's DNA shows up on the envelope that contained a letter demanding the reward money in exchange for the paintings. We also know that Allan is an alleged expert on Degas who runs an art gallery in Carmel. Two months after the robbery, his brother Michael drives a vehicle that seems to match the make, model and color of the one the college kids saw the night of the robbery, onto an auto transport carrier bound for San Francisco. It was the first and only time that the owner of the trucking company ever let the customer drive his vehicle onto the truck. Not only that, Michael puts the keys in his pocket and tells Leonard that his brother has a set of keys and that he, not the driver, would drive the car off the truck."

"It doesn't take a rocket scientist to come to the reasonable conclusion that there may have been something important in the trunk of that car, the Whitcomb brothers didn't want anyone to see or even come close to. We also have hard crime scene evidence that Bobby Datoli was Michael's partner the night of the robbery. His blood and DNA didn't get on that wooden mallet through osmosis; it got there when he used it to break the glass on the two frames that held the Degas prints. At this point, we don't know what the relationship is or was between the Whitcomb's and Datoli. What we do know is that Datoli was friends with David Mercer and that both of them were involved in an attempted art heist at the Museum of Fine Arts back in the 1980s."

"Datoli's involvement seems to be solid since his medical records, obtained by Katharine from his primary care physician, unequivocally establish that for most of his adult life, he was treated for severe anemia consistent with the rare malady agent Cramer told us about." Mullen interjected, "I am scheduled to fly to Charleston, West Virginia to meet with and interview David Mercer. It took a little longer to arrange because his attorney, Ken Leister wanted to be there when I question him. By the way, when I spoke with Leister he informed me that he had heard through the grapevine that the First Circuit Court of Appeal's decision on Mercer's appeal is expected to come down any day now and that Mercer is optimistic that the Court will flip the conviction and order a new trial."

"If I were him, given the First Circuit's conservative leaning in upholding criminal convictions, I wouldn't hold my breath. If it's not overturned, Mercer's going to sit in that federal penitentiary in beautiful, scenic West Virginia for the next fifty years with that dreadful voice in his head repeating over and over again: 'you will not walk out of here, you will leave this place feet first'. Once that bleak reality hits him in the head like a ton of bricks, maybe he'll be looking for something from us in exchange for information from him about the robbery. I think we're right on the money. If we can get across to him that he may rot in prison, maybe he will agree to help us. We know that he was the guy that basically blackmailed Fager, so he is definitely involved. We just don't know to what extent. Katharine ran Mercer's last RMV photo before he was sent to the can." Picking it up to show to Mullen, she continued. "He obviously does not look like either suspect in the BPD sketches. But, as you can see, his eyes are spaced rather far apart and he could pass for being of Asian/Caucasian decent. Correct me if I'm wrong Katharine, but didn't those kids from Emmanuel College tell the police that the guy dressed in a Boston police uniform, who was sitting in the driver's seat in the car parked outside the Palace Road entrance, appeared to be part Asian?"

"They all said that he looked like he was part Asian, that's right," Savage replied. Fowler stood up, signaling that the meeting was over and said to Bryan, "We need to jam this guy as hard as we can and if we're lucky, the First Circuit's decision will come down soon and they hopefully will affirm the trial court's decision.

Then maybe Mercer, will see the light and tell us what he knows." "I'll do my best. I still am going back and forth with Leister about dates. I will check in with you and Katharine around 3:30 PM," Mullen replied. "This time, I am not going to take anything for granted." Prior to heading over to the meeting with Fowler and Mullen, Savage had just finished her research concerning the mysterious note writer's reference to "Strike Force". She learned that it was a special unit located in the United States Attorney's office in Boston back in the late 1980s and early 1990s that dealt with organized crime in New England. The unit, as she understood from what she read, was tasked by the Justice Department in Washington with the elimination of the Italian mob in New England. Its particular focus was the DePasquale family in Boston headed by Sal the Clam and the Maglio family in Providence, Rhode Island, headed by the alleged patriarch of the Mafia in all of New England, Raymond Maglio. She came across a Department of Justice publication that defined organized crime as "self-perpetuating, structured, and disciplined associations of individuals, or groups, combined together for the purpose of obtaining monetary or commercial gains or profits, wholly or in part by illegal means, while protecting their activities through a pattern of graft and corruption.

Organized crime members either "commit or threaten to commit acts of violence or other acts which are likely to intimidate." Much to her surprise, Savage learned that the New England Organized Strike Force, although located within the physical confines of the United States Attorney's office, was truly an independent, autonomous group that operated basically unchecked. Its members did not answer to the United States Attorney but reported directly to Main Justice in Washington, D.C. She also learned that the Chief of the Strike Force in 1990 was Assistant United States Attorney Frank Cullen, now Morrissey's First Assistant.

Chapter Sixty Sanibel Island, Florida, October 3, 2007: "The Epiphany"

McGrath was still watching the Red Sox and Indians game when he raised his backside slowly off the bar stool and started to walk towards the men's room. All of a sudden, he felt his cell phone vibrate in his pocket. He stopped, took it out and flipped it open. He couldn't believe it. It was another text message from Katharine Savage in Boston. It read: "It is not a Fool's Errand! We need your help!" With the phone still in his hand and before he could push the Old West louvered doors open and enter, he felt the unexpected pressure of a firm hand from behind grab him by the shoulder. He was stopped in his tracks.

The two agents from the Fort Myers' FBI field office displayed their credentials and then asked if he was Edward McGrath. He told them that he was. "We have been instructed to transport you to the Bureau's local field office. A subpoena is there for you." It was from the Joint Congressional Committee on Governmental Affairs, chaired by the irascible senior senator from the State of Illinois, Thomas Barton. McGrath had been summoned to appear before the committee on Thursday afternoon at 1:00 PM in Washington.

While the two agents gently escorted him from the Hurricane, he heard cheers coming from the television. Glancing back quickly over his shoulder, he saw that the Red Sox had just won the game. David "Big Papi" Ortiz, with a full count, had crushed a walk-off home run over the Green Monster seats at Fenway Park. As the three walked out into the steamy air of South Florida, a soft rain was falling. Lights from the restaurant splashed across the parking lot, giving the retired agent's face a yellow glow. As he was being helped into the back of the squad car, he looked up at the rookie agent, who didn't look old enough to be his grandson and asked, "What the hell is this all about?" No response.

What he didn't know, but would soon learn, was that item number one on Senator Barton's list for agent Teddy McGrath, the kid from South Boston, was the Isabella Stewart Gardner museum robbery. While driving to the field office the two agents told him what was in store for him in Washington. The young agent in the passenger seat turned around and started to explain what was going on. "You should get to the Congressional hearing room located on the second floor of the Capitol building at 10:00 AM, so you can see how Senator Barton conducts his hearings and hopefully figure out what the Committee members might be looking for. When we get to our office our boss will fill you in with more specifics."

"What are you talking about? Who the fuck is Senator Barton? I'm not going anywhere I'm retired. I'm done with the Bureau. I'm not going anywhere other than back to the Hurricane! Take me back there!" The agent in the driver's seat put McGrath's demand to bed. "Why don't you just shut the fuck up and sit back until we get to headquarters in Fort Myers!" Not another word was spoken until they arrived in Fort Myers. When McGrath and the two agents finally arrived at the FBI field office on West Gulf Drive, they took the elevator to the fifth floor. Still incredulous and fuming, McGrath was led into a small conference room, where Special Agent in Charge, Francis Xavier

Cadigan, a career veteran of the Bureau, greeted him. McGrath felt like he was under arrest without the handcuffs. The two rookie agents closed the door, leaving Cadigan and McGrath alone in the room.

Cadigan shook McGrath's hand and apologized for scooping him abruptly from his favorite watering hole. "At least, I told the two rookies to wait until the game was over or almost over before they grabbed you." McGrath, with his usual charm, gave Cadigan a smirk. "You should teach that red-headed asshole of an agent some fucking manners," McGrath spouted. "I'll speak to him later. Ted, let me fill you in on what's going on. I work out of Main Justice's Internal Affairs Unit. I am a direct report to the Deputy Assistant Attorney General. The powers to be are in a real tizzy about Senator Barton sticking his nose into what went on in the Boston field office back in the late 1980s and early 90s. They are also very troubled about possible inappropriate and even illegal conduct by attorneys in the U.S. Attorney's office at the time. His committee has served subpoenas on people up in Boston and down in Washington. In fact, your subpoena was served through this office," as Cadigan handed it to him.

"Jimmy Kelly, and his relationship with that renegade agent that he grew up with in South Boston, has created a real mess and has been a thorn in the side of the Bureau in Boston, as well as in the Department of Justice for many years. It's really given the Bureau a black eye. Now, on top of all that, Barton is sniffing around about the Bureau's investigation of the Gardner museum robbery. We believe he is of the opinion that the Boston field office was in cahoots with the United States Attorney's office, and, for some reason, may have intentionally impeded the Gardner investigation. I grabbed you from the Hurricane because you and I need to talk." "What the hell are you talking about and why do you and Senator Barton want to talk with me," McGrath pointedly inquired of Cadigan.

"Weren't you the lead agent on the Gardner museum robbery? Cadigan responded. "And, didn't you just recently retire from the Bureau after working that damn case for the last seventeen years?" "That's right, but what do these bureaucratic assholes want with me now. I know I was a failure as an agent because I never solved the fucking heist but it wasn't from a lack of effort," McGrath retorted.

As Cadigan looked at the overweight, grey haired soul sitting five feet across from him at the table, he felt a great deal of empathy for the agent from South Boston. "Hey, Mac, do you want a cup of coffee?" "Yeah, that would be great. It would be even better if it had a little Jameson in it." Cadigan chuckled, I think I can arrange that since I keep a bottle of Irish whiskey in my desk drawer — for medicinal purposes only, you understand." Now it was McGrath who was smiling.

When Cadigan walked back into the room, McGrath knew he was a man of his word. The room now smelled of the nutty aroma of coffee and the unmistakable scent of the Irish elixir. McGrath also noticed that when Cadigan walked back into the room, he was holding a file in his hand. Sitting down at the edge of the table, Cadigan asked, "Have you ever felt that working a case is like putting a puzzle together, trying to fit the endless pieces of all shapes and sizes together, to make sense of it?"
"Absolutely," McGrath responded, "that's what I loved about the job, you had to put the pieces together to get the full picture and it was achieving that goal that I thrived on, that is, until I realized I couldn't close the deal. The Gardner museum robbery is a classic example of that."
Listening to the Boston native, Cadigan felt even more sympathy for him than he did just moments before. "During the seventeen years that you worked the Gardner case, did you ever feel that maybe you weren't given all of the pieces of the puzzle or thought some critical pieces were kept from you on purpose?"
"Never crossed my mind and never occurred to me."

Standing up, Cadigan walked over to McGrath and tossed the file he held in his hand down on the desk. McGrath looked at it and as he did, he read the words in capital red letters "CI 1197/1198-1985 BOS SENSITIVE MATERIAL NOT FOR PUBLIC DISCLOSURE". He recognized the code CI. It stood for confidential informant and the numbers 1197/11981985 corresponded to two separate confidential informants, sequentially numbered 1197th and 1198th. BOS indicated the two were "the property" of the Boston FBI field office. 1985 represented the year the two CIs had been formally recruited and then opened as informants. McGrath also knew that before the local office could bring any CI into the fold, Washington had to first give Boston the green light.

"Teddy, before you open it, let me fill you in on some things. I'm sure you know some of what I am about to tell you and I am equally confident that some you are not aware of. We all know that our director, going as far back as the late 1950s, made it a priority of the Bureau to crush the Italian Mafia in this country. Every major city was targeted, including Boston. He didn't give a crap how we did it, he just wanted it done. As I'm sure you are also aware, that balls-to-the wall policy resulted in some serious problems developing with some of our people. Boston is a classic example. You and I both know that in order to destroy any criminal organization, you need intelligence that can be used to build a case. To obtain information, we, unfortunately, but necessarily, have to rely upon criminals who turn into snitches. The bottom line is that we need informants."

McGrath sat very quietly as Cadigan continued. "In Boston, as you know, the Bureau developed both Jimmy 'The Tooth' Kelly and Frankie 'The Shanks' Martell as government informants to be used against their own partner in crime, Sal 'The Clam' DePasquale and his organization. The Clam is still in the can, as is Martell for murders he committed with Kelly while those two assholes were paid informants for the Bureau. What you or anyone else for that matter couldn't have known, was that several field offices in the country developed a special, secret, elite group of senior agents whose sole responsibility was to develop informants to keep track of the Bureau's existing stable of snitches' activities. Hoover created the Top Echelon Criminal Informant Program or TECIP in the 1960s to squash the La Cosa Nostra like a bug. They were put in place to make sure people like Kelly and Martell while on our payroll, as surrogate employees, were not committing crimes. When the Director made the elimination of the Italian Mafia a top priority, we had to carry out his mandate. However, not at all costs. There had to be some limitations. We needed to keep our existing informants in check and the way Washington believed it could accomplish that was to have each field office put together a select group of reliable sources whose only task, again, was to provide information about other informants. The groups were created because, as you know, an agent working with a criminal turned informant can't be with him 24/7. So, guys like you and me had to be able to rely upon other people, usually scumbag criminals, to help keep a lid on an informant's extracurricular activities. Such a group was created in Boston, but it went haywire when a rogue agent, a childhood friend of Kelly's, unexpectedly inserted himself into the mix. Let me give you an example of how he operated."

"What was the name of that young, go-getter agent who was assigned to work the Gardner case with you"? "Billy Morton," McGrath replied. "Wasn't he working the case one day and the next, they transferred him to the East St. Louis office to hunt down prostitutes and drug dealers? Do you know why they shipped his ass out of Boston?" McGrath shook his head. "He was getting too fucking close to the informants who were watching the hen house."

"Through their extensive criminal network throughout the City of Boston, the two confidential informants came to learn what Kelly and Martell were up to. They learned the two were popping guys off like fish in a barrel all across the city and shaking down local businessmen with impunity. Kelly and Martell were being fed information about who was saying what to agents in the Boston office. The poor bastards that they killed, as you know, weren't choirboys but they had no clue that Jimmy and Frankie were our informants. The worst part is that anyone who happened to be at the wrong place at the wrong time with the guys Kelly and Martell targeted for execution were also killed in cold-blood, all with the knowledge and blessing of our people. Why? To bury 'The Clam' and the Mafia! The two local boys from Boston who agreed to become part of this elite group of canaries were not too pleased with what Kelly and Martell were up to, particularly when it concerned how those two thugs were treating their father."

"They eventually learned that Kelly and Martell were extorting money from their Dad who ran a small business and was just trying to make a living. They developed a real hatred for Kelly because they thought he was just an Irish punk who made his living off the blood and sweat of others. Kelly and Martell had the balls to put the arm on the poor bastard, believe it or not, by grabbing a piece of the action from his tiny business. Every cop in the city knew that the Old Man ran book in the back of the supply store but nobody gave a crap. Anyway, most of his customers were Boston police officers. The sons hated those two bums, Jimmy and Frankie! Agent Morton was closing in on the sons who, he believed, orchestrated and pulled off the Gardner robbery."

"Here's the corker. What Billy Morton and you didn't know was that the two suspects in the robbery were members of that special group of Bureau informants who were keeping tabs on people like Kelly and Martell. Morton, I can assure you, never knew why he was shipped out of Boston. They had to get him out of there because he was zeroing in on the two guys that he truly believed were behind the Gardner heist. If they had pinched the brothers for the museum heist, the Bureaus' dirty laundry on Kelly and Martell would inevitably have ended up hanging out on the line for all to see, including the families of the poor bastards that Kelly and Martell brutally murdered while on the Bureau's payroll. If the brothers ever thought we were going to charge them with the robbery they would have announced to the world what they knew about the cozy, sleazy relationship between your colleagues and those two scum bags, Kelly and Martell. Pretty bad, huh? That's the deal Teddy."

With hesitation and trembling hands, McGrath picked up the file and opened it. There, on the first page was a photograph of Allan Whitcomb. He couldn't believe his eyes. Cadigan, watching him closely from across the table, spoke. "Looks like they didn't give you all the pieces to the puzzle, did they, Ted?"

"I can't believe Allan Whitcomb was a fucking FBI informant," McGrath blurted out with what little air was left in his lungs. "I just can't believe it! Why didn't they tell me? Now I know why that asshole boss of mine, Charlie Quintal, had me write that fucking memo within two months' of the robbery declaring to the world that Whitcomb was no longer a suspect or a person of interest. The only way anyone could have solved this fucking case would have been by outing Whitcomb as a CI." Cadigan nodded." I wasted almost twenty years of my fucking life because my superiors couldn't tell me about Whitcomb. It just can't get any worse than that," lamented the now totally defeated agent shaking his head in disgust. He looked up at Cadigan with a painful grimace, his eyes clearly reflecting how he felt.

"I'm sorry, Teddy, there's more, you need to turn the page." Grabbing the right bottom corner of the page with his left hand, McGrath turned it ever so slowly. There, on page two, was another photograph of Whitcomb. "I don't understand, it's just another photo of Allan Whitcomb." Cadigan gave him a head nod, suggesting that he should take a closer look. McGrath adjusted his reading glasses that were, as usual, placed precariously at the tip of his nose. He again looked down at the page. He felt his heart skip several beats in his pounding chest as he tried to catch his breath. Looking at the top of the page he read: "PROTECT AT ALL COST AND DO NOT DISCLOSE". Further down the page, he read: "CONFIDENTIAL INFORMANT MICHAEL WHITCOMB, DATE OF BIRTH JULY 29, 1948". Cadigan could actually hear McGrath gasp as he turned back to page one, where he read: "CONFIDENTIAL INFORMANT ALLAN WHITCOMB, DATE OF BIRTH JULY 29, 1948".

He removed his reading glasses slowly and looked up at Cadigan, his eyes now welling with tears. Barely able to get the words out, he asked in a soft, shallow voice, "They were fucking identical twins?" He fell back in his chair, grabbed the Styrofoam cup and proceeded to down what was left of the laced Java in one gulp. Crumbling the cup, he tossed it in the wastebasket and, looking again at Cadigan, said, "Frank, I'm tired and I want go home. Could you give me a lift back to the Hurricane to get my car?" Cadigan said sure, and as McGrath stood up he placed his hand on the beaten agent's shoulder, turned the lights off and walked out of the room.

The Bureau had a plan for the Whitcomb brothers. However, they needed McGrath's exceptional historical knowledge of the case to pull it off. "Ted, would you consider coming back to Boston as a consultant to work with AUSA Fowler, agent Mullen and your former intern, Katharine Savage to finally solve this thing and get the paintings back?" Cadigan asked as he looked at him in the passenger seat of Cadigan's Crown Vic. McGrath, still stunned and reeling from what he had just learned, could not believe what Cadigan was asking him to do. Cadigan was firm in his request however.

"I know you must feel awful, but since you retired, the Whitcomb brothers have now become *bona fide* suspects in the robbery. Both DNA results and fingerprints support that proposition. There is more that I can't disclose to you unless you decide to help us out in an official capacity. We now know there was inside help from one of the guards." Cadigan, turning and looking at McGrath as he drove, said, "It was that druggie, Jay Fager. He got himself into a jam with his drug supplier when he started to use the profits from his dealing to buy coke that found its way up his nose."

Hearing what Cadigan had just told him, McGrath looked over at him from across the seat with a look of disgust said, "I knew from the get-go that the kid was no good and was somehow involved in the heist." Cadigan continued to try to sell McGrath on the idea of coming back to Boston.

"We really need your help, Ted. I think the folks at your old office are closer to solving this mess than they have ever been. You know the case like the back of your hand. They believe that the brothers have recently developed a strategy to try to return the paintings to the museum to collect the Five Million Dollar reward and then walk off into the sunset. It actually is a pretty fascinating idea when you come to think of it. If they could pull it off, they could collect the reward money and would not be subject to prosecution. If the return of the paintings were brokered through their attorney, he or she, because of the attorney-client privilege would not be able to disclose where or from whom the paintings were obtained. As you know, the only exception to that would be if their counsel knew or had reason to know that the Whitcomb's sought legal advice to assist them in committing a crime. In that case, the privilege could be pierced and their attorney could be forced to disclose what the Whitcomb's said. Teddy, we are close to breaking this case wide open. We need your help. If you think it was a fucking nightmare getting to where the people in Boston think they are today, getting the paintings back in one piece is going to require a miracle."

"The folks in Boston don't even know that I am even involved. I was directed by the Deputy Attorney General out of Main Justice to jump in once Senator Barton started to serve Congressional subpoenas on Justice and the Boston field office. It's really become a shit storm. No one in Boston has been told that I am now overseeing the investigation."

"If you were to decide to get involved and I hope you do, you will report to me and to no one else. You will not even have to enter the federal courthouse or the Bureau's office unless you want to and will never have to deal with the U.S. Attorney. For all I care, you can meet with Fowler, Mullen and Savage at the bar at the Chart House. We just need your knowledge and experience. Give it some thought, and Teddy, please don't mention our meeting or discussion to anyone. If you do decide to get back involved, you can tell Fowler and her group that you read the Boston papers online on a regular basis and that your investigatory juices started to flow when you saw that the United States Attorney's office had just recently put one of the guards who worked the night of the robbery before a federal grand jury."

"Again, you would only report to me and I would give you *carte blanche* in terms of what you could do to put this case to bed and recover the stolen paintings." As Cadigan finished his pitch to McGrath, they had just pulled into the parking lot of The Hurricane. The two shook hands and then Cadigan, as Ted exited the car, said to the now exhausted agent, "After almost two decades, the kid from South Boston, Massachusetts, may someday realize that his quixotic quest was not a fool's errand! Good night Teddy and good luck in Washington," as he watched him walk slowly to his car.

Chapter Sixty-One: "Betrayal, Deception And Disgust" Washington, D.C., Thursday, October 6, 2007

McGrath was running late. He arrived at the Capitol a little after 10:00 AM. He thought he knew what room the hearing was in, but finding it was another story. Walking the halls of the Capitol, he was transported back to the day he, his brother Tom and his Dad met Speaker McCormack and Director Hoover. He always remembered what Hoover had told him. He, in fact, had dedicated his professional life to the Bureau, fighting crime and putting the bad guys in jail. Still hurt, stunned and confused by what agent Cadigan had told him about the Whitcomb brothers and the Gardner robbery, he was not in good spirits. With some help from several security guards, he finally found the hearing room. As he walked in, he was awestruck by the size of the room and by the number of people who were seated in the gallery, particularly the many press photographers and reporters.

As he took a seat in the back, he was stunned to see who was in the hot seat being grilled by the Chairman, Senator Barton. It was his former boss, Special Agent in Charge, Charlie Quintal. McGrath sat back in his chair to listen to what his old boss had to say, this time under oath. As he looked around the room and up at the massive, dark, oak door, he realized he was in Hearing Room 207, the same room the Director had testified in under oath years ago. Closing his eyes for a moment, a brief wave of sadness washed over him as that remarkable, exciting day played like a black and white film through the folds of his memory. He wished his Dad and brother, Tom were sitting next to him this day. Just as on the first day he was sworn in as an agent and every day since, the Department of Justice pin given to him by Director Hoover, sparkled from the lapel of his suit coat; to him, a true Badge of Honor.

"Senator, I understand you feel that what we did back in the late 80s and 90s was atrocious. However, we had received a mandate from headquarters to do whatever it took to destroy the Mafia in Boston. Since that was Washington's priority, it also became mine. Did we do things along the way that we shouldn't have? We sure did, but we got the job done! The bottom line is that we were successful in destroying that criminal organization. We decimated its ranks, sending all of its members to prison. We accomplished that with snitches and informants. Let's face it, as early as 1965, the Bureau was already conducting illegal wiretaps on mob figures in Boston and Providence. We desperately wanted to develop informants from inside the mob's hierarchy and for that matter, anyone else who could provide details on its innermost workings. If men like Jimmy Kelly and Frankie Martell didn't help us by supplying information that we ultimately used against the Italian mob, we would not have been successful. What we did in the 80s and 90s literally destroyed the mob."

"We did such a great job, that today, in the City of Boston, in fact, in New England for that matter La Cosa Nostra no longer exists! Were there collateral consequences and damage as a result? Yes there were and I take full responsibility for those unintended, yet unfortunate mishaps. Did people lose their lives because of what we knew and did nothing about? They sure did and that's unfortunate. I can't bring them back and I feel for their families and loved ones. As you know, there are at least five wrongful death cases pending in the United States District Court in Boston against the FBI, stemming from what the families of Kelly's and

Martell's victims believe to be our negligence. Let me be frank. I believe those cases have merit and the families should be compensated for their losses."

"However, we weren't negligent! We just didn't care about collateral damage. Why should we have? The people that were getting whacked by our informants, with very few exceptions, were lowlifes anyway, hardened criminals. Did I lose sleep over them getting killed? I did not. I had a job to do and I did it. Does that mean today, their families should not be compensated for their losses? Absolutely not, they should be. Because of my government's policy, people lost their lives and that was wrong. However, I had a job to do and I carried it out to the best of my ability."

McGrath could not believe what he was hearing. How could his colleagues have been so single-minded in purpose, carrying out the policies dictated by Washington, without any concern whatsoever for loss of life? He could not fathom how anyone within the Bureau could have blindly embraced that horrendous mandate that continued, not for years, but decades. He was floored by Quintal's glibness. His old boss, to whom he had reported for years, talked about what he had done, matter-of-factly, without a scintilla of remorse or regret. It was abundantly clear to McGrath that Quintal was not going to apologize to anyone, particularly not the committee members. Sitting there, he heard Senator Barton bring up the subject of the Gardner museum robbery.

"Agent Quintal is it not true that at the time of the Gardner museum robbery in March 1990, the largest theft of art in America's history, you had all of the agents assigned to the case report directly to you? I believe the lead agent was Edward McGrath. Is that correct, Sir? "Yes it is. Agent Ted McGrath was the lead agent on that case from the start. He worked as hard as I have ever seen an agent work a case. He was relentless. Unfortunately, because of circumstances that involved a greater institutional priority, he became part of the collateral damage I just spoke about. As a consequence of our mission to crush the Mafia in Boston, he was, unfortunately, destined to fail. We made sure he was never going to solve the Gardner museum robbery."

"We specifically targeted the Gardner case not to be solved to protect our stable of informants. The director's mandate took absolute precedence over that robbery. I'm sorry to say that, but that's exactly what happened. It's the truth." McGrath hearing what Quintal had just said, had the immediate urge to rise from his seat and go choke his former boss. How could he sit there and nonchalantly tell the members of this committee that he had casually decided to ruin a colleague's career?

The Senator continued. "Agent Quintal, I have in my hand and I believe you also have a copy of it in front of you, a memo from 1990, written by you concerning the Gardner museum robbery. Do you have that?" "Yes I do and I did write it. Those are my initials at the top of the page."

"Well Sir, it states that you possessed information at the time, only weeks after the robbery, that a person by the name of Michael Whitcomb may have been involved in the robbery and you did nothing with that information. My aides, who have reviewed all of the FBI's documents in connection with the investigation, have indicated that there is not one other document in the entire file, other than the one I have in my hand that refers, concerns, or relates to Michael Whitcomb. It appears you took absolutely no steps to prove whether that information was true or false. It's apparent to me that you did no due diligence whatsoever. How can that be?" Barton asked with disgust in his voice. The Senator was now ready to blast the former FBI supervisor with both barrels.

"I am also informed by my investigators that as of this date, neither one of the security guards who were working the night of the robbery have ever been shown photos of any suspects."

Quintal, unfazed by the questions and the Senator's tirade, responded. "Remember when I spoke of collateral damage? Well to be blunt, the museum was also a victim of our stated priority: to wipe out the Italian Mob in the City of Boston. They got the short end of the stick, just as the agents working the case did. At the time, McGrath had a really aggressive and sharp agent, whose name escapes me at the moment, working with him on the case. He was starting to get too close to the Whitcomb brothers, believing they may have had something to do with the Gardner robbery."

"The brothers were both members of what we referred to as our 'elite' group of informants. They were part of a select group of known criminals that we recruited and brought into the fold, to keep tabs on our more difficult tattle-tales, like Jimmy Kelly and Frankie Martell. When the rookie agent started to put two and two together about the Whitcomb's, I uprooted his entire young family and transferred him to East St. Louis to arrest pimps, prostitutes and drug dealers. My priority again, was the Boston Italian Mafia. We knew Kelly and Martell were popping off people left and right and that they were also shaking down other hoods in the City, including the Whitcomb brothers' father, who was a big time bookie in the South End of Boston. We knew all about that. It came down to this. What was more important to our stated mission from Washington? Recovering paintings for a place that had drugged-up college kids babysitting their valuable paintings and, by the way, that was too cheap to insure them, or squashing the Boston Mafia? That was an easy decision for me. If I had to do it all over again, I'd do the same thing. In hindsight, the only thing I would have done differently is that I would never have written this damn memo to the file," as he lifted the piece of paper into the air. "Do I feel bad for the museum? No. Their security was third world when they had the financial wherewithal to have had a first class system. Shame on them! Do I wish they could have recovered the paintings? Sure. That may happen someday. At the time, I had to make a judgment call and I went with what I was told to do by my superiors. It was our number one priority."

"No photos were ever shown to the guards because we knew who was behind it. What were those two punks going to do? Who were they going to complain to? The only person I feel badly about is agent Ted McGrath, a very fine agent, who, for seventeen years, desperately wanted to and tried to solve the case, but because of me, wasn't given all of the pieces of the puzzle to do so. Strictly on a personal level, I will regret that decision for the rest of my life."

"If you, Mr. Chairman and the members of your committee are looking for an apology from me, you are not going to get one. My superiors gave me orders and I followed them out to the best of my ability. That Senator is all I have to say."

Washington, D.C. Several Hours' Later

That night, McGrath, disgusted with what he had heard from Charlie Quintal, sat on a barstool at The Dubliner, a watering hole frequented by members of Congress after long days at the Capitol. He had just spent two hours testifying before Senator Barton's committee concerning alleged improprieties at the Boston FBI office and listening to the incredible testimony of Charlie Quintal.

McGrath thought his appearance was a waste of time since, as he explained to the members of the committee, he was not privy to any of the shenanigans that may have been going on around him in the late 80s and early 90s in Boston. He made it very clear to the committee that he was unaware of agent Quintal's intent to purposely sabotage his work on the Gardner robbery. Had he an inkling of what his boss was doing at the time, he would have done everything within his power to put a kibosh to Quintal's handy work.

He had provided the committee members with a summary of what he had done over the many years trying to solve the Gardner case and in a closed-door session, related what he had been told recently by agent Cadigan. The members of the committee could see, while he talked about how he had not been given all the pieces of the puzzle to solve the case by his superiors, that he was almost moved to tears. "I was just one agent and when I took that solemn oath when I graduated the Academy, to uphold the law and to serve my country, I assumed that my colleagues would do likewise. I guess I was wrong."

As he sat at the bar nursing his pint, disgusted by what agent Cadigan had said, but also torn about what he had been asked to do. He was truly ambivalent. He loved his retirement life-style and had fallen in love with the Sanibel Florida weather. When the wind was blowing, and chilly snowflakes were falling in Boston in February, he could be found on the Sanibel pier with two or three sheepshead in the water secured to a rope fastened to a piling. Instead of being subjected to 20 or 30-degree weather, not including wind chill, he would be sunning himself in an 80–degree tropical paradise. The thought of giving up what he had in Florida to return to Boston to work on the Gardner case was not particularly appealing to him. He was also conflicted about getting back involved because he was now a grandfather and wanted to spend time in Florida with his grandchildren on the shell-covered beaches of Sanibel. His oldest daughter, Lynn had two young daughters and his daughter-in-law, Maureen, was pregnant with twins. After retiring from the Bureau, he had made a vow to rekindle relationships with his three children since he knew in his heart that he had not been there for them when they needed him most. The Bureau had been his mistress and solving the Gardner robbery had been his unrelenting quest.

While the years passed and each and every lead hit a stone wall he drank more, hanging out at the Chart House most nights until closing. He desperately wanted to make amends with his children before it was too late. Taking a long sip from his pint, he started to go over in his head the new and what appeared to be very promising leads and developments. Cadigan had apprised him of how Fowler, Savage and Mullen seemed to have miraculously moved the case along and based upon what he had been told, they now most likely knew who was behind the robbery. He realized that the hardest part now was to figure out a way to find the paintings.

If he decided to return to the fray, he was pleased that he would not have to deal with anyone other than Cadigan, whom he liked and trusted. There was one other thing. He knew that he owed the Bureau nothing and in fact, believed strongly that they owed him an apology for their treachery and deception. He also knew, however, that there was always a political angle to everything in life, including law enforcement. His bosses were following orders and he just so happened to be in the way and became collateral damage of the Bureau's chicanery.

He realized that's how life sometimes worked. He also realized there were two paths he could follow. He could either let his anger eat away at him for the time that he had remaining on God's green earth or take the high road and become part of a team that just might hold the key to this mystery; one that had eluded him for seventeen years. He also understood that what he had just learned from Quintal was a double-edged sword.

On the one hand, he felt a sense of relief. Maybe he wasn't a failure after all. On the other, he felt tremendous anger towards Quintal, and the FBI as an organization. He knew in his heart that since he could not change the past, he might as well look to the future, to right a wrong. Placing the empty pint glass on the bar, he threw down a tip, got up from the bar stool and walked out into Washington's cool night air.

Two Days' Later, Sanibel Island, Florida

McGrath finally made the decision to return to Boston to help with the investigation in any way he could. He was impressed by the new developments and believed that if the stars aligned and they were lucky, they might have a shot at solving the robbery. He also decided not to tell anyone including Cadigan his strategy. Come hell or high water, he was going to return to Sanibel on December 22nd to celebrate Christmas with his three children and grandchildren and would never again travel to Boston to help his former employer, robbery solved or not!

Agent Cadigan had given him his cell phone number, so he called him to let him know his decision. Cadigan was delighted. "I can't tell you how much I appreciate your personal sacrifice to help us out to try and put this case to bed. We should meet in the morning at my office so I can brief you on the current status of the case. The Three Amigo's, as I refer to them, Fowler, Savage and Mullen, don't know and will not know until this case is solved, that I'm involved. You will be my eyes and ears. Main Justice is handling it this way because it appears that some members of the law enforcement community back in Boston have become persons of interest by Senator Barton's committee and, regrettably, by us too. I've had an agent up there for a while and the word we're getting back is that agents as well as several people in the United States Attorney's office, may be dirty or at the least, criminally negligent when it came to Kelly and Martell. The Senator's focus and interest, as well as ours, doesn't concern the robbery itself but rather, what was known by whom and when and, what if anything they did about it. That's all I can say over an unsecured land line."

Chapter Sixty-Two
Federal Courthouse, Boston, October 21, 2007

Fowler walked back into her office. It was twenty minutes to five. She was trying to catch the 5:15 PM commuter boat because her youngest daughter had a music recital at school. She always made it a point to attend her daughters' school and sporting events, despite her heavy caseload at the office. As she was packing up her things, she glanced at the phone and saw that the red light was flashing, signaling there were messages. Reluctantly, she decided to dial the number to retrieve them and was stunned to hear retired agent Ted McGrath's voice. "Hi Attorney Fowler, this is Ted McGrath calling from sunny Florida. I hope you and your family are well and that Ms.

Savage and agent Mullen are also well. I read with interest down here in the Florida papers that one of the guards from the Gardner museum robbery was recently put in the grand jury."

"I know you cannot tell me what he said, but I was interested in speaking with you about him. I have always had this gut feeling that he was the inside help. That he was the guy that gave information and access to those who pulled the robbery off. I also have always believed that the Bureau wrote off Allan Whitcomb way too early but every time I brought his name up, my SAC, Charlie Quintal shut me down. I have some thoughts that I would like to share with the three of you; to help in any way I can."

"In any event, I am pretty lonely down here. The weather is great but to be perfectly frank, I'm bored out of my mind! I am actually seriously thinking about offering my services to you, of course free of charge. I still have relatives in the Boston area and I could rent out my condo here out for the winter to support myself up there. The only thing I ask in return is that I don't deal with the Bureau or anyone other than you at the U.S. Attorney's office. I didn't leave on particularly good terms. So, I would prefer to deal with only you, Mullen and Savage, if she is still there. Here's my cell phone number. Call me any time and I look forward to hearing from you." Fowler was shocked by the message, but was certainly pleased that McGrath wanted to jump in at this stage in his life. She jotted a note to herself. "I'll call him in the morning, run it by Jim London."While trying to relax by listening to songs on her I-Pod on the commuter boat to Hingham, Fowler started to ponder what steps should next be taken to keep the momentum going in the case. "If McGrath comes back, I will meet with him, Mullen, Savage and the new director of security at the Gardner museum, Anthony Fenore, to bring everyone up to speed on where the case stands."

Being a veteran prosecutor, Fowler knew that timing is critical in every investigation, as is momentum. A bad decision by her or an agent at the wrong time could bring a case to a screeching halt or could set it back months. She, as the prosecutor, had to delegate assignments and tasks to Savage, Mullen, and hopefully, McGrath. She had to take the lead, to be the leader who could motivate her troops. She also appreciated the fact that although she had to rely upon the good work of her colleagues, in the final analysis, she was the one ultimately responsible for making a case that could hold water and end up in a conviction. She was less concerned about the possibility of a conviction, than getting the paintings back. The exceptional work by Savage and Mullen had brought the case to a point where, with a little luck, it could be solved. She knew it was essential to keep her group motivated and she vowed to do just that.

Federal Courthouse, Boston, The Next Morning

As she anticipated, London had no problem taking the retired agent up on his offer. As London said to her while she sat in his office, "He knows the case better than anyone in the Bureau and injecting his experience and knowledge at this critical stage might just be the key to solving the case. You seem to have a pretty good idea who was behind the theft. We now need to close the deal by getting the paintings back. It's certainly not going to hurt having Ted back on the team. The one thing we have to be careful of, since the Bureau no longer officially employs McGrath, is that he cannot under any circumstances, be privy to any 6e material from the grand jury. Because of that, you won't have to list him on your 6e disclosure letter to the Chief Justice. When you speak with McGrath, give him the heads up on that and also, thank him for me and give him my regards." Her conversation with McGrath was brief and to the point.

"We would love to have you back and I am delighted that you are willing to help us. When you get here, we will all sit down and I will brief you where the case now stands and figure out what we should do next. Yes, Ms. Savage is still here and both she and agent Mullen, who replaced you, have been working very hard and I think you will be impressed with how they have moved the case along. Savage in particular, has been a tremendous asset to me and she often asks me if I ever hear from you. You taught her well! Now, I not only can tell her that I spoke with you, but also give her the great news that you've agreed to help. She will be thrilled! We look forward to seeing you on Monday morning. I think one of the first things I am going to have you do, is to take a trip with agent Mullen down to West Virginia to speak with David Mercer."

Chapter Sixty-Three: "McGrath's Return" Federal Courthouse, Boston, 9:00 AM

The War Room had become too small to have a meeting with what Fowler now referred to as her "Dream Team," Mullen, Savage, McGrath and Fenore. After catching up on old times with McGrath, they got down to business. Fowler began. "I want to personally thank Ted for agreeing to offer his expertise and extensive knowledge to this very active investigation. It is extremely timely. I also want to thank the museum's Director of Security, Anthony Fenore, for joining our group. He has agreed to attend our meetings each Monday at this time. In the event we need to meet if there is a development in the case, we all should make sure that we have each other's cell phone numbers. I will be the contact person. So, if anyone has a question or issue, you should speak to me and no one else. Okay, with the housekeeping issues out of the way, we can now talk about substance. I think everyone at this table except for Ted, has seen the two videos of Allan Whitcomb on his newly established web site. For Ted's benefit, I downloaded the two videos onto a CD," as she placed it into the carriage of her computer. Clicking the Start button, they began to watch the videos.

The first person to speak when the second video ended was McGrath. From the look on his face, the others at the table could see that he was not pleased. Disgusted, he said, "This guy Whitcomb is full of horse manure. Here he is complaining that the Bureau tormented him and harassed him for years after the robbery. That is absolute bullshit! My SAC at the time, Charlie Quintal, wrote a memo to the file, in fact, I remember the date, May 23, 1990, when he officially eliminated Whitcomb as a suspect in the robbery. That was the last I ever heard of Allan Whitcomb until now. I know for a fact that after May 1990, no one from the Boston office ever contacted him again! I am aware of no other agent ever talking to Whitcomb after I did out at his art shop in Carmel. Once he was off our radar screen we forgot about him. Oh yeah, one more thing. Him saying that his niece saw a copy of the Boston police sketch and believed that her Uncle Allan resembled the sketch of suspect #2, is also a crock of you know what."

"I know for a fact, that the museum never, ever displayed that composite sketch of the two suspects, at any time or any place outside the museum. Something is up with this guy." "I agree, his story sounds really sketchy," Fowler said. "He's offering to broker the return of stolen art to museums around the world, including the Gardner. We now know that it was his or his brother Michael's DNA on the stamp taken from the anonymous letter sent to the museum in 1994."

"I think he either has the paintings or has access to them. I believe he wants the world to believe that the FBI wrongly accused him of being part of the robbery back in 1990. He wants the world to feel sorry for him and now, wants to clear his name and reputation by appearing to act as a savior in dealing with the guys that pulled it off when we know that it was him and Michael," Savage interjected. "If he could facilitate the return of the paintings to the Gardner, he would look like a hero."

"Here he is, returning the paintings to the Gardner, collecting the reward and then walking off into the California sunset to live happily ever after. Not a bad gig if he can pull it off," Savage said. There was prolonged silence in the room. Then McGrath spoke. "I think Katharine is right on the money. I think Allan Whitcomb is trying to pull a fast one. This is a scam! I also believe, based upon what I have now seen and heard, that he has the paintings or either knows where they are or who has them." Fenore then offered his opinion. "I think we need to call his bluff. We need to figure out a way to create a big enough carrot to lure him out of his rabbit hole. He needs some incentive to come forward and tell me, as the museum's representative, that he, or more precisely, his attorney, has been contacted by a third party who wants to return the stolen paintings to the museum and to the people of Boston."

"I believe I can convince the museum's trustees to at least get the word out to the press that the museum is willing to increase the reward, to sweeten the pot, to entice him to come forward with the paintings. I would urge them to do so and also, to put a time frame on the reward. There should be a firm deadline for anyone to come forward with the paintings. We need to bait Allan Whitcomb. If he calls me and tells me he has been contacted by someone who is willing to turn over the paintings to his attorney, we'll have him just where we want, hook line and sinker. From what I see and hear on that video, he doesn't appear particularly bright and if the museum can make it worth his while, we might just be able to beat him at his own game."

"One thing we need to be very careful of, is keeping our eyes on him at every moment from this point on. If he is able to get the paintings to his attorney, who, in turn, deals directly with Anthony, we may never be able to nail him for possession of the stolen artwork. We want to grab him red handed," said McGrath"

"If we aren't able to grab him with the paintings, we might still be able to prosecute him through his attorney," Fowler said. "Isn't that the exception to the attorney-client privilege?" asked Savage. "You're absolutely right Katharine. The courts have said that there is no attorney-client privilege if the services of an attorney are sought or obtained to enable or aid anyone in committing or planning on committing a crime. If Whitcomb intends to use the attorney he refers to in the video clips as a shield or as an intermediary in brokering a deal with the museum, I think any judge in this building would allow our motion to pierce the attorney-client privilege and force his lawyer to disclose any conversations he had with Whitcomb. We would then at least have a good shot at prosecuting him." As Fowler was speaking,

AUSA James London poked his head into the room and excused himself. "Hi Mac, it's good to see you," he said as he shook McGrath's hand.

"Thanks for agreeing to help us out. Amy, I thought you would like to take a look at this," as he handed her some papers. "It's the First Circuit Court of Appeals' decision on David Mercer's appeal. "They affirmed the lower court, so he loses and now will spend the rest of his life in jail." Fowler, taking a quick look at the decision, said, "This might just be the ticket to get Mercer to tell us about the robbery and his involvement. If he has any thoughts about getting his sentence reduced, he better think about becoming a tattletale. Ted and Bryan, can you speak with Mercer's attorney to see if his client has any interest? If he does, you two need to fly down to West Virginia and speak with the lad. "

"No offense Bryan," as Fowler smiled at him, "I think McGrath should do the talking with Mercer, since, as we all know, he can be very persuasive." "I agree. I have no problem with that, he's been doing this a lot longer than I have," Mullen said, laughing. "We need the FBI field office in San Francisco to assign one or two agents to follow Allan Whitcomb's every move." "Anthony, how much time are you going to need to speak with the museum trustees to see if they are willing to crank the reward up to ten million? I'm sure you will make it clear to them that increasing the reward is simply a ploy to entice Whitcomb. Stress to them that they will never have to pay any money to that fool!"

"I think it will take only a couple of days. I will speak to the chairperson today. She and I, along with the museum's director, can then have a conference call with the other trustees to get their input and consent," Fenore responded. "Great. When you know what the trustees' decision is, please give me a call and we can meet to get the word out to the press. I think the museum should hold a press conference at the museum to announce the increase in the reward. Ted and Bryan, you are going to speak with Mercer's attorney and also touch base with San Francisco to get them to put a tail on Whitcomb?" Fowler asked. "Katharine, could you draft a brief on the crime-fraud exception to the attorney-client privilege. I have a feeling that we are going to need that at some point to convince one of our fine jurists in this building that we have a case. Thanks." As Fowler and her group were huddled in the conference room, the First Assistant United States Attorney, Frank Cullen, had just walked into United States Attorney James Morrissey's office, closing the door behind him.

"We have major fucking problems," Cullen said as Morrissey removed his reading glasses and looked up from his desk. "I just learned that Charlie Quintal spilled his guts to Senator Barton's committee in Washington. He told them all about "Operation Elite Informant" and I'm sure he threw the two of us under the bus, probably a couple of times. The word percolating at Main Justice is that Quintal is going to be indicted for obstruction of justice by a special prosecutor and that there is a mole from Main Justice in this office who is feeding information to Washington and Barton's committee."

"If that's true, you and I are both in hot water. We both knew what was going on back in the early 90s with Martell, Kelly and the FBI and we did nothing to stop the brutal killings. Innocent people were killed and I sat on my hands. We were like two ostriches with our heads in the sand," Cullen bemoaned. "The Bureau had given those two free range to commit vicious crimes, all in the name of stomping out the Mafia and neither one of us did anything to stop it. In some respects Boss, you and I have as much culpability as they do. There's no doubt in my mind that Quintal, given his age, will flip to save himself from a long prison term and you and I are going to be in his words," collateral damage" when he starts to sing like a fucking canary. That's problem number one."

"Problem number two is agent Ted McGrath. Remember him? He was assigned to the Gardner heist from day one. As we speak, he is seated ten feet away in your conference room along with AUSA Fowler, her nosy law student Katharine Savage, agent Bryan Mullen and the Gardner museum's director of security, Anthony Fenore. From the looks of it, McGrath has come out of retirement to work on the Gardner case. Fowler and her group, as I understand from Jim London, have made great progress in the case and in fact, now believe they know who was behind the heist. That's very bad for us." Morrissey sat there without saying a word, his face blanched. A protuberant vein from his left temple pulsated visibly as he listened to his First Assistant. "There's also some scuttlebutt from second hand hearsay that McGrath was sitting recently in a bar down in Florida when he was escorted out of the joint by what appeared to be two FBI agents. Now we have him back here on the Gardner case. I have this awful bad feeling that he's agreed to come out of retirement to act as a mole to provide his historical perspective on the robbery that will ultimately be used to bury you and me. I think someone has educated him or he has recently learned about what went on back in the 80s and 90s when you and I were in the Strike Force. Christ, if it ever comes out that we purposely deep-sixed the Gardner museum robbery to protect Kelly, Martell, DePasquale and the rest of our elite informant group, we could face some serious time! We have a major fucking problem!"

"There's not much we can do about it. If Quintal tells the truth to the committee, then we're finished. Main Justice will appoint an outside prosecutor and will indict the two of us for obstruction of justice if not worse," Morrissey said in a fatalistic tone. "We were given orders by Washington to wipe out the Mafia in Boston and we did. If McGrath's career was ruined in the process, too bad! As for the paintings, their recovery was never a priority of the Bureau and to be frank, it wasn't for this office either."

"Those assholes over in the Fenway let pimply faced, nitwit college kids, posing as rent-a-cops without weapons, baby-sit their precious little paintings. Do you know that after the robbery the museum referred to their security system as 'state of the art'? That was bullshit. I think I read somewhere at the time, that the system in place was so poor that they couldn't buy theft insurance. I can't believe this." Morrissey said as he gazed out his large office window and out onto Boston Harbor, his back to Cullen.

"If McGrath really is a mole, what can we do to put the skids on what Fowler and her people are doing? Goddamn it! I never did like that son of a bitch McGrath," Morrissey said in disgust.

Chapter Sixty-Four
Federal Penitentiary, Hazelton, West Virginia, Four Days' Later

McGrath and Mullen could see the sprawling, grey concrete federal prison as they drove down into the valley nestled in the surrounding mountains of Preston County, West Virginia. They had traveled to the sparsely settled area to meet David Mercer, now known as inmate number 15921046. The meeting was arranged with the consent of Mercer and his lawyer. The United States Penitentiary at Hazelton is a high security institution housing only male inmates. Like most other prisons, it has a grey, stark exterior and is constructed of steel reinforced concrete with a massive footprint. It was designed to hold 1600 inmates in its four tiers of cells that surround a centrally located guard tower that has a 360-degree view of all of its guests. As the two walked in, they identified themselves to a guard at the reception desk, who checked their credentials and licenses. Once satisfied, he handed them visitor badges and then, hit the intercom to alert the guard on the other side of the door that it was all right to let them into the inner, secure pod of the facility. As a buzzer sounded, a large, heavy metal door, with what looked like bulletproof grade glass, began to slide open very slowly. Mullen and McGrath were met on the other side by another guard who asked them to follow him. They were escorted to a large room that had many tables and chairs in the center.

The room was painted the usual sterile grey color of institutions. Nothing was on the walls except warning signs reminding the inmates and their guests what constituted permissible and impermissible conduct. A constant hum came from sets of long florescent lights that were the only source of light in the room. All inmates at Hazelton, a maximum-security facility, were serving lengthy sentences. They were dressed in orange jump suits with the letters BOP in black letters printed on the back of their tops. The scene in front of the two agents in the massive room was almost surreal.

Most prisoners were hugging, kissing, and holding hands with their loved ones. Walking through the sea of humanity, a guard brought McGrath and Mullen over to one of the small rooms and then said, "If you need me, I'll be right outside the door." Sitting in the room were David Mercer and his attorney, Ken Leister. The four shook hands and then McGrath got down to business. "David, we want to thank you for agreeing to talk with us. We need your cooperation in connection with the Gardner museum heist. I know you have always denied any involvement in the robbery. We, however, believe you were involved. As I explained to Attorney Leister, we now have what we believe to be solid evidence that several months before the robbery, you approached one of the guards who worked at the museum with a proposition. If he agreed to let two guys dressed up in police uniforms into the museum in the early morning following the festivities of St. Patrick's Day, you would take care of the big problem he had with his supplier of illegal drugs."

"Agent Mullen and I want to hear what you have to say and we have been instructed by the AUSA who is lead counsel on the case, to inform you and your attorney, that, if you decide to cooperate with us, the United States Attorney's office in Boston would give very serious consideration to filing a Motion to Revise and Revoke to have your sentence reduced. In fact, here is a signed agreement from our office formalizing that proposition. If you agree to cooperate with us, we will file the motion with the court."

McGrath, playing hardball now, was ready to throw a fastball right at Mercer's chin. "Let's face it, as it stands right now, after losing your appeal in front of the First Circuit last week, your expected release date is 2036. You and I know that really sucks. You, most likely are going to die in this concrete tomb! I'm sorry, but as that old country song goes, 'I see you're out of aces,' my friend. Agent Mullen and I are now going to step out for a few minutes so you can speak with your attorney." About five minutes later the door opened and Leister nodded that his client had made a decision. Sitting down, McGrath could see the agreement was on the table right in front of him with Mercer's signature on it.

"Excellent. We're very pleased that you decided to sign this." Taking a tape recorder out from his coat pocket, having found an easier way to memorialize a witness's statement without writing it down in a spiral notebook, McGrath turned it on. "This is retired special agent Edward McGrath and I am here with agent Bryan Mullen, attorney Ken Leister and David Mercer. It is Thursday, October 26, 2007 and we are at the federal penitentiary in Preston County, West Virginia. David, do I have your permission to tape record our conversation?" "Yes," Mercer replied.

"Let me be straight with you. We know that you were involved with the robbery. We also know that you and your compadre, Georgie Walsh, a week before the Gardner robbery, forced your way into a home in Stoughton back in 1990 to steal jewelry and cash from a safe located in the basement of the house. When Mullen and I recently looked at that case, there were clear similarities between that home invasion and the Gardner heist. You handcuffed the poor woman to a banister and used duct tape to tie her up just like in the Gardner robbery. What caught our attention about the Stoughton case was the victim's description of one of the assailants. She described him as a white male, 25-26 years of age, about 5'9" and of average build. He had straight, spiked dirty blond hair and looked like one of his parents was of Asian descent. It fit you to a tee. By the way, when I showed your booking photo to the kids who were screwing around on Palace Road the night of the robbery, they all identified you as the guy in the police uniform sitting in the driver's seat. You were in a light colored hatchback parked just feet from the side entrance to the museum. So, instead of me asking questions, why don't you just tell us what you know about the Gardner robbery? If agent Mullen and I have any questions, we'll jump in, alright?" McGrath asked. "That's fine." Mercer responded.

"You're right, I was there that night. I was one of the two guys sitting in the car that those college kids saw parked on Palace Road under the streetlight. I was sitting in the driver's seat. A buddy of Bobby Datoli's and mine was in the passenger seat. My job that morning was two-fold: to act as a lookout and to help the three guys inside with putting the paintings in the trunk without fucking them up. My buddies and I used to hang out at an after hours bar in the South End. They always had good bands playing and it stayed open until four in the morning. I used to hang out with Bobby Datoli, Carmine Martino's younger brother, Stephen, and a few others who weren't involved."

"When we were there one night, I met a guy who had lived in Boston his whole life until he got caught by the feds in some sort of art scam. He told me that he and his wife were forced to move to California where he opened up a shop, selling art and antiques. He rambled on and on to me about how he hated the FBI and the Boston Irish, especially Jimmy Kelly. He seemed like a pretty decent guy, so we had a couple of beers together. That's when the subject of the Gardner museum came up."

"He said that he wanted to get back at the FBI and wanted to really embarrass them. He said that he also wanted to make some money. I think the beers were starting to go to his head, because he then told me that he and his brother were planning on robbing the Gardner. He said they planned to pull it off the morning after St. Patrick's Day." McGrath asked, "Had you ever bumped into this guy before or was this the first time?" "No. This was the first time."

Mercer continued. "He said that he could pull it off because he had a nephew who worked there and could provide inside help. He asked me if I wanted to make a quick score and I said yes. I gave him my cell phone number and a couple of weeks later, he called me and we met to discuss what he wanted me to do. That's how I ended up talking to the guard who played in a band at the club. He told me what to say to him and the rest is history. I found out after the score that this guy didn't just bump into me at the club by chance. I ultimately learned that he and his brother were loosely connected guys and had ties with the DePasquale family in the North End and with Carmine Martino's family. I also found out after the fact, Martino had ties with a couple of made guys from Philadelphia and Hartford, Connecticut."

As he listened carefully, McGrath pulled four photographs from his shirt pocket and handed them to Mercer. He then asked him if he recognized any of them. "Sure. They are the four other guys who pulled this thing off. Allan Whitcomb, his brother Michael, their nephew Elliot Neufeldt and Bobby Datoli, who, by the way, is unfortunately now dead. Allan Whitcomb wasn't at the museum that night but he and his brother, Michael, planned the whole thing. Datoli and I were in the carpenters' union in Boston, Local 67 working out of Dorchester. Both he and I were pretty fucking good plasterers and dry-wallers. I recruited Bobby and he agreed to go into the museum with Michael Whitcomb, while I stayed in the car outside with another member of our union, Tommy Doyle. The robbery went off without a hitch and the paintings were first put into a white van the night of the robbery and then as I later learned, some were transferred to the trunk of a car."

"Michael Whitcomb had me drive to a business located on Cambridge Street. I think it was a car transport business. I parked the car in the fenced in, barb-wired parking lot. He told me to lock it and to place the keys on top of the left rear tire, which is exactly what I did. After the robbery, Bobby told me that he had a hell of a time trying to get that fucking French flag out of its metal frame. He got so fucking frustrated, that he gave up and instead, grabbed the eagle from the top of the frame. I told him he was a stupid fuck because all he had to do to get the flag out was to smash the glass in the frame and then grab the flag. I guess he didn't realize the frame was encased in glass!"

Mercer, now laughing, said, "He was really pissed that he didn't think of doing that. Bobby was never the brightest bulb on the Christmas tree. Oh yeah, he grabbed the Degas sketches because Allan Whitcomb wanted them. He told me that when he was in the Short Gallery, trying to get that flag out of its frame, he gave up and took the eagle instead. Then, when he jumped off the table that he used to reach the flag, he saw the sketches of the jockeys and racehorses and grabbed them. When I asked him how he got them out of the two frames, he told me that he looked around for something to break the glass with and, then saw a fire extinguisher. When he went to remove it, to break the glass, he felt something on the side of it that turned out to be a wooden hammer or mallet. So he used that to break the glass."

"Allan Whitcomb also wanted the vase and explained to us that the husband of a chick he grew up with in Boston, who, I think he said lived in Paris and somewhere down in Florida, wanted the flag because, according to him, it once belonged to Napoleon. Her husband wanted to return it to the French people. Suddenly, Mercer stopped in mid-sentence. McGrath and Mullen were confused as the two looked at Mercer and then at Leister. Mercer then spoke. "That's all I have to say. Now you two have to do what you promised me. I have nothing else to say until I hear back from you through my attorney. Let Leister know when the United States Attorney's office has filed the Motion to Revise and Revoke my sentence." Mercer then got up from the table and knocked on the door. The prison guard standing right outside opened it and then grabbed him by the arm and walked across the room to return him to his cell.

Chapter Sixty-Five
Federal Courthouse, Boston, Three Days' Later

The group had once again assembled in the U.S. Attorney's conference room. Fowler started the meeting. "Ted and Bryan had a good meeting with Mercer and his attorney down in West Virginia. Mercer, as we expected, spilled his guts but did not tell us who has the paintings or where they may be stashed."

"Both Bryan and I are convinced he has more to tell us but won't until we file the Motion to Revise and Revoke. I don't blame him. If I was in his position, I wouldn't say another word to anyone until I saw some real progress on getting my sentenced reduced," McGrath said. "You're right, Ted. It's just like a defendant who might cooperate with us to nail a co-defendant or when someone throws a target of an investigation to the wolves to get a reduction in his sentence after a plea," Fowler said.

"We all know that, whenever we are looking at multiple targets, the first one who walks through the door, after he or his attorney gets a target letter from someone like me, will get the best deal. Whoever wants to cooperate in exchange for being a snitch by ratting out his cohorts, if their information is good enough could end up with a 5K for their assistance. If what they have to tell us pans out, they will luck out by getting a reduction in their prison time. It's no different in this case with Mercer. The only difference is that he's already in the can doing time, while offering information to help us," Fowler said. "One other thing. His story about Allan Whitcomb coughing up his plan to rob the Gardner rings hollow to me. I, don't think he's being entirely truthful on that. Allan Whitcomb was living in California at the time and would not be hanging out at an after hours bar here in Boston. I think he's holding back," McGrath said to the group. "I'm going to head back down there to squeeze him some more to see if he's telling the truth or lying to us."

"That's great Ted. In the meantime, I have asked Katharine to draft the Motion to Revise and Revoke and I will prepare an affidavit for Mercer to sign setting forth what he has already told to Ted and Bryan. I have the tape of the interview and I will also have his attorney come in to help me with drafting it. Ted, you should take a copy of the motion and affidavit with you to show Mercer when you meet with him. At least it will prove that we have started the process and are acting in good faith," Fowler said.

"Since the motion concerns this office's formal request to the court for a reduction in a sentence that has already been handed down by a judge, the United States Attorney needs to sign off on it. Before it gets to him for his review and signature, it has to be reviewed by my Chief, Jim London and by the First Assistant, Frank Cullen," Fowler explained to the group. "Having them sign off on the motion, given what we will in all likelihood get in return from Mercer, should not be a problem and shouldn't cause anyone heartburn," Fowler said with confidence.

Chapter Sixty-Six: Federal Courthouse, Boston, Several Days' Later

After the group had met and decided to move forward with the Motion to Revise and Revoke on Mercer's behalf, having heard nothing back from the front office, AUSA Fowler stopped by AUSA Jim London's office to see if he had gotten it back through the inter-office mail. He was sitting at his desk when she popped her head in. "Good morning Amy, what's up?" "I was wondering if you had gotten that Motion on Mercer back from the front office?"

"I haven't seen it. I reviewed it the day you gave it to me and then I signed off on it. It looked fine to me." "Would you mind checking with the First Assistant to see if he can light a fire under Morrissey to sign off on it?" "No sweat, I'll speak with Cullen today." "Thanks Jim."

When Fowler got to her desk, she hit the call button on her voice mail to see what fires she was going to have to put out. There were the usual calls from agents that she was working with, trying to get some time to meet with her or at least run something by her on pending investigations. Then there were the annoying calls from the front office reminding her that she was late in updating the status of all cases that were on her plate. She hated the pesky, administrative things lawyers in the office had to do. It was bad enough that they were currently down fourteen lawyers because of budget cuts; it was worse that they had to spend precious time sitting at their computers, updating their cases. Fowler knew that when it came to Main Justice, it was always about the numbers. The last message was from Anthony Fenore from the Gardner. He had good news. The museum's Board of Trustees, after his presentation, had agreed to announce an increase in the reward to Ten Million-Dollars. They too, now agreed with the group after seeing the videos of Allan Whitcomb, that, he is in possession of the paintings or knows where they are located. He went on to say that the museum wanted to announce the increase in the reward at a news conference on the front steps of the museum. The director of the museum also suggested that United States Attorney Morrissey, if his schedule allowed, was more than welcome to say a few words at the event. They planned to announce it on Friday at 3:00 PM just in time for the 6:00 PM news.

Hanging up the phone, Fowler walked down the hall to Mary Crespo's desk, located just outside Morrissey's office. Crespo was his executive assistant. "Good morning Mary, how goes the battle?" Fowler asked. "Not bad, but it's still early in the day," she said, smiling. "I received a call from the Gardner museum this morning. They are planning to have a press conference to announce that the reward for the return of the stolen paintings is going to be increased to Ten Million Dollars. They have asked me to attend and would like to have U.S. Attorney Morrissey attend as well. What does his schedule look like on Friday of this week, around 3:00 PM?" Fowler asked. "He has meetings out of the office all day up until 1:00 PM, and then he is available. I'll pencil the Gardner press conference in for 3:00 PM. Just do me a favor. Could you prepare a summary of what is going to be said at the press conference and by whom? If they want him to say a few words, could you also draft some talking points that he could review while driving over to the event?"

"Not a problem, I'll take care of that, thanks again Mary. Oh by the way, have you seen the Mercer Motion to Revise and Revoke come across your desk with the U.S. Attorney's signature on it?" "That's funny, Attorney London just asked me the same thing and I told him that I hadn't. I'll mention something to Mr. Morrissey in the morning."

As Fowler was speaking with Crespo, Morrissey and Cullen were in a closed-door session in the U. S Attorney's private office ten feet away. "I'm not going to sign off on this Motion to Revise and Revoke David Mercer's sentence. I say that for two reasons. Number one, in all likelihood, based upon what I have been told by London and Fowler, Mercer knows where the paintings are, and, number two, he's a cold-blooded killer. We know that over the years he's killed at least three people but based upon the lack of hard evidence, the Plymouth County District Attorney could never make a case stick. They were never able to get witnesses to flip and to testify against the punk. As a result, there was never enough evidence to convince a unanimous jury that he was involved in the murders," Morrissey said to Cullen as he looked out onto Boston Harbor. "I know I told you that we shouldn't thwart Fowler and her group from recovering the paintings, but I've reconsidered that plan of attack. Once Fowler and her crowd find out from Mercer that the Whitcomb brothers have the art work, those two, who will be facing a minimum mandatory sentence of fifteen years under the bill that Senator Kennedy filed, are going to sing like there's no tomorrow."

"Yeah, you're right, just like that bum Charlie Quintal has, Cullen said. "If it's only Quintal who is talking, then we might be able to ride out this storm, since it will be our word against his. If he has in fact told Barton's committee that the two of us knew what Martell and Kelly were up to and, we just turned a blind eye, all we need to do is to deny it. How is that rat ever going to prove it? It's almost twenty years ago for Christ's sake!"

"There is a slight problem with that," Cullen said, "If the Whitcomb boys decide to open their mouths and tell the world about the Bureau's elite informant program and worse, that they told Quintal in 1990 that Kelly and Martell were killing people on our watch, we are going to be in deep do-do."

Morrissey responded, "You need to tell London that I'm not going to sign off on it and if he asks you why, tell him because the guy is a killer and deserves to die in prison." Neither Morrissey, Cullen or anyone else for that matter knew that the night before, Katharine had received a third note that read: "Deve-se estudar para aprender." Unlike the first two encrypted messages, this one was to the point: "MEET ME WEDNESDAY NIGHT AT 7:30 PM UNDERNEATH THE

LONGFELLOW BRIDGE...BRING NO ONE!"
The small piece of paper twitched with the
rhythm of her pulse.

Chapter Sixty-Seven

McGrath once again sat across the table from
David Mercer and his attorney. This time, unlike
the first meeting, when he had been cocky and
sure of himself, Mercer now appeared gaunt and
looked depressed. McGrath figured it was the
likely result of the kid's realization that if the
Motion to Revise and Revoke was denied, he
would rot in jail. McGrath, picking up on
Mercer's gloomy demeanor, got right down to
business. Unlike the last visit, he wasn't going to
throw a fastball under his chin. He was going to
throw a 96-mile per hour fastball directly at
Mercer's head.

"David, I'm going to be frank with you, I don't
believe your story about Allan Whitcomb and
how you got involved with him and his brother
in pulling off the robbery. Allan, at the time, was
living in California and I don't think he was
hanging around Boston and, even if he was, it
wouldn't have been at some after hour's gin
mill. Even if I believed you that he did hang out
at that seedy bar, there is no way that after just

meeting a total stranger, he would shoot his mouth off about robbing the Gardner museum. Now, we can do this the easy way or the hard way," McGrath said in a firm tone. He could see that Mercer wasn't too pleased with where the seasoned agent was going.

Taking out papers from his suit coat pocket, he threw them across the table to Mercer and said, "That's a copy of the Motion to Revise and Revoke along with the affidavit that you signed. We plan on filing this under seal in court in the next couple of days. Either you come clean with me or I'll tear this fucking thing up right now and fly back to Boston. Do not waste my fucking time!" Mercer, looking at his lawyer, asked McGrath to step outside. A short time later, the door opened and Leister asked him to come back in. Mercer was holding the motion and affidavit in his hand. "Alright, here's the deal," he said, as McGrath placed the tape recorder on the table and turned it on to record what Mercer was about to say. "You're right, I haven't been completely straight with you. I was trying to protect a friend. I didn't meet Allan Whitcomb or Michael Whitcomb at the after hour's club. One night when I was there with my buddies, I ran into a kid I played American Legion baseball with back when I was in my teens. We hadn't seen each other for years and so we caught up on old times and just shot the bull. I couldn't fucking believe he had become a Boston cop.

Anyway, he started to hang out with me and my friends and we all would go to the club on Saturday nights."

"One night, when he and I had a real good buzz on, he asked me if I might be interested in robbing an art museum to make some quick cash. When he asked me that question, at first I was like, what the fuck are you talking about, I'm a freaking union carpenter, not an art thief. That's when he looked at me with that funny smile of his, that he's had since the day I first met him on the baseball field years ago. When he smiled like that, I knew what he was saying: 'Hey dude, come on, remember who the fuck you're talking to'. With the smile gone, I knew he was serious when he said, "Weren't you and a buddy of yours a few years back jammed for an attempted robbery at the Museum of Fine Arts in Boston that went south? He was right. What was I going to do, tell him that I wasn't when I knew it was all over the newspapers back then? So I asked him what he had in mind. He said that he and two other guys were planning on robbing the Gardner museum." "When he told me it was the Gardner, I almost fell off the fucking bar stool. He said that he had personal knowledge that the security sucked at the museum and that it would be a walk in the park. He also said that they would have inside help. He told me he was in a real jam with the feds. It had something to do with him and some other

Boston cops taking bribes from some nightclub owners. He said that if he was going down, he had to make a quick fucking score before he landed in the can so he would have some dough when he got out. He also told me that he was familiar with the layout of the museum because he was real tight with a Boston building inspector who had inspected the museum a zillion fucking times. He said the guy knew the layout better than any museum employee including Old Lady Gardner. When I heard him say that they were going to have inside help, I thought that maybe I would get involved."

"When I asked him what I had to do, he told me that I would be the lookout stationed outside, while he and the others entered the museum to grab some paintings. He said that before they could rob the place, they needed me to speak to a guard who worked at the museum, for me to put the fear of God in him so he would have no choice but to let us into the fucking place. He said that the guard actually played in a band at the club where we were hanging out and that he was in a bad jam with his supplier of grass and nose candy. This would give him real incentive to cooperate with us. Somehow he knew that this asshole guard with the coke problem was dealing drugs out of the museum. So he had him by the balls! I told him I would give it some thought and the rest is history. I decided to get involved. I scared the fucking crap out of the kid one night when he was packing up his equipment. He was easy and, about six weeks later, we pulled it off without a hitch. It was like taking candy from a baby," Mercer said with that infamous boyish grin of his now on his face.

"What's the name of your buddy that got you involved in the robbery," McGrath asked. Mercer, taking his time to respond, finally said, "Elliot Neufeldt, who, I found out when this thing went down, also worked at the museum as a security guard. So, the night of the robbery it ended up being me, Tommy Doyle in the lookout car, Neufeldt, Bobby Donati and "Slick" Feldman in the museum. Donati and Feldman were the two 'cops' that were let in. We were dressed as Boston cops too. The other guard never saw us so he never even knew we were there!" McGrath was stunned. "Well I'll be a son-of-a-bitch, that fucking oboe player of a guard was right, there were more than two people 'working upstairs' that night!"

Chapter Sixty-Eight: "The End-Around Plan"

AUSA London was reading a prosecution memo when his phone rang. Looking down at the caller-id, he could see it was First Assistant

Cullen. Picking up the phone, he said "Hey Frank what's up?" "Hi Jim, I need to speak with you on this Mercer matter, do you have a minute?" "Sure, when do you want to see me," London asked. "As soon as possible."
"I'll be right there," London said.

London walked down the hall and into the front office area where Morrissey and Cullen's offices were located. When he knocked on Cullen's door, Cullen opened it and invited London to come in and to take a seat at a small table. The office walls were bare. Absent were the usual family photographs and mementos that most prosecutors in the office would display on their desks, walls and credenzas. Every award on a wall or desk was to a prosecutor what notches on a belt were to a gunslinger, each one representing a conviction or kill. Cullen did not have any on display for two reasons: he was single and in his twenty-seven years with the office, not once had he tried a case. The Department of Justice was Cullen's family and being a career prosecutor was his life. He could be found in his office on weekends and even holidays. Whoever happened to occupy the corner office, he was there to serve and protect the United States Attorney at all cost. If the United States Attorney told him to jump off the nearby Mystic River Bridge, he would follow orders. He possessed that blind, storm trooper mentality: follow orders without question; never give any thought whether it was the right or wrong thing to do; and never, ever be concerned about possible consequences or collateral damage. Cullen was what defense attorneys refer to as a true believer.

"Morrissey is not going to sign off on the Mercer motion. He feels that he is a killer and doesn't deserve any breaks or consideration, including any reduction in his sentence. He is adamant about that and he is not going to budge. You know firsthand what he's like when he's made up his mind on an issue; he's stubborn, like a mule," Cullen said.

"I know he is, Frank, but Fowler and her group are positive that Mercer can lead them to the Gardner paintings. Mercer will not tip his hand if he doesn't get something in return. With his appeal now dead in the water, this is the perfect opportunity for us to jam him so he can help us," London said with some anger in his voice. "This is the closest we have ever been to solving this case and for Morrissey to block our efforts is extremely disappointing and… unfair! How could he do such a thing,? It just doesn't make any sense."

"I understand your position Jim, but he has made his decision and that's that," Cullen said as he rose from his chair, indicating that the meeting was over. "Thanks Jim and I trust you will give Fowler the heads up," Cullen said as London walked out of the office. Fowler and the others were aghast. How could Morrissey have decided not to sign off on the Motion to Revise and Revoke? They were incredulous. "Without Mercer telling us or at least pointing us in the right direction, we're back to square one. The Whitcomb brothers are not going to just hand the paintings over to us, we need Mercer's help," Fowler said to the group who were in the War Room. "I'm going to have to give this some thought to see if we need to bypass Morrissey and make the request to Main Justice directly. I know that is an extraordinary step, but this is our opportunity to blow the top off this case. I'll think about it overnight and we can all re-group in the morning, say 9:30. Okay, thanks everybody and remember, what is said in this room stays here. Understood?" While the group was walking out of the cramped room, McGrath grabbed Fowler and asked if she had a moment.

"Sure Ted, what's up? McGrath asked her if she could keep a secret and she said yes. He told her about his meeting with Cadigan and what agent Charlie Quintal had told Barton's committee. As the story unfolded, Fowler sat in amazement, finding it incredible; not only as a federal prosecutor, but also as a citizen. McGrath explained to her that there was always more than one way to skin a cat and with her permission, he would speak with Cadigan to

inform him of the new developments in the case
to ask his advice and guidance. "You cannot tell
anyone about this. No one in our group must
know, not even your chief, Jim London. Do I
have your word?" McGrath asked her. "Yes you
do, Ted," she replied.

Agent Cadigan was having lunch at the
Washington Deli on K Street, when his cell
phone rang. Taking it from his belt, he could see
that it was Ted McGrath. "Hi Ted, how are you
making out up there in Boston?" "Not too good.
We have a major fucking problem here.
Morrissey is refusing to sign off on the Mercer
Motion to Revise and Revoke for some bullshit
reason. If he doesn't, then Mercer is not going to
talk and we're going to be back to square one.
We need Mercer's help to get the paintings back
or at least try and get them back," McGrath
replied.

"Are you sure he won't reconsider his decision?"
Cadigan asked. "From what I hear from the two
AUSAs handling the case, he will not change his
mind. What I know of the guy, the harder he's
pushed, the harder he pushes back." "Well just
sit tight. Why don't you e-mail the motion to
me? I'll have the Deputy Attorney General take a
look at it. If it meets with his approval, he can
sign off on it and then Fowler can file it with the
court in Boston under seal. That way, we can

bypass Morrissey and get it before a judge. Morrissey doesn't even have to know about it." "By the way, based upon what Charlie Quintal is telling Senator Barton's committee down here in Washington, Morrissey's ass could soon be on the line. If I had to guess, I think he's concerned about what Quintal is telling the committee and he is probably getting a little spooked. I'll e-mail that motion to you this afternoon along with Mercer's affidavit. I'm going to have to let Fowler know what our game plan is; she's going to have to know. Do you have any problem with that?" McGrath asked. "If you think she can keep her mouth shut, then I don't have any objection to her knowing. An AUSA is going to have to sign the motion and file it under seal anyway. It might as well be Fowler," Cadigan said.

McGrath had Fowler meet him after work at the Chart House the next day after faxing the motion to Cadigan. Instead of his usual practice of sitting at the bar, the two sat at a table in a dark corner of the dimly lit room, the only light coming from a candle at the center of the table that cast a shadowy glow upon their faces. There was a musty, worn-out smell to the room but the stout and wine were cold and, as usual, McGrath's favorite bartender, Tony treated both of his guests like family.

"I spoke with my contact at Main Justice about our little problem with your boss, Morrissey. I told him that he's unwilling to sign off on the Mercer motion. He wasn't too pleased to hear that. He suggested that I email him the motion so that he could run it by the DAG. I did that about an hour ago. It can be handled down there and once approved you could file it under seal, totally bypassing Morrissey and Cullen."

With a concerned look on her face, Fowler responded, "What you're telling me is that you want me to file this motion behind Morrissey's back, without his knowledge, after he has already made his decision very clear to London. Is that what I'm hearing? I've been a federal prosecutor for twelve years and if I go along with your plan, I could be fired. I'm a single mom with two kids and if I lost my job over this, it would be a disaster. I feel uncomfortable even discussing this with you."

McGrath in response said, "Look, the Deputy Attorney General will sign off on it and if need be, we can get a letter from him absolving you from any disciplinary action if you agree to participate. Listen. You don't have to go along, but I think you are really close to breaking this case wide open. If Mercer gets what he wants and needs, we will hopefully be in a position to recover some, if not all the paintings. We're so close. I spent seventeen years of my life on this case. As you will soon learn, people within your office and within the Bureau didn't want me to solve it. On the contrary, they intentionally put roadblocks up all along the way. They did everything they could for those long seventeen years to thwart the investigation. They, your boss Morrissey included, double-crossed me   I need your help now and I would ask you to give it some serious thought." McGrath said as he looked at her with intense conviction in his eyes.

"I will think about it. By the way, thanks for the glass of wine. I've got to catch the commuter boat. Good night," Fowler said, as she got up and walked out. McGrath walked to the bar and ordered another pint from Tony.

Several Days' Later

Fowler's message on McGrath's cell phone was short and to the point. She was in. She would not tell anyone about his or her plan of attack but just as a precaution, she asked him to obtain a letter from the DAG in Washington to protect her. He knew her request was not going to be a problem. He finished his coffee and headed to the federal courthouse. Fowler was at her desk when the phone rang. She could see it was reception. "Agent Ted McGrath is here to see you."

McGrath was handed a pass without escort by the receptionist and headed to Fowler's office. She welcomed him and took a seat as she closed the door. Fowler had asked him to arrive early so they could go over a few things before their scheduled meeting with Mullen, Savage and Fenore at 9:30 AM. "I spoke to my source at Main Justice last night. They will prepare a letter for your review to make absolutely sure that there will be no repercussions whatsoever up here with the front office. I appreciate your help on this and I hope it pays off," McGrath said. "I do too," Fowler replied with a nervous smile. McGrath continued.

"Once you receive the letter from the DAG, you can file the motion under seal so the press will not know what we're up to. Hopefully once Mercer sees that it has been filed, he will tell us what we need. He wasn't straight with Mullen and me but finally came around after I told him I was going to tear the motion up right in front of him and head back to Boston."

"What's the next step with the Whitcomb brothers?" McGrath asked. "That's a good question. I've had Mullen check with the Bureau out in San Francisco how Allan Whitcomb is supporting himself. I've asked for surveillance on him, and Bryan tells me they have been doing just that. The same two agents who obtained the cigarette butt for the DNA are watching his every move. Initial reports are that his art and antique business doesn't seem to be making a go of it. I had Katharine draft an I-Order so IRS could pull his federal tax returns for the past five years to see if he has been cooking the books. Despite the fact that business looks slow, I also understand that he and his wife lead a pretty expensive life style, including owning a summer place at Lake Tahoe."

"Once the IRS pulls the returns, we'll take a look at them to see if he's living above his means. If it looks like he is, we'll have the IRS put a scope so far up his ass that we'll know if he still has his tonsils. The more leverage we have on him, including a tax evasion prosecution, the easier it'll be to get him to come clean. At his age I doubt he would want to do a 5-10 stint down in West Virginia with Davey Boy. We need either a big carrot or a large enough stick over his head to get him to talk or call his bluff to broker the paintings' return," Fowler said. "That sounds like an excellent idea. We should probably do the same thing with his brother Michael. There have always been rumors on the street that he launders money and does some loan sharking out of the marina. My recollection is that someone mentioned to me at one time way back when that Michael owned a summer home in Edgartown on Martha's Vineyard and has a palatial place in Chestnut Hill. If his brother doesn't decide to move forward with this cockamamie scam about acting as a broker to return the stolen art, we are going to have to force one or both of them to come forward the old fashioned way, by having a couple of agents from the IRS serve subpoenas on them at home and at work."

"No one in their right mind wants the IRS on their case. Those guys always seem to find something. Hey, that's how the feds ended up nailing Al Capone, through tax evasion. If it worked with him, it could also work on the brothers Whitcomb. I'll call my friend, agent Bill Collier over at the JFK Building to see if he could come by in the morning to speak with us about doing a lifestyle income analysis on the Whitcomb's."

The Next Morning

Agent Bill Collier was a twenty-three year veteran with the IRS. Although 62, his hobby, water polo, kept him in great shape. His hair, cropped close to the scalp in a crew cut style, was a throwback to the 50s and 60s. His quiet nature made him very popular with other agents and federal prosecutors. Over the years, he had worked with hundreds of them on tax fraud cases, including several each with Fowler and McGrath. Like McGrath, he was a seasoned veteran. Born in Oklahoma he had that midwesterners gentle style about him, and was very gracious and humble. His quiet demeanor, however, as everyone who worked with him knew, masked the fire in his belly. When it came to nailing taxpayers, he had a relentness tenacity in the way he approached potential tax cheats. He was like a junkyard dog that hadn't been fed for a week. If you were screwing the government on your taxes, and Collier was assigned to the case, you would undoubtedly become another one of the unfortunate souls who were going to pay the price for their greed. Billy Collier, at the end of the day, was going to make sure the government won!

After greeting everyone gathered in the War Room, Collier, at Fowler's request, gave a little tutorial on lifestyle income analysis. "One of the most intrusive, time consuming and abusive audit methods used by the IRS is the 'lifestyle audit'. It's what we used to call the 'economic reality audit'. When an IRS auditor suspects that a taxpayer may have significant unreported income, they perform a detailed analysis of the taxpayer's lifestyle, looking at what is coming in versus their assets. This might include their spending habits, what cars they drive, how often they travel and where they travel to and what properties they own. We do this in order to compute how much income would be required to support such a lifestyle. If the estimated income is more than the reported income, we presume that the taxpayer has failed to report all of his or her income. The burden in a civil tax case is on the taxpayer to refute our estimates. How do they do this you ask? They are required to provide us with detailed cash receipts and disbursements outlined on a balance sheet, from year to year, to establish that any excess "income" can be accounted for by things other than salary or profit from a business. Items such as gifts, inheritances, and the depletion of assets or assuming liability of a new debt can be shown to explain away our estimates based upon what we computed. On the criminal tax cheat side, the burden is on the government to prove the case against someone who is intentionally under-reporting their income."

"If the loss in tax revenue is large enough, we will refer it to someone like Attorney Fowler to prosecute. The loss amount necessary to trigger a possible look-see by the U.S. Attorney's office is a well-guarded secret and, I'm not going to open my mouth and give any secrets away," Collier said jokingly. "I anticipate receiving both Michael and Allan Whitcomb's tax returns for the past five years in a couple of days and if it's okay with you, our auditors can go through them first thing and then I will let you know what I think. In the meantime, I will draft a summary of their assets and liabilities once I obtain more information from the FBI agents,

who, I understand, have them under
surveillance as we speak."

Chapter Sixty-Nine
Federal Courthouse, Boston, Days' Later

Collier was again back in front of Fowler's group
after receiving an analysis from his auditors of
both Allan and Michael Whitcomb's tax returns.
They also reviewed the balance sheets of their
respective businesses for the last five years. He
started with Michael. "Based upon the numbers
run, this guy is definitely under reporting his
income. It appears even more serious than that.
It looks like he is laundering money through the
business. I have a source over at Boston PD who,
when I mentioned Michael Whitcomb's name to
him, immediately responded that he was dirty.
He explained that his people, in cooperation
with the Feds, have been looking at Whitcomb
for several years for laundering money. "When
my people ran the numbers based upon his
reported income, they came to the unanimous
conclusion that this guy's lifestyle which, by the
way, can only be described as extravagant, can
in no way be supported by his reported income.
If ya'll are looking for a way to put the fear of
God in this guy so that he has no other choice
but use the Gardner paintings to save his butt or

314

buy the keys to Club Fed, you should build a case against him for tax fraud. I believe we can, based upon what we now know make a criminal case against him. Based upon Sentencing Guidelines, which I place at a level of fourteen, if he's hooked on the tax fraud charge alone, he'd be facing 356 months in prison. All in all, Amy, I think if you were to send him a target letter advising him that he is about to be indicted for tax evasion, money laundering and mail fraud, he'd be in here faster than you know what through a tin horn. I'm sure he'd come in with his tail between his legs and with the best lawyer money could buy to negotiate a deal to keep his ass out of jail."

"The problem we have is time, Fowler responded. "To get the evidence needed for a grand jury to indict Whitcomb would take months and we just don't have that luxury. Momentum is on our side and if we can just jam David Mercer hard enough or give him an incentive to cooperate and tell us what he knows, then I think we might have a chance to recover the paintings. Again, Bill, we really appreciate your help and opinion and it probably would work. However, I still think we should give Bryan and Ted one more shot with Mercer down in West Virginia. If that strategy doesn't work out, we will definitely need your help to indict Whitcomb on the tax case."

Fowler then turned and looking in McGrath's direction she was prepared to tell a white lie. "I know Morrissey continues to refuse to sign off on the Motion to Revise and Revoke, so we haven't been able to file it with the court. Maybe Ted can use some of his Irish charm to convince Mercer to cooperate even though we haven't been able to file it," she said as she forced a smile.

Chapter Seventy: "Spilling The Beans"
Federal Penitentiary, Hazleton, West Virginia

David Mercer, this time without his attorney, once again sat across the table from McGrath. Fowler had asked Mullen to stay behind to help her with another matter he was working with her on. At least that's what she used as an excuse to send McGrath down to speak with Mercer alone. Known only to McGrath, Fowler had filed the motion to Revise and Revoke under seal two days earlier. They got lucky when the motion was assigned to Chief Judge Harold Caswell, one of the more liberal judges in the District.

With the tape recorder running Mercer started to talk. "You know, everybody always thought that Allan Whitcomb was the expert in art. Everyone knew that he owned an art gallery in Boston and one in California. Everyone also knew that he has an expertise in the works of Degas. Well, as I understand it, he is definitely an art junky but his brother Michael is an even a bigger collector. His nephew, Elliot Nuefeldt, told me that he has a particular interest in rare paintings. He told me that Michael owns a very impressive art collection. Most of it is in his home in Chestnut Hill but I think he also has some of it in his summer home in Edgartown on Martha's Vineyard. The place in Chestnut Hill is a freak'n estate not far from Boston College's Alumni Stadium." What Mercer next said surprised McGrath.

"I wasn't being straight with you the last time we met. I told you that Bobby Donati was one of the 'cops' let in by Fager. Well, that was bullshit. Bobby was there, but Fager let in Feldman, who was wearing the wire-rimmed glasses. Allan Whitcomb was the other 'cop'. Feldman ended up with the Manet that Fager grabbed while making his rounds. Someone, I think it was Martino, told me after the fact, Feldman's lover was in the can and that he got involved in the robbery to use a painting as a bargaining chip to get him a reduced sentence. That never happened because Feldman met an untimely death a year after the heist. I think he hid a painting somewhere up in Vermont. Because he died unexpectedly, no one knows where he hid

the fucking thing. Talk about fucking bad luck!
Do you have the Boston police sketches with
you?"

"Yes I do, the composite sketches are in my brief
case," McGrath replied. He placed the yellowed
Boston police sketch of the two suspects on the
table and was startled when Mercer reached into
the back pocket of the pants of his prison-issued
jumpsuit and placed a photograph of William
"Slick" Feldman next to the sketch. "Look at that
fucker. Feldman is a dead-ringer for suspect #1
and you already know Michael Whitcomb looks
like a fucking clone of #2. Doesn't Michael also
look just like that guy who played the idiot
Commandant on that prisoner of war sitcom
back in the 70's?" Looking down at the table,
McGrath couldn't believe his eyes. Mercer was
right on the money!

"For some reason that none of us could ever
figure out, you fucking guys at the Bureau never
realized that the Whitcomb boys were identical
twins. Allan flew into Boston on the 15th of
March and flew out the day after he robbed the
museum with the rest of us. His brother Michael
was at the museum a week or two before the
robbery, casing the joint with Feldman. No one
can tell the difference between the two
Whitcomb's. I know I never could."

"Of course Allan had a solid alibi the night of the robbery! His fucking identical twin purposely hung out with Allan's college buddy and his lady friend you guys gave the polygraph tests to after the robbery. Michael covered for his brother all weekend fucking long to give him an absolute bullet-proof alibi." Mercer continued. "Anyway, after the heist, Michael Whitcomb had me and Bobby Datoli build him a room off his den that, unless he told you about, you would never know that it was there. Bobby and I were really good at what we did. We were damn good carpenters and dry-wallers. He wanted us to build the room and since he paid us in cash, we did the job for him. It turned out beautiful. When the wall partition to his secret room is opened, the lights inside go on automatically and it is absolutely dazzling. They light up the whole fucking room! Paintings hang everywhere."

"The special lights that he had us put up over each painting makes the place sparkle. He can open and close the wall panel by pushing a button that's located under the wet bar. As I said, when its open and the lights inside are on, it's quite a sight. It's a huge stash of paintings hanging all over the walls. There's not one inch that is bare."

"He told us he designed it so that when it is open, it looks like it's always been there as part of the room. He told Bobby and me that it was climate controlled and when we heard that, we both assumed that some of the Gardner paintings were probably going to end up hanging on the walls of his secret vault. Now, don't get me wrong, I've never seen the paintings in there. I wouldn't know a fucking Vermeer from a Picasso, but I'd bet my last fucking dollar that some of those bad boys from the Gardner are in that vault. Except for the fuck up with the two Rembrandts, Bobby told me that Michael Whitcomb treated the Gardner paintings like they were his children. Bobby said that he cut out the two Rembrandts because he underestimated how securely they were fastened to the frames and to the wooden stretches behind each. He had no choice but to cut them. The frames were too fucking big to lug out of there. If they had done that and somebody had seen them walking out the Palace road entrance carrying huge frames, the gig would have been up. So, he cut them out with a box cutter. Bobby told me it wasn't pretty but it was necessary."

McGrath was stunned. His thoughts raced through his head. "There is a strong probability that some, if not all of the stolen paintings from the largest art heist in United States history, may be hidden in a secret room not ten minutes away from the Gardner." He got up, shook Mercer's hand and said, "I believe what you just told me and when I get back to Boston I am going to tell AUSA Fowler about your cooperation. That should go a long way with her when she appears before the judge on your motion." As McGrath got up out of his chair to leave, Mercer spoke up.

"I want you to understand one thing. I can get the word to Michael Whitcomb through some of my boys who are still up in Boston. If he has the paintings and I drop a dime before you can get a search warrant, you guys are fucked. You will never get the paintings back, and then instead of being a hero, you will be the pathetic, suck agent you've been your whole career. In fact, I might just let the press know that I was involved in the robbery and that I told you where the paintings were hidden but you and the FBI did nothing with the information back in 1990. As usual, the great FBI sat on their ass and did nothing." McGrath's blood started to boil, as the veins in his neck throbbed. He wanted to jump across the table and throttle the punk. He knew, however, that if he did, it could be the death knell to recovering the paintings. Trying not to explode, he bit his tongue and once again took a seat at the table. Mercer, his eyes now focused on the agent's, wanted to make crystal clear that there was going to be no confusion about his demands.

"I know there is a reward for the return of the paintings. I'm almost positive Michael Whitcomb has a couple of them. I also am pretty sure that his brother Allan has some including the Degas' and the Chinese Ku. Feldman is dead but I think his former lover, who is in the can at Walpole, knows where Manet's painting is stashed. If you guys get any of them back, I want the reward money deposited in my mother's account back in Boston within twenty-four hours after the museum confirms that the paintings are theirs. I want the museum's Board of Directors, or anyone else who has the authority, to send me a written agreement within the next three days memorializing our agreement."

"No letter, and the word goes out to Whitcomb," Mercer said as he reached into his pocket and tossed a dime towards McGrath. It rolled across the table and onto the floor; as a Cheshire grin appeared on the kid's face. Appreciating the significance of the dime, McGrath once again kept his cool and then responded, "I'll see what I can do."

Boston's Federal Courthouse, The Next Day

Fowler and McGrath were alone in her office as he filled her in on what Mercer had told him the day before. They were both apoplectic. On the one hand, she couldn't believe what Mercer had said. If he was actually telling the truth, she could clearly use his information to prepare an affidavit in support of the application for a search warrant. Michael Whitcomb's home in Chestnut Hill would be the locus of the warrant, and the paintings would be the items to be recovered. McGrath and Fowler however knew that they had a major obstacle to preparing an affidavit for Mercer to sign. His demands were totally unrealistic. Mercer, a convicted felon and cold-blooded killer, wanted the reward so he could give it to his ailing mother.

"We have a real dilemma here. If we tell Main Justice what Mercer's demands are, we both know what their response will be. Never mind that I've kept the fact that I filed the Motion to Revise and Revoke from Morrissey. This is a real fucking quagmire. It is because we know what Anthony Fenore would say. The museum in all probability, would agree to Mercer's terms if there were any possibility that Whitcomb has the paintings. We probably have an obligation to the museum and Fenore to tell them what Mercer has told you and what his demands are."
"You're right. We need to speak to Fenore. Let me get him on the phone to set up a meeting for tomorrow morning,"

McGrath said. Fowler, McGrath and Fenore were seated at a table at the Alumni Café located three blocks from the courthouse in Boston's financial district. McGrath spoke first. "I met with David Mercer at the federal penitentiary down in West Virginia a couple of days ago. Amy and I believe he has a pretty good idea where the paintings are, although he is not 100 percent positive. He thinks they are hidden in a secret vault at Michael Whitcomb's home in Chestnut Hill. According to him, he and Bobby Datoli helped build a room off the den in the house sometime after the robbery. We probably have enough from Mercer for Amy to file an application for a search warrant to search the house. However, there's a slight problem. Unless Mercer gets something in writing from the museum promising to put the reward in his mother's bank account within twenty-four hours after the paintings are recovered, he's threatening to get word to Whitcomb that we are about to break the case."

Putting his pen down, Fenore, excitement in his voice, looked directly at Fowler and McGrath said, "I don't think it's a problem at all. As far as I'm concerned and I think the museum trustees will agree with me, it's a win-win proposition for the museum. If the paintings are recovered, we would be more than happy to pay the money to Mercer. If his hunch turns out to be wrong, and, I hope it doesn't, no harm done. We don't pay him a nickel."

"That's the problem," Fowler responded, some tension in her voice. "I'm a federal prosecutor and I have a real concern with any criminal benefiting financially from their criminal acts, particularly a scumbag like Mercer. Plus, the bottom line is that he is blackmailing the museum."

"I understand Amy, but the fact remains that he might be right and if we don't give him the opportunity to be proven right, we could blow any chance of recovering the paintings. I am going to recommend, in no uncertain terms to the trustees, that they sign an agreement agreeing to Mercer's demands. I know you and Ted might have a problem with that but, I am almost positive, the letter of agreement will be in Mercer's hands within twenty-four hours."
And so it was.

Chapter Seventy-One: "The Stranger And The Meeting By The River"

It was one of those nights in Boston when the fog seemed to sweep across the city from the harbor like a blanket, leaving anyone and anything it touched wet and soggy. It was just a small annoyance, mostly to the commuters who were inching their way down the Southeast Expressway to homes in bedroom communities south of the city. Shortly after 7:00 PM, Katharine put on a dark, blue slicker and a Red Sox baseball hat and started to walk east towards the Charles River and the Longfellow Bridge. Walking along Cambridge Street and past the Massachusetts General Hospital, her thoughts were focused on her upcoming encounter with the mysterious person who signed each note she received with the words: 'Deve-se estudar para aprender'.

Since the notes left at her apartment were typewritten, Savage had no clue who it might be or whether the secretive person was a man or a woman. The contents of the notes hadn't given even the slightest hint of the person's occupation or employment. She was completely in the dark. Despite not knowing the note writer's identity, Savage was sure of one thing: whoever it was, he or she, for reasons only known to them, after seventeen long years, was providing information to help resuscitate an otherwise stone cold case. Now, only several blocks from the foot of the Boston side of the Longfellow Bridge where she was to rendezvous with the mysterious note writer and as the noisy trolleys rumbled across the dilapidated span heading to Cambridge, Katharine started to feel uneasy.

Trying to get her bearings while she squinted to adjust her eyes in the dimly lit misty air, she could make out a figure standing off to the left, on the Boston side of the river. The person had their back towards her and light from the nearby lamp, cast scattered, willowy light down on an ankle length trench coat. As she walked towards the dark silhouette, Katharine could feel goose bumps rise on the skin of her forearms. She wasn't sure if this was her target but she was about to find out. Before she could make inquiry, the person turned suddenly and looked directly at her. A colorful silk scarf was strategically placed across the stranger's face. It was bright orange with a small, delicate floral design. "Good evening Ms. Savage. I am very pleased you have taken the time to meet me. Thank you for coming. I trust you have told no one about our meeting?" It was a woman's voice and one that she had never heard before. "No one knows I'm here and nobody followed me. Why have you contacted me and why can't you disclose your identity?" Savage asked. "I still work for people who were involved in this whole cover-up. If they knew I was talking to you, both of us could be in danger. A lot of people have a great deal to lose if the truth about why the robbery hasn't been solved comes out." "Why now? Why have you come forward now?" Savage pointedly asked.

"I knew certain things were going on in the late 80's and 90's at the FBI, but I didn't have an inkling about the extent of the agency's complete lack of loyalty until now. A confidential memo from Washington that was supposed to be read only by the person to whom it was addressed, was mistakenly forwarded to me through inter-office mail. It concerned former Special Agent in Charge Charles Quintal's recent testimony before Senator Barton's committee in Washington. A transcript of his testimony was attached and I read it. I, in fact, have a copy for you," the stranger said as she handed Savage an envelope. "It will open your eyes about what was going on in Boston years ago when the robbery at the Gardner took place. It should help you and your colleagues connect the dots. Although you don't know me, I know you. I have admired your aggressive style and tenacity concerning the Gardner museum robbery. You are on the right track. Continue to follow your instincts."

"As you will see when you read the transcript, they all knew back in the late 80s and early 90s what was going on at the Bureau but did nothing to stop the bloodshed. Focus on the players at the time. Do some digging. Find out who worked in the Organized Crime Strike Force. Many of the Assistant United States attorneys who worked in that Unit back then are still around. Several of them in fact, are still in positions of tremendous authority and power." With that, the stranger turned and started to walk away into the night. All of a sudden, she turned and called back to Katharine, "Be careful, watch your back. You are being watched!" Stunned by the warning, Savage yelled, "Who is watching me...how do you know...tell me who!"

Chapter Seventy-Two
Chestnut Hill, Massachusetts, Three Days' Later

McGrath and Mullen were sitting in an unmarked unit at the end of a long driveway leading up to a Tudor style home located at 180 Morning Glory Lane. Michael Whitcomb had purchased the home shortly after his father died. His mother now lived with him and his wife along with his 135 pound German Shepard, Tron. McGrath and Mullen were there to scope out the layout. If all went well with the search warrant application, they, along with other agents from the Bureau, would soon be descending on the house like a swarm of hornets. There was a wrought iron, electronic gate close to the street that would have to be disengaged before agents could make their way up the cobblestone driveway. The property was densely wooded with many tall pines and American oaks. The lighting was terrible. Except for a light coming from the intercom located at the far left of the gate, the house sat in complete darkness. McGrath took his spiral notebook out and jotted down: "need to neutralize security gate...we'll need klieg lights." The stately dwelling, according to the town assessor's office, had five bedrooms and six baths. Its assessed value about Four Million Dollars.

There was no indication, when the two agents checked with the building department, that Whitcomb or a contractor on his behalf had ever pulled a permit to renovate or add a room any time after the robbery. If Mercer was telling the truth about creating the secret vault, Whitcomb in all probability, had added it without pulling a permit to keep it from the eyes and ears of the neighbors and building inspector. As the two sat there, McGrath's cell phone went off. Taking it from his shirt pocket he could see it was AUSA Fowler. "Hi Amy, Bryan and I are doing some surveillance of Michael Whitcomb's house over here in Chestnut Hill. The place is like the Taj Mahal."

"Ted, I have some good news. I wanted to let you know that the judge just signed off on the search warrant. We're ready to go on it. We need to meet to coordinate when you, Bryan and the other agents are going to effectuate the search warrant. I think we should do it as soon as possible. When you decide on the date and time, I will ride with you in the unlikely event some technical legal issue comes up concerning the nature and extent of the search. Since Katharine Savage has worked like a dog on the case I am going to ask her to ride with us along with Fenore. Any objection to that?" Fowler asked. "Absolutely not. I don't anticipate any trouble but if it develops, you three will be far enough away from the house anyway until it is secured. They deserve to be part of the take down."

"The first thing we need to do is to find someone in the office who can bypass the electric gate without Whitcomb knowing that its been disarmed. In fact, we are heading back to the office to meet with an agent who Bryan tells me can take care of the gate. Why don't we all meet on Friday afternoon? By then we should have a good handle on the date and time of the raid. We will also know who is going to participate in the take down," McGrath said.

Boston's Federal Courthouse, the next Friday

The group was again gathered in the cramped War Room. "We are going to go in on Monday morning at 6:00 AM sharp. There will be six agents armed and dressed in full riot, tactical gear who will participate. Since I am technically not an "official" agent, Bryan is going to lead the search. He and I will serve the search warrant on Whitcomb and two other agents will secure him and the immediate area of the house. The other agents will secure the perimeter to make sure no one comes in or goes out. Once in we will go directly to the den, and if Mercer is right, we should find the buzzer behind the wet bar to open the secret panel. If all goes well, it should be over in a matter of minutes. Probably a lot shorter than what it took this guy and his cronies to pull off the robbery in 1990. I've waited seventeen long years for this and we are not going to fuck it up," McGrath said with determination in his voice.

"Between now and Monday morning I don't want anyone to say anything to anyone about this take down, including Morrissey," Fowler said, as she glanced around at all in the room. "Alright everyone, I need to speak with Ted for a moment. Please remember what I said about keeping our mouths shut." Fowler shut the door and sat at the other end of the table from McGrath. With her head in her hands for a moment, she looked up and said in a shaky voice, "I can't sleep at night over this. If these paintings aren't where we think they are and we come up empty-handed, I will be out of a job Ted. Morrissey will prosecute me and I will lose everything. I know what Main Justice has said but if the proverbial hits the fan and Mercer is wrong, and we all have egg on our faces, Washington will never back us up. I know how they work. I've seen it first-hand. When the press turns the heat up, the powers-that-be shrivel like grapes in the sun. They can't stomach controversy. I will be the scapegoat and they will move on and I'll be screwed!"

"I understand how you feel," McGrath said quietly. "I have Cadigan's word that the Deputy Attorney General will protect you. That might not be of comfort to you at the moment, but I believe him to be solid and a man of integrity. Let me say this to you. We are going to get the paintings back and it's because of your hard work. I promise you Amy, I will not let you down."

Chapter Seventy-Three: "The Assault"
Boston FBI Headquarters, the following
Monday, 4:30 AM

Darkness still shrouded the city as McGrath, Mullen, and four other agents stood together at McGrath's old desk, putting on their snug bullet proof vests. The smell of burnt coffee filled the air. The only sound in the room was a low hum from the heating system. As the veteran agent from South Boston loosened the belt on his vest, he could see the many multi-colored pins that were still pinned to the panel along with the collage of the missing works of art. Seeing them again, he felt a sense of sadness. At the same time, he also felt an emotion that he had not felt in a very, very long time: exhilaration. He felt the most alive he had in years.

It was not lost on the grey haired, retired agent from Southie that, he and his colleagues were possibly on the verge of closing the book on the Isabella Stewart Gardner museum robbery. In a few short hours, if they were lucky, most if not all of the stolen art would hopefully be in their possession and soon after, in the hands of the museum's director of security, Anthony Fenore. He could only hope.

As the six of them finished securing their gear, Mullen had each of them once again go over their individual responsibilities when on site. Mullen and McGrath would attempt to serve the search warrant at the front door while the others secured the perimeter. No one was to be let in or out. Intelligence received from other agents posted in the area of Whitcomb's residence earlier in the morning, indicated that he was home along with his wife and mother.

The six checked the time and synchronized their watches. Neither Mullen nor McGrath, unlike the other four, were in full tactical gear consisting of full riot helmets with face shields. The agents in tactical gear also held fully automatic MP- 5A3 sub machine guns. Looking at each other, Mullen asked if anyone had any final questions and hearing none, he said, "Ted and I are going to head over to the courthouse to pick up Fowler, Savage and Fenore. Estimated time of arrival on site will be 5:42 AM. We will all meet at our checkpoint on Compass Landing, two streets over from Morning Glory. Once at that location McGrath and I will transfer to another vehicle, leaving Fowler, Fenore and Savage at a safe location. We will be able to communicate with all of you and them on frequency 107.88. There should be no communication until we have Whitcomb in our presence and the area secured. All right, why don't you head on over to Compass, we'll be right along."

While Mullen was speaking with the others, McGrath had walked over to his cubicle; realizing he had not taken down a quote that he had pinned to it years before. He took the pin out, grabbed the piece of paper, crumbled it up in his hand and threw it into the wastebasket. It was from that greatest of Irish poets, William Butler Yeats McGrath's favorite. It read: "The indigenous character trait of the Irish is an abiding sense of tragedy that sustained people through temporary periods of joy." He knew it by heart!

On the short ride from the Bureau's office to the Federal Courthouse, McGrath called Fowler on her cell phone. "We're about two minutes out. We'll meet you, Katharine and Fenore out in front of the building." Once the three got into the car, after brief good mornings were exchanged, no one said a word. You could feel both the tension and the excitement that emanated from the five occupants. McGrath was first to break the silence.

"Bryan and I will change vehicles when we head the few blocks over to Morning Glory. We will communicate with you on this radio," as he turned in the front passenger seat and handed a radio to Fowler in the back seat. "Once the scene is secure, I will let you know when to drive over. You three will be able to hear everything that is going on and if trouble develops, under no circumstances are you to come to the site." They all responded that they understood. "This guy Whitcomb has a lot to lose if we grab him with the paintings, so he may become violent or act irrational. We hope not, but being Irish, we need to think the worst but hope for the best." With that, Mullen pulled onto Compass Landing.

Light from the agents' idling Ford Victorias'
headlights reflected off pooled rainwater in the
street. It seemed to bounce off the nearby Million
Dol1ar homes in a wavy, yellow glow
appearance. Pulling up behind the last vehicle,
Mullen and McGrath started to get out when
McGrath glanced back at Fowler with a
confident reassuring look. She, Fenore and
Savage wished them luck and told them to be
careful. Everyone looked at his or her watch. It
was 5:51 AM. Fowler and Savage got into the
front seat while Fenore stayed in the back and
watched the others leave the area.

From their radio, they heard Mullen ask if agent
Thomas, who was responsible for disarming the
security gate, was in place. He responded that he
was and given the command he could open it at
any time. As Mullen's vehicle rolled slowly to a
stop twenty-five feet from the gate, they could
see agent Thomas trying to blend in with some
of the large rhododendrons to the left of the
entrance. Mullen looked at his watch, which
now read 5:56 AM. "OK, let's hit the lights,"
Mullen barked into the microphone pinned to
the front of his blue jacket.

In a flash, the still, murky dawn transformed
into a brilliant, blinding sunny afternoon.
Mullen again barked, "Let's go," as he and the
others walked up to the gate, which in a fraction
of a second was pushed open by agent Thomas

as the others walked up the driveway. They could hear a dog barking inside the house. The klieg lights flooded the area down below the residence and as the truck traveled up the serpentine driveway with agents in front, the letters FBI in yellow clearly visible on the back of their jackets. Two of the agents took positions outside the front entrance, on the finely manicured lawn; the other two walked behind the large structure near the massive brick patio that extended as far as the eye could see. In the early dawn light the patio appeared to meander down to a large pool situated next to a cabana. McGrath knocked on the door and after several moments it opened ever so slowly.

A dog barked angrily from the other side. Fearing that someone might be standing in the atrium with a weapon or firearm and, given the presence of the German Shepard, both Mullen and McGrath pulled their 9MM Glocks from their holsters. McGrath had done the same on that misty morning when he first entered the Palace Road entrance to the Gardner museum. As the door finally swung open, a man who looked to be in his sixties who was dressed in a silk robe over red pajamas, stood looking perplexed in the doorway. His German Shepard, Tron was struggling on a leash at his side and was obviously very unhappy. The grey haired man shielded his eyes from the klieg lights. He then heard someone yell, "Turn the lights off."

All of a sudden, appearing still to be groggy from being awakened from sleep, he looked at the two agents and said with a concerned yet quizzical look on his face, "What the hell is going on here and who are you?" Mullen displayed his badge and told him they were members of the Federal Bureau of Investigation and had a search warrant to search his home. When the now startled looking man asked them what they were searching for, McGrath responded in a cocky tone of voice, "a couple of paint-by-number masterpieces," a smart ass grin appearing on his face. He then asked the gentleman his name. He responded, "Michael Whitcomb." Fowler, Savage and Fenore were listening to the exchange when they heard Whitcomb say, "You're not searching a fucking thing until my lawyer gets here." Seconds later, loud voices could be heard over the radio and then a scuffle and a dog barking wildly.

Amy, Katharine and Anthony became so concerned that Fowler started the car and, against McGrath's specific instructions, bailed from the secure location and headed towards the house, blue wigwags flashing from behind the front grill. She stopped for just a moment at the gate to give a nod to agent Thomas and then sped up the driveway, tires squealing. She threw the car into park, as it lunged forward jumped out and hurried towards the door.

When she entered she could see Whitcomb in handcuffs sitting on the floor, his mouth and nose bloodied. One of the agents standing guard on the lawn had somehow restrained the dog that was now off to one side. Two women stood near Whitcomb, both of whom were crying hysterically. McGrath and Mullen stood over the bloodied Whitcomb, who had been pushed up against the wall by Mullen. An agent with her MP-5A3 at ready stood in the doorway in full tactical gear. Whitcomb kept yelling to his wife to call his lawyer at his home in Belmont, even though it was only 6:08 in the morning.

Chapter Seventy-Four: "Exoneration?"

While the yelling and chaos continued, Mullen stood guard over Whitcomb as McGrath, Fowler, Savage and Fenore went to find the den. "I thought I told you three to stay away until the place was secured," McGrath said with some tension in his voice as they walked down the hall. "We couldn't help ourselves," Savage shot back with a smirk. Walking through the majestic rooms laden with paintings, they finally came to one that had a massive stone fireplace that rose 30 feet into the air.

To its left was a gigantic high definition television and across from that were three or four leather lounges and tables. The walls were decorated with what looked like watercolors, bright pastels, pinks, greens and light blues, giving the room almost a springlike feel; several palm trees climbed almost to the cathedral ceiling. The bar was in the right-hand corner of the room. There were at least twelve stools and a portrait of a nude hanging front and center, the young woman's ample breasts on display for all to view. McGrath walked over to the bar, found the light switch and turned it on. In a flash, the whole bar was illuminated. They were now ready to locate the button to open the secret panel to the hidden vault. "That son of a bitch Mercer was right. If there is a secret room, where the hell is it?" McGrath queried. Savage, who had walked around to the bar with Fowler, was now leaning over pointing to something near the sink located underneath the dark, granite slab.

"I think I found it," she exclaimed excitedly. McGrath, Fowler and Fenore walked over to where Savage was now squatting and pointing a flash light up under the wet bar. It looked like a small buzzer that could be picked up at any local hardware store. It was labeled "skylight switch". As they all looked up at the ceiling, they could see a massive skylight with what appeared to be an electric shade that could be opened and closed.

They all thought the same thing without saying it: "That's a damn peculiar place to put a skylight switch." McGrath was about to press it to see what would happen, when he heard an angry voice coming from the other side of the room. "What the hell is going on here and how did my client get bloodied?" Looking up from behind the bar, McGrath recognized the man approaching. It was Attorney Ken Leister.

Thoughts raced through McGrath's brain. "David Mercer, who was also represented by Leister, must not have told him that I spoke to him just a couple of days ago. Leister must not know that Mercer threw Whitcomb under the bus or maybe, he never even told Mercer that he also represented Whitcomb. That would be a significant conflict of interest!" Seeing Leister, Fowler came out from behind the bar, walked over to him and handed him a copy of the search warrant. "It's a perfectly valid warrant and as you can see from the attachment, we're here to search for the art work stolen from the Isabella Stewart Gardner museum," Fowler said. Leister's face blanched as the prosecutor's words registered. "There must be a mistake," his face now transformed to a beet red. "My client was not involved in that robbery. You have no proof!"

Hearing what he had just said to Fowler, McGrath yelled out from behind the bar, "That's bullshit," veins throbbing in his neck "You and I both know that your other client, David Mercer was involved in the robbery and that this darling of a client," pointing to Whitcomb, who was now standing behind his counsel, "was one of the two thieves who went into the museum and ripped the paintings off. I think you have known that for fucking years," as he scowled at Leister, who appeared to be in a state of shock. With that, McGrath turned away, bent down and pushed the button.

All of a sudden, a low-pitched drone that seemed to come from a section of the wall closest to the fireplace, filtered through the room. The room actually shuddered. Then, a section of the grass-papered wall started to slide away from the large, grey fieldstones. Everyone in the room except Whitcomb and Leister stood in place, in silence, spellbound by what was happening.

They gazed with utter amazement at the gaping hole that was now part of the room. No one moved. Brilliant dust- filled opaque light, filtered from the room. McGrath turned his gaze to Leister who appeared dumbfounded as he looked at his client. McGrath walked from behind the wet bar towards the light coming from the room. It reminded him of a massive bank vault. Savage, Fowler and Fenore, purposely a few feet behind him, started to do the same. They walked to the entrance where they all stood for a moment trying to adjust their eyes to the blinding light. Then, they walked in. As Savage entered, her cotton jacket brushed up against several of the fieldstones of the fireplace, revealing something shiny attached to her belt. It was an agent's gold badge and read: "Federal Bureau of Investigation". Clearly inscribed at the bottom, if anyone happened to notice, was "Special Agent Katharine Lynn Savage".

Entering the vault, looking left and then right, countless paintings hung at various levels on perfectly plastered, museum quality walls. It was an incredible sight to behold. There in the brilliant light were works by Picasso, Renoir, Dali and others. An extraordinary collection of masterpieces! Continuing to walk further into what looked like a gallery in a world-class museum, the three stopped dead in their tracks. There on the wall were Vermeer's "The Concert" and Rembrandt's "A Lady and Gentleman in Black". They were all speechless. They stood motionless, temporarily suspended in time. McGrath had tears in his eyes. They told his story. He smiled at Fowler as he gently placed his hand on her shoulder. His story ending in exoneration, fulfilment and achievement in an otherwise tattered, bruised and beaten man. Their collective delight however, was about to turn into dreadful despair! Someone else had just entered the vault.

Chapter Seventy-Five: "Hoodwinked?"

"Yes, aren't they indeed exquisite and yes, they are priceless," a man with a Boston accent declared from behind the group. McGrath and Fowler recognized the voice immediately. Both looked like they had just seen a ghost. Mullen and Fenore turned to see a figure standing in the dusty light. It was First Assistant United States Attorney Frank Cullen. "Oh it is such a splendid morning. I must congratulate all of you for what has been a magnificent piece of detective work. There is however one colossal problem," pointed sarcasm in his voice. "What just transpired here is an illusion; it never took place. Let me say it again, your quest has been for naught!"

Fowler felt like she was going to faint, while McGrath, Mullen and Fenore were in a state of shock. "What do you mean its been for naught?" Fenore demanded. "You keep your mouth shut!" as he pointed his finger at Fenore. "I'll tell you why! The search warrant that you just used to gain entrance into this house and the vault where you stand was not obtained legally. It was never signed off by United States Attorney Morrissey. As a consequence, anything and everything obtained as a result, including the Vermeer and Rembrandt, cannot be used as evidence against Whitcomb. He can't be prosecuted for possessing the stolen art!"

Fowler turned and looked at McGrath. The color in her face had turned a cadaverous grey. She did not have to speak, her eyes spoke volumes. "How can this be happening? You promised that you would protect me. My career is over and I will lose everything." Numb and devastated by what Cullen had just said, she didn't hear what Whitcomb was screaming at the top of his lungs. While Morrissey's hatchet man threatened everyone with prosecution, David Mercer lay flat on his back staring at the ceiling from his government-issued cot at BOP-Hazelton, West Virginia. He held his cell phone in his right hand at his side.

As he anticipated, the slight vibration signaled a text message had been received. He held it up and tapped the face. "The Eagle has landed and the goods are safe. Now we hold all the cards!" Finished reading the short but unbelievably encouraging text, a Cheshire smirk once again morphed on the face of the kid from Avon. He turned, placed the phone next to him and fell back to sleep. He realized that he just might have grabbed the keys to his freedom. Once asleep however, he would not become aware of who next appeared at 180 Morning Glory Lane. He wouldn't find that out until he received a very unpleasant phone call from McGrath later that day!

Chapter Seventy-Six: "Honor, Loyalty, and Integrity"

Katharine Savage, a recent graduate of the FBI Academy in Quantico, Virginia, had been assigned to the Special Investigations Unit of the Department of Justice in Washington. Agent Francis Xavier Cadigan was her direct report. When Senator Barton started to hold hearings to look into shenanigans that took place in the Boston FBI field office in the late 80s and early 90s, the Deputy Attorney General had called upon his trusted confidant, veteran agent F. X. Cadigan to find someone who could act as a mole in Boston. Savage was chosen to be that person. She was determined to serve in that capacity with distinction and failure was not in her vocabulary. While her law enforcement partners and Fenore looked like they were next in the queue to climb the gallows, Savage seemed cool as a cucumber. Why? Because she knew what was going to happen next!

The room suddenly shuddered with a deep baritone voice. "Good morning Ted and Amy. I'm sorry I left you hanging on the line a little bit too long this morning. My apologies. I just wanted to make sure I got all of this," as he held up a CD and winked at the two of them. By the way, nice work agent Savage!"

Agent F.X. Cadigan, two heavily armed agents at his side, stood front and center in the doorway of the vault. "This is sure going to make for some interesting reading by the Attorney General." Turning to Cullen, "Well Frank, its been a long time. Let's see, I think the last time I saw you was at United States Attorney Morrissey's swearing-in here in Boston," he said as he walked over to Cullen and handed him a piece of paper. "I think your not-so-well thought out scheme, as one of my colleagues said many years ago, has just gone from the precious, gold wine goblet of Midas, to the chaffy lead of a poison'd chalice.

He then walked up to McGrath and Fowler and embraced them. Their eyes' once again, said it all! Savage also embraced McGrath, looked into his eyes and said, "I guess it wasn't a fool's errand after all agent McGrath," as the grey haired kid from Southie, grinned from ear to ear. "You all made it happen and injected us with a can-do attitude. We have two paintings back and now our work begins to recover the other eleven pieces. Thank you for your help," Cadigan said with gratitude.

While standing outside the vault, the sun had risen in the East, peeking through powdery morning clouds over Boston Harbor. The glass façade of the federal courthouse sparkled with an orange glow. This morning, something big was about to go down across town. Real big!

Two other agents from FBI Headquarters in Washington, specially assigned to Senator Barton's committee, sat in a vehicle outside the entrance to the courthouse. Their two partners were walking down the corridor leading to the United States Attorney's office. Morrissey was already sitting at his desk. As the two entered the large waiting room in the executive suite and walked by the desk of Mary Campo, Morrissey's long time Confidential Secretary, they noticed something draped across the back of her chair. It was a very colorful, bright, orange scarf from 'Hermes of Paris'! Agents for the Committee on Governmental Affairs were there to serve a subpoena on United States Attorney James Morrissey officially requiring his presence in Washington, D.C. on Thursday morning at 10:00 AM. He was summoned to answer questions, under oath. Number one on the Senator's agenda: the Isabella Stewart Gardner museum robbery that took place on March 18, 1990 in The Fens.

Retired FBI agent Ted McGrath would, once again, be seated in Hearing Room 207. This time, without the Department of Justice pin shining from his lapel!

EPILOGUE

This is a work of fiction. In reality, some twenty-two years later, the robbery remains unsolved. In recent months, through the Herculean efforts of the museum's Director of Security, Anthony Amore, the theft has received significant publicity through both print and electronic media. Getting what primarily has been a local story out to more people will hopefully result in someone coming forward with information that will lead to the recovery of the stolen art. IF YOU HAVE ANY INFORMATION CONCERNING THESE WORKS OF ART OR CIRCUMSTANCES OF THESE CRIMES, PLEASE CONTACT: www.fbi.gov or the Gardner Museum at aamore@ISGM.org

Marshfield, Massachusetts, May 5, 2012

Artful Deception may be purchased at Amazon.com in Kindle format and in paperback. McGovern may be contacted at jjmcgovern29@verizon.net

James J. McGovern is a New England native, a Suffolk University Law School graduate, an active member of Boston's legal community and a committed Red Sox fan. While serving with the United States Attorney's Office in Boston in 2006, McGovern was given the extraordinary opportunity to take a second look at the FBI's cold case of the Gardner Museum heist, the largest art theft in US history. *Artful Deception*, a work of historical fiction, was written with the specific intent to turn what has been largely a local story into a worldwide, electronic appeal for assistance in recovering the stolen art. McGovern introduces FBI agent Ted McGrath to help solve the incredible story of this real-life who-dun- it in the City of Boston.

Born and raised in Providence, Rhode Island. He is a member of the Sons of Irish Kings has three grown children and lives with his wife and a persnickety calico named Frankie. McGovern is currently working on his second novel, *Proximate Justice*, a medical mystery.

Made in the USA
Lexington, KY
02 May 2013